The MAKE UP

HAILEY GARDINER

This is a work of fiction. Names, characters, businesses, places, and incidents either are the product of the author's imagination or are used fictitiously. Any resemblance to actual persons, living or dead, events, or locales is entirely coincidental.

Copyright © 2022 by Hailey Gardiner.

All rights reserved.

No portion of this book may be reproduced in any form or by electronic or mechanical means without written permission from the publisher or author, except for the use of brief quotations in a book review.

Cover design by Yummy Book Covers

Editing by Heather Austin and Jenn Lockwood

www.haileygardiner.com

To my fellow friends with scoliosis—you are worthy of all good things, just the way you are.

Chapter 1

Chloe

"Five minutes, snitches!" Jax, our production assistant, calls up through the open trailer door.

"Almost ready!" I reply.

I'm Michelangelo, meticulously painting the cupid's bow of Sarah's upper lip with a thin, sharp pencil. Her lips are full—unnaturally full, if you ask me—so it's already hard to tell where the natural shape of her mouth ends and where the injections begin.

Using a delicate hand, I'm able to create a rosy-hued outline around her lips. I've got every word to "Cry, Baby" memorized and could probably sing it back verbatim if they needed someone to perform it live at the shoot today. This freaking song has been playing on repeat, back to back, over and over, during the time I've been applying Sarah's makeup.

She says it's to help her get into character. I say it's to drive your makeup artist to drink copious amounts of tea to cope.

Aside from her nitpicky requests about the volume of her eyelashes and the amount of highlight needed to accent the perfect tip of her nose, I'd say things have gone pretty smoothly.

But that all changes when Sarah decides to abruptly sneeze.

Now, this isn't some dainty, nose-plugging sneeze that sounds like a door squeaking or a mouse making a timid request. No, no. This is a *man* sneeze. A violent sneeze. A sneeze that sounds like rapid laser fire pummeling through space from a *Star Wars* X-Wing.

Sarah's head slams forward with the momentum of the ear-splitting explosion erupting from her nose. I'm stunned and can't move my little hand out of the way fast enough before it hits her face.

Lip pencil, meet Sarah's peach-fuzz mustache. Mustache, pencil. I gasp as a blotchy red spot appears where the sharp tip collided with her skin.

"Oh my goodness!" I breathe, gently dabbing her upper lip with a tissue. "I am so, so sorry."

"It's alright." She gives me a dangerous glare. *Clearly, it's not, in fact, alright.* "How bad is it?"

I assess the growing red spot on her 'stache and keep my expression pleasant. "It's fine. Nothing a little concealer can't fix."

"I really can't afford to have a blemish today," she says firmly, shaking her long, blonde hair back over her shoulders. "Not today."

"I'll get you all taken care of. Don't you worry."

I hurry to cover the spot, dotting concealer and foundation strategically to minimize the redness. I dust some powder over the concealer as it dries and pray that she doesn't have any closeups on the shot list today.

Sarah leans toward the mirror and tilts her head from side to side. "Is that the best you can do? It's still so obvious."

Deep breaths, Chloe. Long, slow breaths. I'm trying not to let her words send spikes through the already paper-thin wall of patience that's fluttering between us.

Maybe if you hadn't suddenly become aggressively allergic to something invisible, your upper lip would have come out unscathed.

"I don't want to use too much product on it," I finally say, managing to keep my voice even. "I think if I leave it like this, the redness will go down in a few minutes, and no one will be able to notice."

"I just got stabbed with a pencil. You think nobody is going to notice that?"

Cool and calm. Cool and calm. That's me right now. Iceberg cool. Snoop Dogg calm.

I turn toward my brushes and palettes that are splayed out across the counter.

"Nobody's going to want to watch a music video featuring a girl with a massive hole in her face," she pouts.

This woman.

Why is SHE the girl Hunter decided to cast in this "Cry, Baby" video? I've just about had it with her.

He *had* to have gone on a date with her at some point. That's the only explanation. He couldn't resist her pageant-worthy, voluminous hair or her doe-like lashes. He took her out to dinner. And then they probably spent a good portion of the date macking in his car parked outside her apartment before he called it a night.

But I know her type. Vain. Perfectly proportionate. And expendable. Hunter could find fifty other girls just like her after one night in town.

What irks me most is that she's implying that I've somehow managed to singlehandedly end her country-music-video career. That *her* ill-timed, *Star-Wars*-sound-effect sneeze is now my fault.

I select another fluffy brush to dust some more powder over her spot. It's barely visible, but I'm all about giving her the placebo effect.

"Well, Miss Sarah, I've done my best." I swallow and force myself to meet her eyes in the mirror over her shoulder. "You look stunning," I say, and I mean it. I didn't just spend hours enhancing and perfecting every inch of this woman's face for nothing.

She drops her lips into that toddler-esque pout and slinks out of her chair. "This is so embarrassing."

"It's going to be a great shoot," I say brightly, impressed at my own stamina. My cheerful tank is running on fumes. "Let's get you off to set before Hunter comes up here looking for you."

Sarah pushes past me in a huff, without so much as a thank you.

Snoop. Be like Snoop. Snoop wouldn't be ruffled by a model-slash-actress on a country-music-video set. No, sir. He'd be talking her down in that even tone of his until she had no choice but to concede to his level of chill.

I'm unruffled. Unbothered. Everything is great.
I love my job. I love my job. I love my job.
I also NEED my job.

I follow Sarah down the tiny stairs that lead out of the trailer and take a slow, deep breath at the bottom. The sun is peeking up over the treeline, the birds are singing, and I'm about to go bathe myself in that placid water. It's so inviting.

I take a moment to drag the cool, autumn air into my lungs.

The shoot this morning is taking place at Radnor Lake, a state park made up of thousands of acres of lush forest surrounding a picturesque lake just outside of Nashville, Tennessee. Miles of unpaved trails meander through the woods and around the water. Hunter's vision for this video includes lots of nature shots. With the leaves showing off with vibrant shades of blood orange, rust, and gold, he's sure to capture some epic shots today.

Which should be only *slightly* marred by Sarah's battle wound should the cameras pick up on it.

I trail along after her to where the first shot of the morning has been set up. Hunter's crew is small but mighty, mostly made up of his fellow film-school-dropout friends who've stuck by him since the days when Hunter was still shooting weddings. I like working with Hunter's crew. We have a way of doing things, a flow. I'd like to think that, as the hair-and-makeup artist, I'm an integral part of that flow.

Hunter's standing at the end of a boardwalk that juts out over the misty lake, laying out the shots with his main camera man and the star of this music video. He's in creative mode, his faded baseball hat resting backward over his dark hair, the sleeves of his navy crewneck pushed up his forearms. He's walking Connor Cane through his paces, demonstrating how he should move down the boardwalk for this first shot.

A smile teases at the edge of my lips as I watch Hunter blocking out the shot. The ironic thing about this country-music-loving, music-video-directing man is that he can't sing worth crap. He couldn't carry a tune in a bucket if it were made out of vibranium from Wakanda. I'm the only person who's allowed to tease him about his severe lack of musical ability, and that's only because I've earned it over the fifteen years we've known each other.

Hunter tells me that he's sure God will compensate for his lack of a singing voice in the next life. He's certain he'll be appointed to be the director of His heavenly choir.

Hunter's voice carries over to where I'm standing behind the rest of the crew, and as I suspected, he's rhythmically speaking the words to the song. I start humming along, bracing myself to have to hear this song on repeat throughout the entire day.

Hate to break it to you, Connor, but your next single has already been overplayed before it's even hit the radio.

Sarah is preening off camera, ready to receive her instructions from Hunter as soon as he's done with Connor. If homegirl were an animal, she'd be a peacock—all fluffed feathers and swaying hips.

Hunter finally turns around and notices Sarah and her desperate attempts to draw his attention.

"Well, good morning to you!" he says. "You look gorgeous."

His eyes then find mine, and he gives me a little nose-scrunch grin that I'm pretty sure means, '*All thanks to you, Chloe. What would I do without you?*'

Either that or '*I need a donut and STAT. Blood sugar's starting to dip.*' Not really sure.

He places his hand on Sarah's mid-back and leads her out onto the boardwalk to Connor, where he begins talking through the shot with the two of them.

I pull my cardigan tighter over my body, chill bumps breaking out over my arms as a breeze dances over the places where my bare skin is exposed.

"Cold, honey?" Jax asks from beside me. "Can't have our makeup artist blowing away in the wind. With you gone, who would do Sarah's touch ups?"

I bump him with my shoulder. "You. You would do them."

"And lose the entirety of my self-worth with one of her barbed comments? No, thank you."

I snort. "She is a piece of work."

"They all are."

"Why does he cast girls like her, Jax?"

"Honey, I wish I had an answer for you. I really do."

"Jax?" Hunter's voice crackles through the walkie-talkie on Jax's belt. Jax is technically the PA on Hunter's shoots, but he works more as the-guy-who-doth-Hunter's-bidding.

He sighs, lifting the walkie up to his lips. "Yes, your highness?"

"Hey, has craft services shown up yet? I could really use a donut down here."

Ahh. Cryptic message decoded. It was the blood sugar.

"Because you're paying me, I'll check on that for you. Though, you really should be choosing to fuel yourself with something more nutritious," Jax preaches to Hunter, who's still standing at the end of the boardwalk. "I'm going to start ordering oatmeal instead."

"Thank you, Jax," Hunter says, his voice thick with sarcasm.

"Sure, sweet cheeks." Jax sighs, turning back to me. "Can I get you anything while I fetch his lordship's pastries?"

"I'm good for now. Thanks, though."

"Suit yourself," Jax sings over his shoulder as he departs.

I turn my attention back to the blond, built man who's doing vocal warmups at the end of the boardwalk as if he really intends to sing along to the song instead of lip sync like everyone else does. Connor Cane is Back Road Records' latest up-and-coming artist. His first single went platinum last year, and he's been building up to the release of his debut album in a few months by dropping radio hit after viral hit. I have no doubt that "Cry, Baby" is going to be a chart-topper.

Hunter's first shoot he'd booked with Connor had been much more low-budget, a gamble the label was taking on a relatively unknown artist. But now? We get trailers, craft services, and more zeros added onto our paychecks.

"Alright, I think we're ready to roll!" Hunter rubs his hands together. He's like a kid on Christmas morning. I can't help but love the energy he brings to his work. It makes it such a positive experience for everyone involved—including Sarah, apparently, who no longer looks like her mere flesh wound is of any degree of importance.

I settle into my spot behind the shot, where I belong. Behind the scenes. Somewhere quiet where I can observe the shoot and go unnoticed until someone needs a new coat of lipstick or a dusting of powder to cover up some forehead shine.

Hunter cues up "Cry, Baby", and I'm honestly about to shed a few tears myself as the opening chords of the song fill the air, echoing over the glassy surface of Radnor Lake.

But I will bear this discomfort, along with the discomfort of long days spent on my feet that make my spine ache and my feet swell. I'll do it all if I get to be in the same room, the same car, or the same forest as Hunter Ward.

He and I are a package deal. One and the same. You want one, you're going to get the other.

We are the very best of friends—which is starting to feel less like an honorable designation that I'm happy to accept and more like a death sentence meant to torture me until the blessed day the good Lord calls me home.

Because here's the thing about Hunter and me...we are fine just the way we are. And if he were to ever find out that my feelings run a whole lot deeper than friendship, I would risk losing the truest love I have ever known. He would find another Sarah to replace me like *that*, and I would rot away as a spinster for the rest of my days, trying and failing to find a man who could measure up to all that Hunter is for me. I couldn't bear that.

So, I hide my feelings as best as I can. Button them up under the guise that we are, and always have been, the best of friends.

But I'm living a lie, day in and day out. Hunter is the one man in my life that I truly love, and it's taking everything in me to keep my heart from fastening itself onto my sleeve for everyone to see.

Chapter 2

Hunter

I'm hovering over the box of donuts at the craft services table when my hand is subjected to a sharp slap.

"Dude!" I hiss at Jax, who has apparently taken it upon himself to be my unwanted dietician. "Lay off me!"

"You've had three already this morning, dearest. But if you'd like to throw away your chances of living a long and healthy life, be my guest and stuff your face with another sugar bomb."

Chloe's hand shoots across my body from the left, lifting a donut from the box. "I think you already touched this one, so I'll eat it on your behalf."

"A sign of true friendship," I deadpan.

The three of us huddle together at the end of the table. The crew is hurrying to set up our next shot in the nearby woods before we lose our mellow morning light. I had escaped to the refreshment table for another donut, but I force myself to pick up a bottle of tasteless, sugarless water instead. I take a long draw from the bottle just to appease Jax. "Staying hydrated. Just for you, pal."

He rolls his eyes at me. "You're still nowhere near your needed water-intake level for the day. Keep guzzling. Can't have our director passing out from dehydration."

"What about hunger?" I say, watching Chloe take slow bites of what should have been *my* donut. "This is torturous."

And I'm not just talking about the donut. Chloe's lips are the forbidden fruit in my personal Garden of Eden—but we don't talk about Chloe's lips.

Never, ever.

Because the closest I'll ever get to kissing Chloe is drinking after her from the same glass or taking a bite from a fork she used.

Sometimes (read: pretty much all the time these days) I wonder what it would be like to pull Chloe into my arms, to feel her lips on mine. I imagine that her kisses would taste like summer strawberries, both tart and perfectly sweet.

But I'm pretty sure I'm never going to satisfy that craving because, up until recently, I have made it entirely impossible for Chloe and me to be anything other than friends.

Since the day I turned fifteen, I've never *not* had a girlfriend. I've bounced from one relationship to another, permanently attached to someone at all times.

Chloe's dated other guys, too, but at what I'd consider to be a normal rate. I've had my relationship status dialed in as *perpetually taken* for as long as I can remember.

Until last summer, when my dad passed away.

Losing my closest friend, my greatest example, caused me to do some serious self-reflection. I broke off my on-again/off-again relationship that same day, needing space and time to process the waves of grief that threatened to pull me under.

A little over a year later, and I'm still not *officially* attached to anyone.

That's not to say that I haven't gone out on dates—because I have. But the longer I try to deny my ever-growing feelings for my best friend, the more every other woman I interact with pales in comparison. Nobody can measure up to Chloe. Nobody.

And that's also what makes her seem so untouchable. Too good and pure-hearted for any man to claim as his own.

Chloe sighs, dusting crumbs off the front of her tee. "Now THAT...was a donut."

"You're telling me," I mumble.

"You'll thank me when you're thriving at ninety-nine, bombing down mountain trails like you did back in high school," Jax says.

"I'll never be that fast again. Chloe and I have accepted our fate as has-been cross-country phenoms."

Chloe snorts, tossing back her short, light-brown hair. "Speak for yourself. I'm a speed demon on the track these days." She fidgets with the buttons on her cardigan. "Which you would know, if you ever decided you wanted to come run with me again."

I grimace. "About that..."

"What's your excuse now?" Chloe jabs a finger into my chest. Barely over five feet tall, she has to tilt her head back to meet my eyes. "Summer's over, sweetheart."

"Don't I know it." I peer up at the overcast skies overhead. "These clouds are killing my light for this shoot."

Jax shrugs. "It's moody. I like it."

Chloe gives my arm a squeeze. "Come run with me, Hunter. You need it. We all know you're stressed out over these back-to-back shoots. You could use the emotional outlet."

"And the exercise." Jax gestures to my stomach. "No offense."

Uh, OFFENSE. Much offense taken.

"I'm well aware of the fact that I haven't been keeping up with my cardio lately, but that doesn't mean I've let myself go," I say. "I'm proud of the state of my abs right now, thank you very much. I'd be happy to show them to you if you'd like..." I start to peel up the edge of my shirt and glance over at Chloe, who's suddenly very occupied with the colorful leaves that are slowly falling around us.

Jax tsks. "Abs with *your* eating habits? *So* unfair."

"Fine. Chloe, I promise I'll come run with you."

Her brown eyes brighten. "Really?"

"I think you're right." I eye Sarah and Connor who are chatting it up outside his trailer. "I could use a little stress relief after dealing with *her* all morning."

Jax and Chloe share a disbelieving glance.

"You mean you're not gunning to make her your soon-to-be plus-one?" Chloe scoffs.

I remove my ball cap and run a hand through my messy hair. "Sarah? *Heck* no."

Chloe is now zeroing in on me, gearing up to telepathically read my mind. I keep my gaze firmly fixed on the waterfront, aware that she's probably rifling through my thoughts right now like she's entitled to know all of them.

Which she totally is. She has stuck with me since our freshman year of high school, when we were assigned to be lab partners in chemistry class. We know almost everything about each other—*except* for the off-limits thoughts I've had about Chloe since the day we met. The thoughts that turn my stomach inside out and make me wonder what my life would be like with the stunning, humble, ever-steady Chloe by my side.

"You kissed her, though."

Goodness, this woman is good. I'd never told her about my date with Sarah a few months back.

I squint down at Chloe. "I did."

"Totally made out with her."

I drop my head down to my chest, ashamed. "I did."

"How'd those massive lips feel?" Chloe teases. "I'm sure it was like kissing a pair of nice, golden twinkies."

I bark out a laugh. "Twinkies? Disgusting."

"I mean this in the most non-judgmental way possible, but you really should be more selective, Hunter," Jax says. "She's not worth your time."

"Obviously I know that now."

I push my hands into the pockets of my jeans and rock backward on my heels. Chloe gives me her signature *I-told-you-so* look that I have the pleasure of seeing after every NCMO (non-committal make-out) I sign up for.

For the record, I haven't gone on a second date in over a year. And that's not because the girls I take out don't call me back. It's because I can't bring myself to commit to another relationship when the only woman I really *want* to date is completely off-limits.

Chloe is everything to me. My confidant. My standing weekend brunch date at our favorite biscuit spot. If I were to try to put the moves on her, she'd shut me down so fast I wouldn't even have time to explain myself. She's a no-nonsense kind of gal. She wouldn't trust that my feelings are real, and I don't blame her, based on my past dating record. It speaks for itself. *Unstable. Non-committal. Womanizer. Player.*

I've had years to perfect the art of picking up women, showing them a good time, and then putting the kibosh on things when they want to get serious.

But after Dad's passing, something shifted. I'm not satisfied with casual dating. I don't just want to be liked, for a woman to laugh at my jokes and validate my wit. I want to be known, to be seen.

I want the chance to love and to be loved.

But there's only one person who comes to mind every time I start wandering down this mental path.

Chloe.

It has to be Chloe. I've spent half my life dating other women, trying to find someone who makes me better the way she does. All I've proven to myself is that there is literally no one else in the world like her.

And after a year of failed first dates, I desperately want a chance at love. And I want it with Chloe.

"You're a good guy, Hunter." She gives me a little pat on the arm.

A good guy. She's more than generous. That's something she'd say about her UPS delivery driver or the dude who fixed up her car at the shop.

"But you're a terrible casting director."

There it is. Between Chloe's honesty and Jax's bluntness, I'm going to need to book an appointment with my therapist STAT.

"You need to start casting girls who are much more pleasant to work with." She shudders, nodding over at Sarah. "Or I'm going on strike."

I gasp and clasp her hands in mine with desperation. "Please, no. Chloe, we need you here." Her eyes widen as I squeeze her fists in my hands, but she doesn't make a move to pull away.

"We *cannot* replace your feminine energy," Jax agrees.

"Then let me help you cast the next music video," Chloe says.

I let my thumbs travel over her hands, over each ridge of her knuckles. Her skin is angel soft on mine.

"On one condition…" I say. "You have to let me pay you for it."

She rolls her eyes and finally eases her hands out of mine. "Uh, no."

"Chloe," I say sternly. "If you want to be the casting director, you have to be compensated fairly. It's the law."

"I'm perfectly happy with my current compensation, thank you very much."

Back Road Records is generous with their video budgets, so I know Chloe is making good money on these shoots, but not enough to ease her workload in the way she needs it.

"Look, if I bill the label for your work, then there's nothing you can do about it."

Chloe crosses her arms. "Don't even think about it. I just want to help you next time, for the sake of everyone involved."

"Hear, hear," Jax chimes in.

"I'd love your help," I say. "I *need* your help."

"Clearly." Chloe tries and fails to suppress a smile.

"And I will ensure that you get paid fairly."

"Hunter, I don't want your pity money—"

"Ready on set!" a voice crackles through Jax's walkie-talkie, interrupting our argument.

"Alright, crew!" I clap my hands together. "Shot's ready. Let's get back to work."

I gesture for Chloe and Jax to follow me into the woods.

I'm the luckiest son of a gun to get to work with the people I do. I wouldn't be able to do my job without Jax's organizational skills and structure. And Chloe's warmth and artistic eye are invaluable.

And so is her time.

Chloe tries to hide it, but I can tell when she's feeling the pain. When the discomfort starts to kick in and she needs to sit down.

She's been on her feet since 5 a.m., and I know she's probably needing a break right about now. As soon as we locate the rest of the crew, I drag a camp chair over behind the cameras.

"For you," I say, patting the seat for Chloe.

She smiles at me gratefully, her eyes wrinkling at the corners. She eases into the chair and sighs. "Thank you, Hunter."

"Can I get you anything? Water? Another donut?"

She waves a hand through the air. "Stop worrying about me. I'm fine."

"Alright," I say, squeezing her shoulder gently. "Just relax, put your feet up, and enjoy watching me do all the work."

"Oh, believe me. I will."

I'd like to think that Chloe's eyes follow me as I walk away, that they dip down to my backside as she says to herself, *'Mmm, mmm, mmm.'*

But when I glance back over my shoulder, she's got her head tipped back and is watching those dang leaves fluttering in the trees overhead instead.

How am I supposed to compete with Mother Nature's wondrous transformation into fall?

I adjust my cap on my head and gear up for the next shot.

Chapter 3

Chloe

Fifteen years earlier...

I'm nervously gnawing on the end of my mechanical pencil, the eraser barely surviving between my teeth.

My first day as a freshman at Ridgeview High has gone exactly as I anticipated it would. Totally WHACKED OUT.

I'd been shuffling around the halls first thing this morning, face buried in the printed map I'd received at new-student orientation last week, when I'd heard shouting. I'd dropped the paper, looked up, and immediately wished I'd kept my head down.

Students were lined up against the lockers on either side of the hall, chanting, "FIGHT! FIGHT! FIGHT!" Two angry-looking older boys were facing off RIGHT in front of me, about to go at it. When I realized that I had literally walked into the middle of their soon-to-be brawl, I squealed and shuffled out of the way before anyone started throwing punches.

Who are these Neanderthals beating each other up on the first day of school?

Day one, and I already feel like an outsider in this foreign world they call high school.

Once I finally found my first-period classroom, I hurried to fill an empty desk near the back of the room. I'd barely slipped into my seat when Mr. Pike started his introductory spiel, indoctrinating us on the rules of his chemistry classroom.

"I've assigned each of you a lab partner. You'll be partnered for the entire semester, so you'd better learn to get along," he says in a thick, Southern mumble. The back of the classroom makes it easier for me to go unnoticed but heaps harder to understand what the heck the man is saying.

He starts calling out our names in pairs, assigning lab partners. Each pair stands up and takes their places at one of the lab tables situated around the perimeter of the room.

"Chloe Paulson."

I tentatively raise my hand. Mr. Pike peers over his glasses at me.

"You'll be partnered with Hunter Ward."

A dark-haired boy seated a few desks in front of me raises his hand. He's sitting next to what has to be his clone, almost identical in their features aside from the other boy's shorter hair. The short-haired boy gives Hunter a fist bump as he stands up to leave.

"Find yourselves a table, please."

I sling my bookbag over my shoulder, watching Hunter do the same. He meets me near the back of the classroom.

"Should we take this one?" he asks, his voice already deepened, unlike most of the freshman boys at our school. He's tall—way taller than me—and his floppy dark hair is shiny and smooth, like he combs it out with leave-in conditioner every night.

"Sure." I shrug.

I struggle a little bit to get up onto the stool waiting for me at the lab table. My lack of height and prosthetic back brace majorly limit my upper-body mobility, and I feel my cheeks redden as I clumsily hop up onto my seat. I pray that Hunter doesn't notice my rigid posture—or, heaven forbid, that he catch a glimpse of the thick, white plastic brace I've got on under my clothes.

I take out my planner and pencil, intent on writing notes on the syllabus Mr. Pike handed out.

"Wow, you're so organized," Hunter's low voice rumbles in my ear, startling me, sending my pencil flying out of my hand. It clatters onto the floor, earning us a squint from Mr. Pike from his perch on his desk.

I feel my stomach plummet to the depths of my toes. Dropping a pencil is literally one of my recurring nightmares.

Bending down to pick up something you've dropped is easy for most people. But *most people* don't have a piece of armor hidden under their shirt, preventing them from simply bending over. My face burns red hot as I realize I'm going to have to hop down off my stool and try to climb back up again without drawing attention from the rest of my class.

Deep breaths, Chloe. It's not a big deal.

Yeah, OKAY, inner monologue. You try taking deep breaths with a thick, hot plastic corset pressing against your stomach and rib cage twenty-three hours a day. That one hour you get out of the brace? That's spent going on a run and taking a shower. And right now is *not* your freedom hour.

I exhale slowly, stretching my toes in preparation to hop down off the stool. They've almost reached the ground when Hunter quickly slides off his own stool, picking up my pencil.

As he's standing back up, his elbow knocks into my stomach, a hollow sound echoing through the classroom as his bones collide with my brace.

His eyebrows dip down, and he glances over at my torso. I'm horrified. Done for. Dead to the world.

Five minutes into the first period, and my lab partner probably thinks I'm a cyborg.

I ease back into my seat, and he hands the pencil to me with a crooked grin. His eyes are hazel brown, rimmed in long lashes. He's cute. Super cute. Cutest boy I've seen at Ridgeview thus far.

"Thank you," I whisper.

"Chloe, right?"

I nod, swallowing.

"I'm Hunter."

I nod again, my voice apparently taking a lunch break.

"What kind of shield are you hiding under there?" He grins, gesturing to my stomach. "I won't be picking a fight with you anytime soon."

My blush deepens. The last thing I want to be talking about with the cute boy sitting next to me is my scoliosis in all its crooked glory.

"You don't have to tell me if you don't want to." He leans closer. "But I promise I'll keep your secret."

I look up at him from under my lashes. Cute *and* nice? I think I hit the lab-partner jackpot.

I shrug, trying not to look embarrassed but feeling thoroughly humiliated as I hear the words pour out of my own mouth.

"It's a back brace. I have scoliosis, so it's supposed to help prevent the curve in my spine from getting worse while I'm still growing."

Hunter's eyes widen in genuine interest. "Dope."

Uncomfortable? Yes. Unusual? Absolutely. But *dope*? Never would I ever label my idiopathic scoliosis as dope. Or awesome. Or literally any other positive adjective. Ever since my diagnosis in the middle of eighth grade, I have resented and tried to hide this part of myself.

And here I am, talking with a stranger about it, who isn't making me feel weird for having a crooked spine or having to wear a prosthetic under my clothing.

"Just so you know," he says. "I'm happy to help pick up anything you might drop this semester. Consider it a part of my lab-partner contract I'm obligated to fulfill."

I fight to hold back a smile. "What's this contract say about my end of the deal?"

"You guarantee to get us at least a B-plus on all our assignments. You look smart. I need your smarts."

He holds out a hand for me to shake. I press my lips together, trying to hide my smile as I slip my hand into his and give it a firm shake up and down.

"Deal."

Chapter 4

Chloe

Pink...blue...pink...blue...

I hold up the two sweaters against my body one after the other in front of the mirror, feeling like I'm in an early 2000's makeover montage. These cropped cardigans are totally a nod to my childhood wardrobe from Limited Too. I was MADE for the comeback of the claw clip and glossy lip. Now all that's missing are a couple of best friends to watch me emerge from my closet and strut around my bedroom until I nail my outfit.

I pause, taking note of the way the dusty-blue cardigan complements the clear, autumn skies outside my window. It's a vibe. I slide my arms into the sleeves and fasten the buttons, leaving the low-cut triangle of my exposed neck bare.

In just a few minutes, I'll be headed to Sunday dinner with the family.

Not my actual family, seeing as I'm an only child and my parents are divorced, both currently living out of state. I'm talking about my *real* family—the Wards.

More specifically, Mama Ward and Hunter's twin, Luke, who is celebrating his recent engagement to my new sister-from-another-mister, Lainey Helms.

Like any pair of brothers, there's always been a good-natured rivalry between Hunter and Luke. I've wondered if watching his twin get married first bothers Hunter at all, if he feels like he's falling behind.

My phone buzzes on my vanity table, and I swipe it open, holding it up to my ear.

"Hey!"

"Hi, uh, Chloe? Miss Chloe Ward?" Hunter says in a clipped English accent.

"How may I help you, sir?"

"Yes, um, I was just calling to confirm your supper with Mr. H. Ward this evening."

"Ooooh..." I suck in a breath. "Tonight, you say?"

"Why, this very hour!"

"I'm so sorry. I may have to cancel."

"Whatever FOR?!"

I have to pull the phone away from my face so that Hunter doesn't hear me snicker.

"You're getting pretty good at that accent, I'll give you that."

"You're *too* kind," Hunter says stiffly, like an obnoxious actor in a period drama. "Your carriage awaits you out front, my lady."

"Be right out."

I smooth a few stray hairs back into my claw clip and slip the chain-link strap of my slim purse over my shoulder before heading to the door.

I'm not the only woman to experience the phenomenon I like to call The Hunter Effect. He can be extremely hard to resist, but I'm proud to say that I have.

My past few boyfriends always felt threatened by my friendship with Hunter—and for good reason. Whenever I'm in the same room with him, it's like everyone else just melts away, and he and I are alone in our own little bubble of inside jokes and years of bonding.

A phone call from Hunter soothes my worries far more than any conversation I've ever had with a boyfriend. Our weekly brunch dates hold more laughter and fun than any dates I've forced myself to go on with other men. I've made a valiant effort to put myself out there, to date, to find connection. And what do I have to show for it? Nada. All those other men have come and gone, and when the relationship inevitably goes south, Hunter is always, *always* there as a safe place for me to land.

Some people in my life (ahem, my estranged mother) have judged me for my longtime friendship with Hunter. She says we've only stayed friends for this long because we're comfortable with each other. To go our separate ways would require too much *work*. She implies that our relationship is unhealthy, that we're stunting each other's growth.

Of course, years of therapy have helped me to filter out the emotionally damaging projections my mother tries to toss my way, but she couldn't be more wrong about Hunter and me. He's the only person I truly trust. The one person I know will never judge me and will always listen. He shows up for me every single day, not only through the words he says but also in how he acts.

And I love him for that.

And if I don't stop letting myself skip down this romantic, wildflower-lined path in my mind, he's going to see my feelings written all over my face in five seconds when I hop into the passenger seat of his car.

"Darlene?" I call out once I'm at the top of the basement stairs. "I'm heading out! You sure you don't want to come have dinner with us tonight?"

She appears in the open doorway, apron on, drying her hands on a towel. Her dark copper skin contrasts with her striking silver hair, and her brown eyes twinkle down at me through her glasses. "Quit worrying about me, Chloe girl!"

I place my hand on the stair railing. "You sure? I can bring you some leftovers if you'd like."

Darlene waves a hand dismissively. "I can fix my own Sunday supper, ma'am. Now get out there before your man comes knocking at my door."

"He's *not* my man."

"You keep telling yourself that, sweetheart." Darlene peers down at me over the tops of her glasses before shooing me back down the stairs. "Don't forget to lock up."

"I won't." I give her a wave over my shoulder.

"Have fun, darlin'."

I tramp back down to the basement, being sure to double check the lock on the door to my apartment as I exit. After taking the steps up to the side yard, I follow the paved path that winds around and connects to the driveway at the front of the house.

Hunter still drives the same white Jeep Wrangler that he drove in high school. I can't even count the number of ice cream cones I've dripped on those floor mats or how much popcorn I've accidentally dropped on the seat. I even keep a pair of my sunglasses in the console—*that's* how often I'm riding shotgun.

I yank the door open and have to use both hands to hoist myself up into the seat. I wish his car had one of those fancy steps that makes climbing into a tall vehicle easier for someone vertically challenged like me.

"Hey, Chlo," Hunter says, flashing a grin in my direction that makes my heart go into shock. Every. Single. Time. You'd think after years of taking shot after shot of his charisma, the effect would wear down, but I swear his charm just gets more potent with time.

He wears glasses while he drives, and he always reclines back in his chair so far that his hands barely reach the steering wheel.

"Are you trying to nap and drive at the same time?" I ask as I snap the door shut and pull my seatbelt on. "If so, I'll drive."

"You can't reach the pedals."

I shoot him a glare. "Rude."

"But true."

I roll my eyes as he starts to back out of the driveway, his head tilted up at the rearview mirror.

"You didn't even do a shoulder check, Hunter," I say, stepping into my role as his designated backseat driver. "You could have hit someone."

"But I didn't." He gives me an appreciative onceover, making my mind go completely blank. Busy tone. *Chloe is currently unavailable. Would you like to leave a message?* "You look...nice."

I place my palms over my bare knees to cover them, feeling vulnerable under his gaze.

"Thanks." I scrunch my nose up as I look his way. He's got one of my favorite sweaters on. Gray-blue. Fitted and slim.

I shake my head at him as I lean my elbow on the side of the car window. I press my knuckles to my lips, watching the space between the houses grow wider and wider as we drive through the suburbs of Franklin.

"How'd your edits go today?"

Hunter shrugs. "Fine. Those shots in the woods turned out really cool."

"I can't wait to see the finished product."

"How's Miss Darlene today?" Hunter asks.

"Oh, you know..." I rest my chin in my hand, getting jostled as Hunter speeds over a bump. "She's good. Just her usual sassy self."

An old friend of my grandmother's, Darlene is a seventy-three-year-old widow with enough pep in her step to keep her spritely until she's at least one hundred. I've lived in her basement apartment in Franklin for nearly five years now. After her husband passed, she couldn't bear to leave the home she'd raised her children in, so I'd offered to be her roommate, to pay rent, and to help take care of the place so she could stay. She has the coziest kitchen where we spend a lot of time together, chatting over tea and whatever dessert she's taken the time to whip up that day.

Darlene is darling. The most purehearted, loving woman I've ever known. She's like family to me, too.

I count my blessings every day for the good people I have in my life to love and be loved by. Love wasn't something that was in abundance in my childhood and teenage years, but as a grown woman, I now hold on with a fierceness to the ones I love. Darlene and Hunter make up the top of my list.

"Did you ever read that book she gave you?"

Hunter grimaces, a guilty expression on his handsome face. "Oops...must have gotten moved to the bottom of my TBR pile."

I give him a nice smack on his shoulder. "What TBR pile? You mean the stack of mail you keep on your kitchen counter?"

"Did *you* read it?"

I shift in my seat. "Well...no...but..."

Hunter gives me a pointed look. "Don't go throwing rocks from a glass house."

"I was hoping you could give me the SparkNotes version, just like I did for you in English class back in the day."

"Even if I gave you the summarized version of every book I read for the rest of my life, I still wouldn't be able to read enough books to pay off my debt to you."

"You're right. I saved your high-school career. You know you owe all your good grades to *moi*."

"You were the best tutor I ever had." Hunter flashes me a smile as he makes a right turn. "And also, a know-it-all. Some things never change."

I scowl at him. "Just like how you refuse to eat a burger with anything on it besides ketchup."

"I'm a simple guy, ok?" Hunter raises his hands defensively. "Speaking of burgers, I'm pretty sure Luke's grilling tonight. Might be our last chance before the weather turns."

I peer up at the cornflower-blue sky, the fading sunlight flickering between the trees as we drive. "Good. I'm making you a Chloe burger, then—with all the fixin's."

"Hard pass."

"Hunter, if you never try anything new, you will never find out if you *like* other things!" We've had this conversation a thousand times. I've yet to get Hunter to try sushi, or Brussels sprouts, or even guacamole. He insists that he doesn't like things before he even tastes them. Sometimes his stubbornness drives me bonkers.

And then he looks at me with those eyes, the color of iced coffee with a pour of cream, and my plans to change him float away like dust on the wind. Because all of Hunter's quirks, his insanely boring burger order, his ever-growing mountain of mail that he refuses to sort through...all of it adds up into the sum of who he is. And I accept it all.

And I want it all.

Insert tragic sigh.

Maybe, in the next life, we'll come back as different people, becoming each other's soulmates through a series of kismet cosmic events. Because the chances of Hunter and I moving out of the friend zone are so, so, slim. Next to none. Non-existent.

At least...that's what I tell myself to keep my heart from getting trampled.

Naturally, we're the last to arrive at family dinner. In Luke's mind, five minutes early is already late.

Hunter pulls up the driveway behind his twin brother's glittering black Porsche, leaving a minuscule amount of space between his bumper and the Jeep's fender.

"Ooooh..." I whistle. "Bold move."

"It's what I like to call precision parking." Hunter throws the Jeep in park and gives me a saucy wink.

"Your precision might just cost you your relationship with your brother. He's going to lose it when he sees how close you came to hitting his precious car."

"Nah, it'll be alright."

Hunter jumps down out of the Jeep and circles around back to open my door, just like he has since the day he got his license.

His mother, Maggie, let him take his driver's test first thing on the morning of his sixteenth birthday. He was so proud, pulling into Ridgeview High's parking lot in his blinding-white, brand-new Jeep. He made me promise to let him drive me home from school that day. I'll never forget the way he opened the door for me to climb in like he was my hired driver.

"That's what you said before you ran that stop sign the day you got your license, remember? And look how that turned out."

I swing my legs out the car door and hop down, bending my knees to cushion my landing. When you're as short as I am, you've got to take all the precautions you can when jumping from dangerous heights.

"I swear to this day, that officer was just trying to fill his daily quota," Hunter insists, shutting the door behind me. "Or he was bored out of his mind. That ticket was totally undeserved."

"Consider yourself warned," I say. "Luke's not going to be happy about your parking job."

"Chloe, Chloe, Chloe..." Hunter wraps an arm around my shoulders, pulling me into his side. The temptation to slide my arm around his lower back, to feel the muscles around his perfectly straight spine is so powerful that he must feel me tense up in an effort to resist him. "Just relax. Quit worrying so much."

The smell of smoke from the grill greets my nose as we walk together to the backyard, bringing with it vibrant memories of summer, baseball games, and cookouts by the pool. The early autumn wind brushes over the back of my neck, signaling the coming change in the seasons. I love the transition from the heat and wild energy of summer to the coziness of fall.

Hunter unlatches the porch lock and pushes it open for us to pass through. The Ward family home sits on several acres of land, complete with a massive sports court and a pool. The white fence that surrounds their yard is lined with tall cottonwoods that have matured over the twenty-five years since Hunter's parents first built the place.

"I challenge you to a round of tetherball before the night is through," Hunter says.

"Challenge accepted." We give each other a firm handshake, nodding sharply.

"You're going down, Shortstack." His dark eyes glitter in the fading light.

"Not tonight." I point one of my toes, lengthening my leg out with impeccable form that would have made my ballet teachers proud. "I've got my platform sneakers on."

"Shoot. I'm done for." Hunter smirks. "After you." He lets me walk ahead of him up the back porch steps.

I've made it to the third step when I feel his hand land on the small of my back, gently pressing into my spine—my very crooked, S-shaped spine that I blame entirely for my lack of height. I won the genetic lottery from my maternal grandmother, whose scoliosis was so severe that it gave her a hump in her back.

Thankfully, my curvature was never serious enough to require surgery. I've, instead, experimented with a plethora of treatments to help relieve my discomfort from the time I was diagnosed at thirteen years old.

I like to keep my upper body fully covered and my back hidden from most people, so they would never know about my deformity. Even as an adult woman, I still sometimes carry the fear of judgment from others should they catch a glimpse of my misshapen upper half.

But Hunter? He's always known about my crooked spine and has never made me feel weird about it. In fact, his hand is making itself right at home along the twisted curve of my lower back right now.

I tune into the warmth of his palm through my sweater, my skin breaking out in a rush of chills as if there's nothing between his hand and the skin of my back. He closes the space between us, trailing right behind me as I reach the top of the stairs.

I'm half tempted to close my eyes, cross my arms over my chest and do an impromptu trust fall to see how attentive he is to the fact that we're touching.

But I remind myself that Hunter's gesture feels sweet. Friendly. He knows his way around women, so I try not to read too much into the placement of his hands whenever they come within a five-mile radius of my body.

Heaven help me. He's making it hard not to analyze every moment of contact when my skin and heart react as if his touch is intentional, giving me a sign that he potentially sees me as someone other than his best friend.

Take it down a notch, Chlo. Enough wishful thinking. I've seen Hunter in action. He hugs everyone. Touching me is probably the equivalent of high-fiving one of his bro friends. Totally tame, totally platonic, and totally not flirtatious.

Chapter 5

Hunter

As soon as we reach the top of the porch steps, Chloe takes several swift strides away from me. I drop my now empty hand, wishing I had a real excuse, or at least permission, to keep my hand plastered to the small of her back.

"Hey, hey!" Lainey calls out, waving to us from the table she's seated at on the deck.

"Look who decided to show up," Luke says from his designated perch at the grill. He's wearing a Duke apron, and I know it's just to spite me because I'm a Tar Heels fan.

"Miss me?" I give my brother a slap on the back. "Nice apron."

"You like it?"

"Hate it."

"Hey, now..." Lainey says, rising from her seat. "Watch yourself, Hunter. That apron was a gift from my daddy."

I back away, hands raised in innocence. "I've got nothing against your daddy, Lainey—except maybe his terrible choice in sports teams."

The back door swings open, and my mother steps out, her arms loaded with a stack of plates, linen napkins, and cutlery.

"Hey, you two!" She smiles brightly.

"Hey, Mama." I plant a quick kiss on her cheek before shifting the plates into my grip.

"Miss Chloe. Looking beautiful as always." Mama wraps Chloe in a warm embrace. "So glad you could come tonight."

Family dinner wouldn't be the same without Chloe here. She's been spending most Sunday nights with our family since her parents' divorce in high school, and I wouldn't have it any other way.

"How are you?" Chloe asks, tenderness in her voice.

"Better now that you're all here." Mama's smile doesn't reach her eyes. Has she been crying? Maybe someone said something to her at church today, and she's missing Dad a bit more tonight. I give my mother a squeeze with my free arm, and we share a knowing look.

"Burgers are almost ready," Luke says.

There's a hustle that lasts a few minutes as we all pitch in to get dinner on the table. Once we're settled in, Luke says grace, and then we start passing food around.

Chloe has the audacity to immediately slap a pickle onto my bun.

"Not today."

"It's now or never," she whispers. "Man up, and eat your pickle."

I wrinkle my nose at the sour, circular object that's dampening my bun. "I can't do it."

She rolls her eyes, snatching the pickle up and tossing it into her mouth. "You are missing out on *so* many flavors in life."

"I like my flavors. My flavors are just fine," I say, squirting ketchup onto my plain burger. "In fact, my flavors are offended."

"Tell your basic flavors to suck it up."

"Basic?" I snort. "Try *simple*. I'm a simple man, Chloe. 'Bout time you accepted that fact."

She's about to retort when Luke cuts in, causing us both to turn in his direction.

"How'd the shoot go yesterday?" Luke takes a bite out of his burger.

"It was great," I answer. "Chloe *loved* the female lead I chose."

Chloe stomps on my shoe under the table. I click my tongue at her.

"Oh no." Lainey fixes me with a curious smile. "Was she a diva?"

"Something along those lines," Chloe says, her face hidden behind her napkin as she chews.

"Chloe, why don't *you* ever step out in front of the camera?" Mama asks, and Chloe nearly chokes on her food. "You're more beautiful than any of those girls I've seen in the music videos."

HEAR, HEAR. I have never heard a truer statement in my life.

"Oh, Mama Ward, you are too sweet to me." Chloe collects herself by taking a sip of her drink. "But I could never act the way those girls do in front of a camera."

Lainey laughs, covering her full mouth with her hand.

"What are you making those ladies *do*, Hunter?" Mama asks, eyebrows raised sharply.

"Oh, no...that's not what I meant..." Chloe's face reddens. She's so cute when she's embarrassed. I just want to snuggle her up and smooth away the flush that's growing on her cherry-red cheeks. *Come 'ere, you...*

"She means that she's not cut out to play the part of a diva," I explain. Chloe throws me a look of relief. "She's too down to earth."

"But that's exactly the type of girl these country singers are writing about, aren't they?" Lainey points out. "The girl next door. The take-back-home girl."

"Every artist has a different vision for the girl they feature in their video," I say. "Connor Cane, for instance, wanted someone who looked like a heartbreaker for 'Cry, Baby'."

"Sounds like he got one." Luke snorts.

"Just curious. If you were a singer, what kind of girl would you cast in your music video, Luke?" I grin. "What kind of woman could play your love interest? Lainey Helms, reincarnated."

"What music video?" Luke laughs, saving himself from having to label his fiancée. "You know I can't sing, bro."

"Runs in the family, I'm afraid," Maggie says apologetically. "Sorry, Lainey."

"Hey, that's alright." Lainey smiles over at Luke. "He's got lots of other great qualities that I'm sure will be passed down to our children."

"Whoa..." I say loudly. "Already talking about children, are we? Plural."

Lainey rolls her eyes, and Luke tosses a grape at me, which I lean over to catch perfectly in my open mouth. I stand up, arms outstretched, waiting for someone to acknowledge my impeccable grape play.

"Back to the original topic of conversation..." Mama says, patting my back from her seat at the head of the table next to me. Aaaand that's my cue to sit down. "You really should cast

Chloe in one of your next videos. I think she'd do a beautiful job."

Chloe's eyes widen, her cheeks full of burger.

"What do you think, Chlo?" I nudge her with my shoulder. "Wanna star in my next cut?"

She gulps. "I could *never*. I'd get so nervous I'd throw up or trip, embarrass myself somehow."

"Chloe *did* agree to help me cast the next video, so I'm sure our next actress will be much more satisfactory for all of the opinionated people at this table."

Lainey nods her approval. "'Attagirl. Find someone cool!"

The conversation shifts as Lainey starts recounting funny stories about Ella Mae, her songwriter roommate, and her celebrity encounters in Nashville. I tune out, my thoughts circling back to my mother's comment about casting Chloe in a video.

I watch Chloe roll her shoulders back, straightening in her chair. She must be uncomfortable already. I can't imagine how much pain she's in after the end of a long shoot like yesterday. If she didn't insist on booking herself out all day, every day, she'd actually have time to go see a chiropractor or a massage therapist to help relieve some of her discomfort.

I know I'm partially to blame for the fact that Chloe doesn't have a lot of spare time to take care of herself. She always prioritizes my shoots and then fills in the rest of her time with referrals or clients who find her via social media, and then back-to-back weddings every weekend. The girl never stops. While I admire her work ethic, my concern about the condition of her back is growing every time I see her wincing in pain or stretching out when she thinks no one is looking.

My wheels are turning now. Sarah definitely made more money on Connor's shoot yesterday than Chloe did. I know the general ballpark of what actors in these music videos make, especially on shoots that are backed by a major label. That kind of money could be the bump Chloe needs to hire a second makeup artist. An assistant. It's a goal she's been working toward for a while now.

She's swirling a French fry through ketchup on her plate, the stacks of delicate rings on her fingers twinkling in the glow from the porch light. I swallow, listening to her laugh at something Lainey said. Chloe never complains. She doesn't draw attention to herself, even when she might be struggling or in pain. I would love more than anything to help ease some of her burden so she can get more massages, more time to read, and more time to rest.

But I know Chloe. And I know that she'd never agree to something like that. Reserved, shy, quiet Chloe would wilt under the blazing lights and stares of a crew on a music-video set. Not to mention having to play the part of somebody's love interest on camera. That would do her in. And probably me, too. I'd hate to have to watch her get cozy with some hotshot country bro.

But this isn't about me. This is about Chloe. And I'm going to have to be very strategic in how I pitch this idea to her.

I can picture her shooting me down immediately, then darting away like a frightened deer. She'd probably ghost me for a few days, afraid that if she let me see her, I'd drag her off to star in some music video against her will.

I'll have to suggest it at an opportune moment, when she's open and willing to receive it.

Chloe stands up, helping to clear plates from the table. I follow suit, and she eyes me warily as we walk together into the house.

"Why are you so quiet?" she asks cautiously. "Usually when you're quiet, you're either stressed about something or you're plotting."

"Just thinking," I say, loading my plate into the dishwasher. "Congratulations."

I thin my eyes down at Chloe as she joins me at the sink. "Ha-ha. You ready to get crushed in a game of tetherball?"

She juts her chin out. "Ready to defeat *you*, as always."

We finish the dishes before heading out to the backyard. The tetherball is bouncing against the pole with the wind, the rope frayed from years of use. Chloe and I used to spend hours battling it out on the tetherball court as teenagers, then refueling with ice cream from Rosie's down the street. The tradition continues whenever we have the chance to squeeze a few games in.

"Loser buys the goods tonight," I say, extending my hand for her to shake as we take our places on either side of the tetherball court.

She slips her hand into mine and gives it a jostle. "Looking forward to my triple scoop, on you."

I clap my hands together, rubbing my palms to warm up. Chloe cranks her neck from side to side, swinging her arms back and forth a few times. You'd think we were getting ready to run a cross-country meet like we'd done together countless times in high school.

"I think, to make it fair, you should play on your knees," Chloe says, grabbing the ball with a smirk.

"Even if I were to reduce myself to the size of a hobbit, I would still beat you."

"Them's fightin' words, Mr. Ward."

Chloe walks to the back corner of her side of the court. She pushes the ball up into the air and knocks it with all her might around the front side of the pole toward me.

My height certainly gives me an unfair advantage. I easily knock the ball back in her direction. Chloe palms the ball, swinging it at an upward angle so that it cruises right over my head and back around to her side of the pole.

"Who's the hobbit NOW?" she taunts.

"Still you!" I return the ball, and it clears Chloe's outstretched hands, once, twice...

Her fingers catch on the rope before I can fling it around a third time, and she chucks it back at me. We toss the ball back and forth a few times before I get it over her head again.

The rope shortens with each turn around the pole until Chloe doesn't stand a chance of reaching it. The ball knocks against the coiled rope, signaling my win.

"Hey-o!" I call out.

"You got lucky," she mumbles, slapping the ball around the pole to unwind the rope.

"Don't be a sore loser, Chloe." I grab the ball from her, holding it close to my chest as her eyes flash up at me. "Remember what Coach always taught us."

"To let the pee flow if we've gotta go mid-race?"

I bark out a laugh. "Well, that and the other sound piece of advice she gave us."

"To lose..."—Chloe flutters her hand through the air and drops a flourishing curtsy—"with grace."

"Not that you ever had to experience that in cross country." I return her curtsy with a bow. "Miss State Champion."

She rolls her eyes. "Whatever. I lost plenty of times."

"Not as much as I did." I fling the ball into the air, starting our second game.

Chloe takes the W on round two, and I win our third game.

Chloe places her hands on her lower back and bends from side to side. "Darn. I was really looking forward to splurging on your dime tonight."

"We could order the kitchen sink. If we finish it in ten minutes, then it's free, and neither one of us has to pay."

"Hunter, when have we *ever* been able to finish the kitchen sink?" She laughs as we make our way back to the house.

"We were *this* close last time. Maybe we could convince the lovebirds to come help us out."

"I really admire your optimism. But it's not humanly possible to consume that much ice cream in one sitting."

"I beg to differ."

Luke and Lainey have already got their shoes on and are embracing Mama on their way out the door.

"Who's buying tonight?" Mama smiles, wrapping her arm around Chloe, who grudgingly points a finger at herself.

Mama tsks at me. "Nonsense. I raised him better. He will buy you as much ice cream as your heart desires. I'll make sure of it."

Chloe leans into my mom's hug and grins. "Don't you worry about his chivalry, now. He always offers to pay, even if sometimes I refuse to let him."

My turn to hug Mom comes, and she pats me on the back before pulling away. "You drive safe now, you hear me? No running stop signs with my Chloe in your passenger seat."

"Alright, Mama. Love you."

We trail after the engaged couple out to the driveway.

Luke stops dead in his tracks when he sees how close I pulled up behind his car.

I grin wickedly at Luke in response to his glare.

"Told you," Chloe mumbles.

"You really need to learn how to park, Hunter," Luke says, his eyes full of threats he's not daring to speak out loud in front of our company.

"And you really need to learn how to lighten up." I give him a salute from behind Chloe's door I've opened to let her into the Jeep. "See you at Rosie's?"

"Not tonight," Luke says. "But you kids have fun."

I grab Chloe's elbow, helping her hop up into her seat. I climb in on the driver's side, and Chloe huffs as she tugs her seatbelt on. "I can climb into your car all by myself, thanks."

"You sure?" I grin. "You seem a little out of breath."

"Still recovering from that grueling tetherball tournament."

"Ice cream's on me tonight," I say as I throw the car into reverse.

"As it should be." Chloe crosses her arms. "You totally cheated."

"Prove it."

She rolls her eyes at me, settling into her seat. I had beat her fair and square, but Chloe's competitive spirit runs free and wild when she loses.

I almost wish she had won, just so I could have seen her victory dance. She busts out into the running man or a Michael-Jackson-worthy moonwalk. But it's probably for the best that I didn't see her dance tonight, because it would have gotten me all hot and bothered. I would have been overflowing with the desire I feel for her, the desire I keep bottled up and hidden at the very back of my shelf of feelings, where no one can see it.

Every so often, I let myself take a little sip. Soak in her beauty. Let my gaze linger on her beautiful features, her soft skin, the adorable tiny overlap of her two front teeth.

But tonight is not one of those nights, I remind myself. I've got to play it cool if I want to have any chance of her accepting my offer to step into the role of lead actress in my next music video. It's the least I could do to help lighten the load the girl of my dreams insists on carrying.

Chapter 6

Hunter

Fifteen years earlier...

"Alright!" Coach Cline, our gym teacher, claps his hands to get our attention. "Everybody get over here to the starting line."

The group of moody freshmen shuffle their feet, arms crossed and grumbling. Eventually, we all make it to the starting line. I start hopping up and down to warm up in the chilly spring air.

"I want four laps. One mile. Ready...go."

A couple of the bulkier dudes in our gym class take off running like their life depends on it. Everyone else moans and groans, easing onto the track at Ridgeview High in a mass of imploding hormones and bitter teenage angst.

I'm somewhere in the middle of the pack for the first lap, but I find that my long legs are able to carry me without much effort until I'm ahead of everyone but a few of the other boys. I find my rhythm, legs striking the track in an even tempo. I try to keep my breathing even, focusing on reaching the next landmark in front of me. A tree. A fence pole. A sign post. Once I pass it, I fix my eyes on the next one.

As I round the corner, I notice that there's one student left sitting alone on the bleachers. Not running. Exempt from the mile today.

I draw closer, glancing over as I cross the finish line.

Chloe Paulson.

She's sitting a few rows up, legs crossed at the ankles, hands resting on her knees. Her posture is impeccable, and I'm probably one of the few people who knows the real reason why.

I throw her a wave as I run by, and she raises her eyebrows in surprise before giving me a shy wave in return.

We were lab partners for an entire semester, and yet, every time I see her, she still acts like we barely know each other. It's like I have to crack the Chloe code anew every single time we run into each other. She'll warm up to me after a few minutes, but she's not a talker like I am.

I've known about her back brace for months now, but it honestly rarely crosses my mind. Chloe to me is just...Chloe. Pretty. Smart. Witty—once she's comfortable enough to speak up. It hadn't even occurred to me that she'd have to sit out of gym class because of her scoliosis. I wonder if she's embarrassed, worried about the questions and teasing she's going to get from our peers because we're all out here running while she's on the bleachers.

I pick up the pace so I can get this mile out of the way and talk to Chloe. I'm not really thinking too much about it, just lengthening my stride, pumping my arms at my sides.

Mr. Cline whistles as I cross the finish line on my final lap. I slow down to a walk, breathing heavily as I circle back to where he's sitting.

"You ever run before, Ward?" he asks, holding up a stopwatch.

I shrug. "I mean, not really. I play baseball."

He works a piece of gum in his mouth, popping it in his back teeth. "My wife and I coach the cross-country team. Tryouts are next week. You should come out. Your mile is wicked fast."

He jots down some details on a scrap of paper and hands it to me. "Thanks, Coach. I'll think about it."

"You do that."

I hike up the bleachers until I reach Chloe, plopping down next to her on the cold metal bench.

"Nice view from up here."

She glances over at me, giving me a shy smile. I don't miss the way her cheeks turn pink at my comment.

"Sure is."

I lean back, placing my elbows on the bench behind me. "So, how'd you get out of running today?"

"Doctor's note," she says softly. "I can only take my brace off for one hour a day, and I'd rather not use up that hour at school."

She meets my eyes for a moment. "But I wish I could. Believe me. I'd rather be out there running right now than sitting here doing nothing."

I take a deep breath, trying to slow my heart rate. "Coach Cline said cross-country tryouts are next week. We should go together."

Chloe shoots a nervous glance my way. "Oh, no...I'm not, like, a fast runner...I just like to run for fun."

"Me, too." I shrug. "Might be fun to just try it and see what happens."

I hand her the slip of paper Coach had given me, and she reads it over.

"My dad ran cross country," she says. "In college, too."

"No way," I exclaim. "Chloe, this is your birthright. You have to come try out with me."

She chews on her bottom lip. "I guess I could find somewhere to stash the brace after school...just for a little bit."

"I'll help you," I offer. "My locker is by the gym. We could put it in there."

She gives me a tentative smile. "Really?"

"Yeah, I'll come find you after my last class. We can change together."

Chloe reddens again.

"I mean..." I backpedal. "Not, like, change together, but like...we can get ready in separate locker rooms and walk out here together."

"Uh-huh."

We're quiet for a moment, watching most of the class walk at a leisurely pace around the track.

"Next time we have to do this," I say, "I'll walk with you so you don't have to sit here alone."

"You can't do that." She knocks her shoulder into mine. "I saw how fast you were running out there. It would kill you to walk."

I wave my hand dismissively through the air. "Nah. I'd be fine."

She gives me a grateful smile. "If you wouldn't mind walking, I'd like that."

"Me, too." I grin back at her.

Chapter 7

Chloe

Is there such a thing as an ice-cream hangover? Because if so, I think I'm in the thick of one.

Hunter had made the call to order Rosie's massive "kitchen sink" again last night, convinced that, this time, we'd be able to polish it off and get our money back. But just as I'd predicted, he's out fifty bucks, and I'm out of every good thing that used to exist inside my gut. So much for trying to diversify my microbiome.

I told myself that it would be worth it if I got to extend my evening with Hunter.

What I didn't consider was just how hard it was going to be to get up and run at 7 a.m. the following morning.

At least I'm not alone in my sugar overdose. Hunter is clearly dragging, moving about as fast as a turtle toward the track at Ridgeview High.

"You good?" I call out to him, lifting my leg into a quad stretch at the starting line.

He raises a hand in response, his hood pulled up over his head. The air is brisk, almost too cold to be comfortable standing still. But I know just how refreshing it's going to feel flowing into my lungs once we're off and running.

"Well, good morning, sunshine!" I say as Hunter shuffles toward me. "And how are you feeling this fine morning?"

He squints at me, sleep still in his half-shut eyes. "Someone's chipper."

"How could I not be?" I gesture to the sky overhead, painted a pale blue with the risen sun. "It's a glorious morning!"

"That may be so, but I'm still suffering from last night." Hunter clutches his stomach and grins at me. "It tasted so good at the time. I can't even be upset about it."

"You gonna be alright?"

He grunts something unintelligible.

My hand finds the curve of his shoulder muscle, and I give him a squeeze. "You'll feel better once we get moving."

He nods, shifting his hood from off his head. Hunter's dark hair is swept over to the side, looking like he's already styled it. Other men would have to use tons of product and styling tools to achieve Hunter's version of bedhead.

"So, how far are we going today?" Hunter pats his legs to warm them up. "Half mile?"

I shrug. "Three. Maybe four."

His jaw slacks. "You serious? I haven't run in months, and you're going to make me start off with a 5k?"

I roll my eyes. "Says the man who could run ten miles without breaking a sweat back in high school."

"Keyword: high school."

"That's two words."

"Whatever."

I tap my watch, starting the timer that will help me pace my miles.

"I'm just messing with you. I usually run two and then see how I'm feeling."

"How about we start with one?"

"Come on, Hunter. Be a man, and run your two miles. You ready?"

Hunter shrugs noncommittally. I throw him a smile and then dart down the track, leaving him to kick himself into gear behind me.

My short legs are no match for Hunter's long, muscled ones. He catches me in a few strides. We fall into pace with each other and run in silence until we're halfway around the track.

"Man, I haven't been here in forever," Hunter says. "It's like nothing has changed."

Those same silver bleachers I'd sat on during gym class are still there. So are the pennant flags painted onto the brick walls of the school, noting state championships won by student athletes over the years.

"This track is so much nicer than the old one." I gesture to the field in the center of the track. "And the turf. It's so plush."

Hunter takes a few theatrical bounding leaps forward, arms pumping at his sides. "So much bounce."

"Right? Would have been nice back in the day."

I try to keep my breathing even as my heart rate picks up and we cross the starting line.

"One lap down. Seven more to go."

I glance over at Hunter. His eyes have brightened up, and his lips and cheeks are flushed red from the morning cold. He's enjoying this. I can tell.

"See?" I say. "Doesn't it feel good to run again?"

He sighs dramatically. "Nuttin' like the fresh sea air to get your soul a'soarin'." His Irish accent is spot on, and I let out a breathless laugh.

"Stop!" I clutch my side. "Ugh, now I've got a stitch."

Hunter snorts. "A *what* now? You *still* call it that?"

"Because that is what it's called!" The pinching in my side intensifies as my side cramps.

"Everyone else on the planet calls it a side ache," Hunter says matter-of-factly. "But you have to go and be different and call it a *stitch*."

"So what?"

"Chloe, that's a Disney character, not a running-induced condition."

"Tomato, tom-ah-to," I say, feeling the tingling in my legs increasing as I push them to keep up with Hunter. I may be more conditioned than he is, but I still have to take two strides for every one of his.

"So, what do you usually do when you're here running by yourself?" Hunter asks.

"I throw my headphones in and get pumped."

"Sorry to make you run without music. That's way harder."

"Why don't you provide the music for us?" I suggest.

"Happily."

Hunter peels off his sweatshirt, pulling his workout shirt up with it. I try not to dwell on the fact that the lines of his stomach are defined, etched into his smooth skin. I force myself to look ahead down the track as Hunter untangles himself from his sweatshirt.

"I'm...too sexy for my shirt..." he starts singing in a low voice.

I try to hide my smile from him by glancing across the turf to the opposite side of the track. "Next song, please.'"

"It's tearin' up my heart when I'm with you…and when we are apart…"

I bust out laughing, nearly tripping over my feet at Hunter's off-key attempt at a classic NSYNC song.

"I've changed my mind," I say, my voice high and breathy from laughing—and not at all because I'm reading too much into his song choice and how it might apply to our relationship. "No more music from you."

"I'm insulted!" Hunter shouts. "If NSYNC ever needs some ghost background vocals, you know my voice would blend right in."

I shake my head, my body warming as we near the end of our fourth lap. We pick up the pace as we kick off our second mile. I can feel Hunter's energy returning, his muscle memory kicking in as his feet pound the track in a steady rhythm alongside mine.

Running with Hunter on this track brings back a flood of memories from high school. Watching him smoke the other boys on the team during warmups and practice drills. Proudly wearing our Ridgeview High Cross-Country t-shirts along with the rest of the team on meet days. The exhilarating feeling of pushing myself past what I thought were my limits, running longer, harder, and faster than I'd thought I was capable of.

Trying not to peek at Hunter's muscular upper legs in his itty, bitty cross country shorts. GULP.

There are also a few memories sprinkled in that I've tried to stuff down into the depths of my mind. Like Hunter's steady stream of cheerleader girlfriends he played through like a deck of cards. Our horrible health teacher whose idea of curriculum included forcing us to watch episode after episode of *Criminal Minds* during our class period—gave me nightmares for an entire semester.

And of course, the divorce.

The months of uncertainty during my junior year as my parents dissolved their marriage and our family.

Hunter would walk with me on the track during gym class when I'd still had my brace and couldn't run. Sophomore and junior year, we'd kept up the tradition by lingering long after practice was over, walking in endless loops. We'd spend those late afternoons just talking. Those talks with my best friend were a major part of what helped me get through that heartbreaking season.

I'm not sure if Hunter will ever know how much it meant that he so generously gave me that time, night after night, week after week. Looking back, I wonder how his girlfriends didn't hate me for stealing him away so much. Maybe they did. I'd probably been too wrapped up in my own problems to notice theirs.

The second mile passes much more quickly, and Hunter sprints across the finish line about five seconds before me.

"Whoo!" he pants. "Daddy's still got it!"

"I've gotta admit..." I say, trying to catch my breath. "I'm impressed by your mad dash at the end there."

Hunter's an Energizer Bunny now, bouncing on the balls of his feet, high off of endorphins.

"Should we go again?" He twirls his finger around. "One more mile?"

"If you're up for it, I'm down."

He immediately takes off running, leaving me in the dust. I roll my eyes and put my head down, lifting my knees higher in an effort to catch up with him.

I'm almost on his tail when, mid-stride, I feel a painful pinch in my lower back, shooting sharp daggers down my tailbone. I take a few more steps before I'm forced to wheel my legs to a stop.

I plant my palms on my lower back and bend over, trying to release the cramped muscle. I can feel it locked up and knotted under my hand.

"You okay?" Hunter calls out as he jogs back toward me.

I take a step, wincing as pain shoots up my right side again. "Yeah, but I think my age is starting to show. I tweaked something in my back."

Concern fills Hunter's eyes. He skirts around me, his warm palm resting on my back where my hands had just been. "There?" He gently presses a thumb into my lower back, and I hiss as the nerves along my spine zip hotly in response.

"Oof."

"Sorry, Chlo." He slowly applies pressure to the cramped muscle with his thumb, easing into the part of my back that's tighter than a ball made from rubber bands.

I can feel his breath on my hair, slowing with mine as our heart rates come down. I close my eyes and breathe deeply, trying to send relaxing breaths to my bunched-up lower back. The pressure from Hunter's hands is easing the tension, and little by little, I feel the pain start to lessen. He patiently moves his fingers over my crooked spine, gently kneading and pressing into the tight spaces. Chills break out down my arms, and I don't think it's from the cool autumn breeze moving through the spaces between us.

"Is that better?" he asks, his voice low and soft in my ear.

"Yeah, actually." I place my hand over his and give it a squeeze as I turn to face him. "Thank you."

I'm surprised by the line that's creasing his forehead, the way his brows are dipping down as our eyes catch. I can see the unguarded worry held there, and knowing that he's this concerned about me makes my heart start picking up again.

"I'm fine, Hunter," I say, giving his hand a little pat. "My spine will live to see another day, thanks to you."

He's not satisfied with my casual dismissal of this little episode. "How often does this happen to you now?"

I shrug and press my lips together. "I don't know, a couple times a day?"

Hunter's eyebrows shoot up. "Every day? You throw your back out like this *every day*?"

"Pretty much. But thanks to your fancy massage technique, my recovery time will be much shorter."

Hunter glowers down at the track and huffs out a breath. "Chloe, that's not normal, you know that? To have your muscles freak out like that every day?"

I prickle at his use of a word that has haunted me since the day I was diagnosed with scoliosis at thirteen years old.

I lift my chin and cross my arms. "Yes, Hunter. I am well aware that my back is not *normal*."

His eyes soften. "Oh, Chlo, you know that's not what I meant."

I sniff and glance over at the bleachers.

"I'm trying to say that you need help. A chiropractor or a massage therapist. You don't have to live with this kind of pain."

I know he's trying to be helpful, that he's worried about me, but anytime my back is brought up, I feel the need to throw on ten extra-large sweaters and hide every inch of my body from him. It's a reminder that I do not—and never will—have a body like the perfect women he's dated before. The kind who don't have to think twice before throwing on a two-piece swimsuit. Women who can stand up perfectly straight or sit for extended periods of time without losing their minds. Women who look very, very different from me.

"I can handle it, okay?" I say, my tone barbed. "I've dealt with this every day since I was a kid, so I think I'm going to be alright."

"Chloe," Hunter says, exasperated. "Why is it so hard for you to admit that you need to see a doctor? Give me the number of the chiropractor you saw a couple months back. I'll call them myself and make you an appointment."

I grumble and cross my arms over my chest. "I *can't* see a doctor right now, Hunter."

"Why not?"

I sigh. "Because I haven't paid off the bills from my last visit yet."

Hunter furrows his brow. "I thought you said they had a new-patient special. That it was cheap."

I shift on my feet. "I didn't go to the chiropractor that day, Hunter. I went to the emergency room."

He lowers his chin, his expression serious. "You went to the hospital? And you didn't tell me?"

I take in a deep breath. "You were super busy on set. I didn't want to worry you."

Hunter's eyes soften and search mine. "What happened? Why did you go to the ER?"

I feel a blush crawling up my neck. "It's so embarrassing. I haven't told anyone about it because I feel so stupid."

"Chloe."

I grit my teeth together. "I feel like I'm being scolded by a parent right now."

"As you should be! Tell me what happened."

I toe the track with the tip of my shoe. "I thought I had something really wrong with me. I thought my lungs were collapsing or something really dramatic was happening." I swallow. "They did a bunch of tests on me—blood draws, a CAT scan, an X-ray."

Hunter's eyes cut between mine, his mouth pressed into a thin line.

"Turns out it was just a good ol' fashioned panic attack," I say, my voice small.

Hunter is quiet for a moment.

"And now, because of my time in the hospital and all of the useless tests they did on me, I have a massive hospital bill to pay off." I glance up at Hunter. "So, I'm sorry that I'm always making excuses as to why I can't just make an appointment. I literally can't pay for it right now."

I'm waiting for Hunter to lecture me, to tell me that I should have called him instead of driving myself to the emergency room.

But he doesn't say a word. Instead, he slips his arms around my shoulders and pulls me to him. He embraces me, warm and damp from our run, but I don't mind. I allow myself to sink into him.

"I'm so sorry, Chloe," he says. "I didn't know your anxiety was flaring up so badly again."

I'd struggled with anxiety a bit during high school but had never experienced the consuming, gripping fear of a panic attack before, hence why I thought I was *surely* dying when it happened a couple months back.

"It's ok," I insist. "I'm ok."

Hunter releases me, deep concern still present in his expression. "Let's get you back to your car."

I walk slowly, my lower back pinching with every step. But I keep moving, trying to hide the fact that I just want to lie down on the track right now until the pain subsides.

I don't want Hunter to feel sorry for me. I want him to see me as a perfectly capable, strong woman who can handle a little muscle spasm in her back or a panic attack. People deal with these things every day, right? I can handle it.

Tears prick at the edges of my eyes as I near my car, and I suck them back in with every ounce of strength I can muster so Hunter won't see just how much I'm hurting.

Chapter 8

Hunter

There's nothing I hate more than early mornings.
Scratch that.
What I hate even more than waking up before the sun is up is watching my best friend suffer.

Chloe may be soft spoken, but that woman is tough as nails. She's able to hide the constant discomfort from her scoliosis from most people, but she's never been good at hiding it from me. As we've gotten older, the natural health issues resulting from her crooked spine have been piling up at a rapid rate. I wish she hadn't hidden her panic-attack/ER episode from me. I could have been there for her. I could have tried to comfort her, support her in whatever way she needed it.

It's clear that Chloe wants me to think she's got a handle on all of this, but I saw her watery eyes and her pinched expression at the track this morning. She was hurting, and though I tried to help her relieve some of the pain, it was like putting a Band-Aid on a bullet hole. She needs professional, consistent treatment for her back. She needs time off to tend to her mental health. And I'm going to help her get it.

After showering and changing into jeans and a long-sleeve tee, I head to my home office, aka the Ikea desk I've got against one wall of the living area of my tiny one-bedroom apartment. This desk houses my desktop monitors, a literal mountain of hard drives, my noise-canceling headphones, and a laptop. I plop down in my swivel chair, pull out my phone, and dial Connor Cane's number.

He answers on the second ring.

"My man!" he says.

"Hey, Connor." I hold my phone between my shoulder and ear, freeing up my hands to type in my password on my computer.

"How's the 'Cry, Baby' edit coming along?"

I open the Adobe Premiere project for his music video. "It's looking awesome, man. I'm going to work on it some more today. I should have a cut for your label by the end of the week."

"Sick. I'm stoked to see it. You always do such good work."

I smile into the phone. "You're our favorite client. You make it easy."

Connor laughs.

"Hey, so, I had some thoughts on the next shoot I wanted to run by you."

"You got the song I sent over?"

I click open my email and scroll until I find an unopened message from Connor. Subject Line: "Make Up".

"Yeah, I've got it right here. I'm sorry I haven't had a chance to listen to the song yet."

"Oh..." Connor says, and I hear the surprise in his voice. "But you already have ideas for the video?"

I grimace. "A few."

"Man, you're good."

I take a deep breath and glance skyward, praying for forgiveness for going behind Chloe's back. She's going to murder me when she finds out what I intend to do.

"I found the perfect girl to play your love interest in this one."

"No way."

"Yeah, she's a little bit more..." I pause, trying to formulate adequate words to describe the most amazing girl in existence on this planet. "Chill. Down to earth, you know?"

Connor laughs again. "Dude...I can't even tell you how relieved I am to hear that."

I lean forward in my seat. "Really?"

"I mean..." Connor sucks in a breath through his teeth. "I wasn't going to say anything, but the last couple of girls you've cast have been...uh...interesting."

I snort. "Yeah, so I've been told. Sorry about that."

"So, how did you find this one?"

Let's see...I was partnered with her in chemistry class freshman year of high school, and the rest is history.

"Uhh...well..." I stammer. "You've actually met her before. Her name's Chloe. She's the makeup artist I've used on all my shoots."

"Oh, right," Connor says, putting the pieces together. "Dude, she is drop-dead gorgeous. I always wondered why she was working behind the camera."

I feel a knot forming in my stomach at Connor's assessment of Chloe, a wave of possession washing over me as I picture Connor and Chloe canoodling on camera. Holding hands. Smiling at each other sweetly. Connor leaning in, brushing

Chloe's hair back off her shoulder, sliding his hand around her neck. Chloe tilting her head up, their lips brushing together...

NO. A THOUSAND TIMES, NO.

How am I supposed to watch the woman who has my heart act like she's head over heels for someone else? Just the thought of seeing her in a music video with country music's hottest star has my stomach churning. There's no way I can do it. No way I can coach them through take after take of love-dovery, and then watch hours of replay footage as I edit. I drop my forehead into my hands.

Love is patient. Love is kind. Love is putting someone else's needs before your own.

This is not about you, Hunter. This is about Chloe. So, suck it up, and tell the man you've got her locked in for the video.

If I truly love her, then I will selflessly help her, right? I will set her up for success by casting her in Connor's video. I will ensure she's paid fairly, enough to help her pay off her bills and hopefully hire an assistant.

Chloe needs this money. This is the only way I can make that happen for her. And because I love her, I will put my own desires and feelings aside, and I will work with her on the shoot just like I would with any other girl who'd been cast.

I'm about to open my mouth and tell Connor I'm going to send over some headshots of Chloe to the label for approval when he starts speaking.

"So, I actually wanted to run a different idea by you."

"Go for it."

"As much as I love being the actor in the music videos, I feel like, for this song, I want to just be me. Connor the songwriter. Connor the singer."

"Right." I nod, unsure of where he's going with this idea.

"So, maybe we could cast a couple to be the actors in the video, and I could just do my thing. Performance shots. Just me and my guitar."

"Hmmm..." I hum. "I like this. It would be different from all the other videos."

"That's what I was thinking."

I rap my fingers on the desk. "Let me listen to the song a few times and get some ideas together. I like the direction this is going."

"When you hear it, hopefully you'll understand why I feel like somebody else should tell the story on screen," Connor says. "It's one of my more personal songs, and the best way I can express how I feel is through singing it. That's what I'm hoping to do in the video."

"I totally get it. I'm looking forward to hearing this one."

Connor and I chat for a few more minutes about "Cry, Baby" before hanging up.

Most people get in over their heads when they taste success in the music industry. But Connor has remained level-headed and authentic even as his fame has skyrocketed the past year. He seems unaffected by the glitz and glamor, and he's a genuinely good guy.

I open his email and throw my headphones on, listening to "Make Up" for the first time.

The ambient electric guitars at the beginning automatically sound different from any of his other songs I've heard. A steady beat kicks in, pulsing in the background as Connor's soulful voice enters my ears.

I close my eyes as I listen, allowing my mind to conjure up whatever images feel natural to me. Usually, after I listen to a song a few times, I can visualize the entire music video, shot by shot, in my mind. This one is no exception.

I can tell after the first chorus that this is a girl-that-got-away song. The song tells a story of a relationship gone off the rails. Connor's listing his regrets, the things he did wrong. The chorus hooks listeners in with a line about how all he wants to do is make things right with this girl he's lost, do everything he can to make up for the things he's done wrong, to make up for the time they've lost.

It's a song about second chances, and I guarantee that any girl who hears this song wouldn't think twice before giving Connor that chance he's begging for—not if it meant they'd get to kiss and make up.

But one thing I've learned about songwriters is that they are sensitive souls. It's clear that Connor wrote this song for one woman, someone he still clearly has deep feelings for. Every word came straight from Connor's heart, and I want to make sure I do it justice with the video.

I want to honor his idea, but if Connor doesn't want to be the leading man, that means I'm going to have to cast someone else to act alongside Chloe.

I exhale slowly. "I can do this," I mutter to myself. "It's just business."

The real issue is going to be getting Chloe on board with this. I'm going to have to pitch it to her just like I'd pitch a concept to label executives. Maybe that's exactly the route I should go.

I open Powerpoint on my laptop and start designing a killer presentation I'm going to give to Chloe. I'm going to make it so enticing, so convincing, that she can't possibly reject my proposal.

Laying out the pros and cons in the form of Powerpoint slides, I have to resist adding my own personal cons to the list. *I can't make this about me.*

Pros:
- Chloe gets paid big bucks.

- Chloe has fun trying something new.

- Chloe gets relief from having to work 24/7.

- Chloe can hire a killer assistant who will lighten her workload while still allowing her to grow her list of clientele.

- Chloe can add the term "actor" to her resume and book other jobs, should she enjoy it.

Cons:
- Chloe will have to act in front of a camera and a small crew of friends.

- Chloe will not be able to visit the craft services table as often as she usually does.

- Chloe will have to do her own makeup for the shoot. I ain't hiring someone else because she's the best of the best.

- Hunter will lose his shiz watching Chloe with another man.

- Hunter will NOT lose his shiz watching Chloe with another man. Hunter will maintain his usual professionalism and will help Chloe feel comfortable on camera with a complete and utter stranger.

I slap my hands down on my desk and stand up, rolling my chair back. Keeping my feelings out of the equation feels impossible—like trying to put socks on a rooster.

Chloe has dated other guys, and up until last year, I was always busy constantly dating other girls. Why do I feel this growing sense of responsibility for her that extends way beyond the boundaries of friendship we've kept in place for so many years? I've always cared for Chloe, being her closest friend. But things are shifting in this particular season, and I'm not just talking about the leaves transforming from green to shades of yellow, red, and orange.

I feel restless. Unsettled. Normally, when something is eating away at me, hijacking my concentration, I call Chloe. Unless she's in the middle of work, she always answers. Always listens. Always offers sound advice and a solution to my problems.

BUT I CAN'T FREAKING CALL CHLOE RIGHT NOW.

Chloe *is* my problem.

I feel relief sweep over me as I realize that there's someone else I can call. Someone who will always give it to me straight. Someone who might be able to help me with this situation.

I dial Luke's number and press my phone to my ear.

"I'm not paying your bail."

I snort. "Shoot. I'm flat broke, and you're my last hope, elder brother."

"What can I do for you, Hunter?"

I sigh, standing up to stretch my legs for a second. "I'm in need of a little...guidance."

"Hunter," Luke says, warning in his voice. "What did you do?"

"Nothing." I open my fridge, fishing around for a Mountain Dew. "I haven't done anything for fifteen years, and that's the problem."

"I see. This is about Chloe, isn't it?" Luke pauses. "Like I always tell you, it's never too late. But I'm curious as to why you're finally getting the guts to go after the girl now."

I explain the Connor Cane situation to my twin, ending with my conundrum of wanting to help Chloe but finding myself unable to stomach casting someone else opposite her.

"Hmmm..." Luke says thoughtfully. "You've got yourself in a tight spot there."

"You're telling me. What do you think I should do?"

"The solution is so obvious I'm shocked you haven't thought of it yourself."

I take a swig of my soda and swallow. "Despite your obvious condescension, you've got me curious. Do tell."

Luke clearly relishes in having come up with a brilliant idea and remains annoyingly silent on the line.

"Luke?"

"Still here."

"Talk to me, bro."

"Just waiting to see if your brain can compute this one on your own, or if I'm going to have to spell it out for you."

I roll my eyes. "Dude. Quit being an as—"

"You sound like Lainey." Luke chuckles. "Alright, here's what you're gonna do…"

He lays it out for me, his genius plan that gets both Chloe and I the win. I nod and jot down a few notes as he talks, feeling confident that Luke's solution is the way to go.

"What would you do without me?" he asks.

"Get into a lot more trouble."

"Speaking of which…"

Uh-oh. Did I do something stupid recently that I've already forgotten about? Leave my debit card in the ATM machine again? Accidentally send my DoorDash to the wrong address?

"I chatted with Mom this morning, and she wants to talk with us tonight. Can you come by her house?"

"Yeah, I can do that. What time?"

"I'll talk to her in a few minutes and get back to you."

We close out the phone call with some brotherly pleasantries, and I let out a deep breath.

Per usual, my level-headed brother comes through for me. I immediately settle back at my desk and start drafting an email to Back Road Records.

Chapter 9

Hunter

When I pull up to my mom's house later that night, I'm sure to leave a healthy six inches or so between the front of my Jeep and the back of Luke's Porsche. I decided to take Chloe's advice and not rattle him with another one of my 'precision parking' jobs.

I take in the cool evening air, the mist hanging over the trees surrounding the yard. I notice the ever-thickening carpet of leaves covering the grass that I need to help my mom clean up sometime soon.

I let myself in through the open garage.

"Hello?" I slip off my shoes, leaving them in the middle of the floor like I still live here. Old habits die hard. Meanwhile, Luke's shoes are neatly shelved. We may be twins, but I did not automatically inherit my mother's tidying skills.

"In here!" Mama calls out from the kitchen.

Luke and Mama are seated at the kitchen island, a plate of Mom's chocolate chip cookies between them.

"Oh, blessed day." I sink my teeth into a warm cookie. "Takes me right back to the good ol' days."

"These *are* the good ol' days, sweetheart," Mama says, giving my arm a squeeze.

"Brother." I slap Luke on the shoulder. He grimaces.

"Try breathing between bites. You're going to choke on a cookie and meet your untimely demise."

I shrug, polishing off a second cookie. "They don't call me two-bite Hunter for nothin'." I rest my hands on the backs of their chairs. "So, what is the purpose of this family meeting?"

Mama and Luke exchange a somber look. I slow my chewing and add my frown to the mix. "What's that all about?"

Mama pats the table, giving me a tight-lipped smile. Her eyes are red rimmed, and I notice a crumpled tissue peeking out from her fist. "Why don't you take a seat."

I snag a chair across the table, and Luke slides the plate of cookies toward me. I narrow my eyes at him. "Why do I feel like I'm being bribed?"

"Because you are," Luke says. "Everyone who knows you knows that you'll do anything for a plate of baked goods."

"Valid." I savor the perfect balance of salt and sweet in my next bite of cookie. "So, what do you guys need me to do? Throw on my old cross-country shorts and dance with a sign outside your office?"

"How about"—Luke swallows and frowns, the lines around his mouth deepening—"you help us pack up this house and get it ready to sell?"

My jaw drops open, and a bit of cookie falls out, hitting the table. "What?"

Mama sniffles. "I think it's time."

I rescue the dropped cookie crumbs, popping them into my mouth. "Time to sell the house? Why?"

"Look around you." She gestures to the great room, every inch of it pristinely clean. Not a piece of furniture even slightly out of place. "I don't need all this space."

I'm in shock, fighting the waves of emotion that are flowing through me right now. After we lost Dad last year, I knew that the day would come that Mom would want to downsize. But for some reason, I'd thought we still had years to enjoy this house, to make memories with our family and with our future families. I'd always pictured having kids one day who'd get to enjoy the magic of visiting Grandma and Grandpa's house for the holidays. *This* house.

"Mom and I were talking the other day," Luke says, "and she finally admitted to me that it's getting to be a bit much to try to take care of this place on her own."

"But," I say in disbelief, "you have *us*, Mom. We're here to help you with anything you need. I'll come over this weekend and rake the leaves for you."

Mama shakes her head. "It's not that simple, Hunter. Luke is getting married soon. He's going to have a family of his own to worry about. I don't want you boys to be tied down to Franklin just because I'm here in this big, old house all by myself."

I feel anger rising in my chest and fight to keep it tampered down. I'm usually pretty good at letting things roll off my shoulders, but this feels like a personal attack on me.

"What am I, chopped liver?" I say. "I'm still here. I can be here in five minutes at any given moment to help you clean, or take care of the yard, or—"

"Hunter." Mama's voice is calm, but her tone is dead serious. I settle back into my chair. "I need you to listen to what I'm trying to say."

I nod, working my jaw as I pick at a splinter in the table.

"It absolutely breaks my heart to think about losing this place. This house is a living memory of the life Dad and I built together for you boys." Mama swipes at her eyes with a tissue. "But aside from our Sunday dinners, I'm here alone most of the time. I watch TV alone. I cook meals for myself. I play my Celine Dion CDs almost every evening just so I don't have to sit and listen to the silence."

Guilt mounds in my gut. Luke and I glance at each other, and I know he's feeling it, too.

"I want to live in a smaller, more manageable place. Somewhere with more people in my..." She sighs. "Situation. People I can talk to, who understand."

I swallow. "I'm sorry I don't visit you more often. I'll be better about that."

Mama pats my hand. "I appreciate that, but this isn't about you, Hunter. This is about what I need."

Luke's staring out the window, his eyebrows drawn low over his dark eyes.

"It sounds like you've already made your decision," I say flatly. "When are you wanting to list the house?"

"That's what Luke and I were just discussing when you came in. I'm hoping to have it ready within the next month or so. I'd love to sell it by the new year."

I let out a whoosh of air and sit back in my chair. We're nearing the end of September, so that means the house could be gone in a matter of months. "That seems...quick."

"The market's wild right now," Luke says, cutting his eyes back to me. "Mom could sell this place tomorrow, if she wanted to."

I glance around at the kitchen, taking in a lifetime of memories made in this space. Mom cooking dinner, littering every single surface with the ingredients she's using. Dad grabbing two IBC root beers from the fridge and sliding one to me across the countertop, the bottle leaving a misty trail in its path. Movie nights in the living room with my buddies—and Chloe. Always Chloe. I can't help but mentally scroll through a list of all the girls I'd kissed on that couch...Chloe not being one of them.

I straighten in my chair, taking a deep breath. *This is not about me.*

"If you feel good about this, then I am here to support you however I can."

Mama smiles at me tearfully. "How did I get so blessed to have you boys as my sons?"

I shrug. "I don't know. I think God was trying to get rid of some of his overflow stock of rowdy kids and sent two of his top troublemakers your way."

Luke raises his eyebrows.

"Okay, fine. One troublemaker and one perfectly responsible child." I reach for another cookie. "These will never taste the same if you make them in a different kitchen."

"Yes, they will. Love is my secret ingredient, and I've got a lifetime supply of that with me no matter where I live."

"Have you already found a new place?" I ask.

"Luke's got a couple apartments that he thinks might work. We're going to go look at them together later this week."

I snort, resisting the urge to roll my eyes Chloe-style. "How convenient."

Luke gives me a questioning look. "You think this was my idea?"

"You're the real estate guy, aren't you? The investment guy," I say, trying not to raise my voice. "Isn't this what you do?"

Luke snorts. "Kick mothers out of their family homes?"

Mama shakes her head, her white-blonde hair shifting around her chin. "This was all me, Hunter. We haven't been plotting behind your back."

"Kind of feels like you have been."

"You forget that we work together," Luke says calmly. "Mom and I sometimes have time to talk at the office."

"Yeah, I know." I take another deep breath, willing myself to calm down. "It's going to suck not being able to come here anymore."

"You can take the tetherball pole, if you want." Mom smiles. "Maybe Darlene would want it in her backyard."

I sigh. They're taking the tetherball away from me, too? Not cool, family. Not cool.

"No, no," I force myself to say. "I'm sure the family who moves in would be stoked to have that stay here as part of the deal."

We're quiet for a moment, each lost in our thoughts. I fill the uncomfortable silence by grabbing another cookie.

"So, what's the first step?" I finally ask around my mouthful.

"Dude, how many is that?" Luke asks.

"I've lost count."

Luke slides the plate back and grabs a cookie for himself. "Scarcity mindset is real."

"It would be helpful if you two could go through your bedrooms," Mama says. "Sort through your childhood things and take what you want. Pack up the rest to donate."

I nod. "We can do that."

"My room's practically empty." Luke gives me a pointed look. "I went through my stuff before I moved to Atlanta."

"And mine's a time capsule," I deadpan. "An exhibit, if you will."

"I can come by this weekend with Lainey," Luke says.

I pull out my phone and swipe to my calendar. "I'll figure out a day that works sometime soon."

"Thank you," Mama says. "But for now, let's enjoy this place while we still have it. You're all coming for dinner on Sunday, yes?"

We both nod.

"And maybe we can do something over here for Halloween next month."

"Sounds fun," I say, swallowing down the feelings that have been swelling in my chest at the thought of losing our family home.

Nothing about this is my definition of *fun*.

Chapter 10

Chloe

Tuesday morning dawns gray and stormy. The kind of morning that makes you want to burrow in a cocoon of blankets and spend the day reading and drinking hot tea.

As much as I would have loved to stay cozied up at home, I had to get Harper Jackson, a rising country music star I work with, ready first thing for a local TV appearance. I then spent my afternoon doing makeup for one client's engagement shoot, and then getting another client ready for her bachelorette party.

Driving to appointments in my trusty Honda Civic with nothing but my massive makeup kit to keep me company felt a little anticlimactic for this moody autumn day. I threw on some James Bay, letting his mellow music create the soundtrack to the gorgeous scenery outside. The leaves tumbling across the road and the steady fall of rain throughout the day warranted something special, so I called Hunter after finishing up with my last client to see if he was up for an afternoon coffee date.

And by *date,* I mean casual meet-up. Two friends grabbing coffee and catching up.

I owe him an apology for lying to him about my panic attack. What better way to say *I'm sorry* than in food form?

I'm the first to arrive at The Toasted Bean, so I place our orders. Is it pathetic that I have Hunter's memorized, down to the flavor of cake pop he loves? I'd like to think of it as thoughtfulness. Not stalkerish. Or romantic. For sure, not romantic.

I settle into a seat near the window, drawing my oversized sweater closer around my body. Every time the door opens, a burst of cold wind travels over my skin, sending chills down my arms and legs. The crisp air doesn't bother me as much as it should. Soon, I'll be warmed right through by my drink and Hunter's company.

I rest my chin on my fist, tilting my head to look out the foggy window.

A couple walks briskly by, huddled together so closely under an umbrella they're practically one person. I see another elderly couple shuffling hand in hand across the street. I glance around the coffee shop. Amongst the usual crowd of college students rapping away on their laptops or staring down at their phones are even more couples. Smiling and sipping. Arms around shoulders. Fingers intertwined. Lips locking.

I swallow, not wanting to stare at the couple going to town in the corner booth at the back of the shop, but I can't help but steal glances their way. I'm fascinated by the fact that they are so completely engrossed in their kiss it's like no one else in the world exists. I don't think I've ever kissed someone like that in my entire life.

"Chloe?" the barista calls out my name, and I snap to attention. I slide out of my seat and hustle to grab our order.

I can't hold the slices of pumpkin bread and cake pops along with our drinks, so I have to take two trips.

I'm concentrating on not letting a single crumb of my lusciously thick pumpkin bread drop to the floor when I feel a hand settle onto my back.

I glance up and meet Hunter's eyes, warm and golden. My gaze drops down to his lips, full and apple red from the cold. I feel a rush of nerves as I wonder what it would be like to kiss him in the corner booth, to feel those lips press against mine. What would he taste like? Golden cider, rich dark chocolate, swirls of cinnamon...

"You didn't..." he says, taking the pumpkin bread from my hands in reverent awe.

I flash a tight smile his way, hoping that my thoughts about his lips and corner booths were not easy to read in my expression.

"Oh, you bet I did." I wave the cake pops in front of his face. "And I got you these. Compensation for yesterday."

Hunter follows me to our booth, sliding across the table from me. "You spoil me."

I slide his drink across the table, and he takes it from me, his fingers brushing over mine, featherlight.

"Hunter," I say softly. "I'm really sorry about keeping my ER visit from you."

He shakes his head, strands of damp, dark hair clinging to his forehead. "You don't need to apologize. I understand why you didn't tell me."

I fiddle with the cup sleeve, sliding it around and avoiding Hunter's gaze. "I do, actually. I was embarrassed, and I'm sorry."

"Promise me you'll tell me if you feel like you're going to have another panic attack," he says, his voice low. "I want to be given the chance to help you, if I can."

I nod.

"Good."

He takes a sip from his cup, focused on something out the window. He looks troubled, his eyebrows drawn low.

Our eyes meet, and his lips curl up into a grin, all traces of his worry gone in an instant. He laces his fingers together and hunches over, his broad shoulders raising as he leans toward me.

"I need to talk to you about something."

In the brief moment that he pauses, my heart starts thudding in my chest. I allow myself the indulgence of jumping to outrageous conclusions. Maybe Hunter's going to reach across the table, take my hands gently in his, and then ask me on a real date.

"I need to pitch something to you," he says, scrunching his nose up like he always does. I mentally pat my disappointed heart on its tiny, little head. *Sorry, sweetheart, no desperately romantic confessions for you today. Maybe next time.*

"Oh..." I say. "Of course."

Hunter pulls his phone out and starts tapping. I take a bite of pumpkin bread and wait for him to collect himself.

"I haven't got all day, you know," I tease. "Time is of the essence."

"Trust me..." Hunter runs a hand through his hair, making it look effortlessly cool. "I know."

He flips his phone around, showing me a Powerpoint slide titled "Make Up".

"Here we have a nice little presentation I've prepared for you." Hunter's entering salesman mode, tossing a cheeky grin my way that makes me feel like I just swallowed warm cocoa laced with melted cream. "For Connor Cane's newest song, 'Make Up'."

I give him a gentle golf clap. "Please, do continue."

He clears his throat and looks back at me. This time, there's no swagger in his expression, no confidence. He looks genuinely nervous, almost like he'd rather not show me what he's about to present after all.

He takes a deep breath and swipes to the next slide.

"I want you to think back to a couple nights ago, when we had dinner with my mom. Do you remember what she suggested at the dinner table?"

I furrow my brows. "She agreed that you should have tried the pickles on your burger."

Hunter snorts. "Not that suggestion."

I shake my head. "What, then?" I ask, urging him to continue his pitch.

"My clever mother pointed out that you are..." Hunter pauses, his eyes searching mine. "Beautiful. That you shouldn't keep hiding behind the camera."

BRB, currently trying to ignore the whirring alarms raging in my heart in response to hearing Hunter call me beautiful.

"Hunter, I *like* being behind the camera."

He raises a hand to stop me. "I know that. But I'd like to propose that you do something a little out of your comfort zone..."

He passes me the phone across the table. I inspect the mood board he's put together for this new video. Shadows cast from couples embracing. A museum filled with sculptures. Grays, dusty blues, and blacks. Then, I spot a photo in the mix that makes me almost drop his phone.

It's a photo of me, one that Hunter took last summer at Radnor Lake. I'm blocking the sunlight from my eyes with one hand, carrying wildflowers I'd collected on our hike in the other. The photo is sunbleached, just like the faded tee I was wearing that day. My lips are pressed together in a soft smile, a rare capture of my true feelings for Hunter. They're written all over my face. I'm suddenly embarrassed that he froze this particular moment we'd shared in a photo.

"Why am I on your mood board, Hunter?" I ask slowly.

"Chloe..." he says, his voice dipping so low that I have to lean closer to hear him. "I pitched you to Back Road to be cast as the love interest in Connor's next music video. The executives and Connor thought you'd be a perfect fit. The job is yours, if you want it."

Well, shoot. Enter panic attack number two. My throat feels like it's closing up.

"What?" I breathe. "You did *what*?"

He settles his palms on the table. "I cast you in my next music video."

I flop back into my seat, swiping to the next slide on his Powerpoint. It's a list of reasons why I should take the job.

Chloe gets paid big bucks. Chloe has fun trying something new. Chloe gets relief from having to work 24/7. Chloe can afford to hire an assistant.

"Why are you doing this?" I suddenly feel hot, my neck burning up underneath my sweater.

"Isn't it obvious?" Hunter gestures to his phone. "I want to help you, Chloe."

I exhale sharply. "Hunter, this is all very nice of you, but I'm not an actress. I can't do this."

"I know, Chloe. I know," he says impatiently. "I knew you would hate this idea. But just hear me out."

He plucks his phone out of my hands and swipes to a different app before handing it back to me.

"This is the contract they sent over." His eyes are wide and open now, almost pleading with me to stay, to listen. "I want you to see how much they're offering to pay you for this shoot."

My eyes scan over the document until they land on a nice number with several zeros. My eyebrows raise a fraction.

I feel my eyebrows rising despite my efforts to clamp them down. "Is this typical pay for actors?"

Hunter shrugs. "It depends on the project, but for Connor's videos, yeah. This is what the label is willing to pay for a two-day shoot."

"So, you're telling me..." I feel the wheels turning in my mind. "If I agree to be in this music video for two days, I'll make..."

"Literally eight times what you usually make." Hunter shifts in his seat. "You'll still be the makeup artist on the shoot, too, if you'd like, so this would be in addition to what you'd take home for your makeup services."

I blow my next breath out of my lips. "But I'm not an actor, Hunter."

He rolls his eyes. "Yes, you keep saying that. But you wouldn't have to figure it all out on your own. I'm the director, remember? I'll tell you exactly what to do and how to do it."

My mind is racing. I've been saving up for months in the hopes of eventually hiring an assistant, but my hospital bill derailed my plans. This gig would allow me to pay off my bill and allow me to bring on a second artist, to train them, and get them their own custom makeup kit identical to mine.

I've known for a while that I need a break. I need time off. I need fewer clients that are willing to pay more. I want to be more selective around the jobs I'd take on myself without risking the loss of my current clients.

This is the opportunity I've been waiting for. I wouldn't have to wait six more months to start spacing out my gigs. I might actually be able to take an entire week off during the holidays for the first time in years. I could do it now.

I scroll through the rest of the contract, not really soaking in the rest of the legal jargon.

Hunter's biting his lip when I look his way. "What do you think?"

"I don't know." I sigh. "I can't believe you did this behind my back."

"Please don't hate me."

"I don't hate you right now." I shake my head. "But I might if I go through with this. The thought of being in front of all those cameras makes me want to die."

He reaches across the table, holding out his hand for his phone. I place it back in his palm, and he deftly takes my hand in his other empty one.

His thumb skates over my knuckles, and my breath catches in my throat.

"I'll be there to help you. I won't make you do anything that you're not comfortable with."

I'm lost in his eyes now, not daring to breathe as I feel the gentle motion of his thumb across the back of my hand.

Hunter and I have touched countless times, but this feels different. Charged. Meaningful.

"There's one more thing I need to tell you about this music video before you make your decision."

"Oh?" I shift in my seat, careful to not tug my hand away from his. I'm savoring every moment of his lingering touch. "What's that?"

Hunter tightens his grip around my hand, as if he's trying to keep me from running away.

"Connor wants to approach this video differently. He only wants to be featured in the performance shots."

"Mmmhmm..." I hum.

"So, that means Connor won't be acting as himself in the video. I had to cast someone else as your love interest."

I suck in my cheeks. "Oh no...who is it? Can I at least see a picture of him before I agree to this?"

Hunter lets out an uncomfortable chuckle. "Well...uh..." He clears his throat and looks up at me, squinting. "It's someone you know—pretty well, actually."

I lean in, desperate to know who this mystery love interest is.

"It's me, Chloe," Hunter says. "I cast myself in the video."

Chapter 11

Hunter

She's not screaming. She's not running away. She also hasn't attempted to slap me across the face from her side of the booth. All good signs.

Right?

I saw something flash across Chloe's face when I told her I'd be playing her love interest in the music video—a glimmer of something I couldn't name. But that disappeared just as quickly as it had appeared. And so had her hand. She'd slipped it out of my grasp so quickly and dropped it into her lap.

Now, her cheeks are flushed raspberry pink, and she's taking the longest sip of coffee known to man. I swear the cup has got to be down to the dregs by now, but she's still going strong, staring out the window, at the baristas bustling behind the counter, at the other customers in the shop. Anywhere but at me.

I'm not sure how to interpret this reaction. Her brown eyes are wide and doe-like as they finally land on me.

"Let me get this straight," she says, her voice cracking. "You and I are supposed to act like...like a couple? On camera?"

I wince. Doesn't sound like she's chomping at the bit, ready to take my hand and run off into the night. It occurs to me that maybe it's not the acting she's worried about. Maybe she just really hates the idea of doing it with *me*.

"How are we supposed to do that, Hunter?" she asks, her lashes fluttering as she blinks rapidly. "I've seen the couples in your music videos. They're all over each other."

I shrug. "Like I said, I'm the director. We wouldn't have to do anything you're not comfortable with."

Cracks are starting to form in my reasoning. Fault lines are breaking up my solid resolve. I was trying to cure my jealousy by inserting myself into the video as her on-screen boyfriend.

Don't wanna watch Chloe cozy up with some random dude? Why don't you be that dude? Cuddle Chloe yourself. Fill up on a lifetime of Chloe cuddles.

When Luke had suggested this idea to me, I'd thought he was brilliant. Inspired. But now?

I feel like I was sold a faulty product. I fell for his sales pitch—hook, line, and sinker. And I'm feeling my confidence die a slow and painful death as Chloe fiddles with her cup and pinches at her pumpkin bread without taking a bite.

If Chloe was hesitant before, it's obvious that she's completely terrified now. I couldn't bear it if she had another panic attack because of something I'd done.

"Ahh man..." I run my hands through my hair, dropping my gaze down to the table. "I really thought this was a great idea, Chloe. I'm sorry."

Her lips quirk up into a shy smile. "You're so thoughtful, Hunter. Do you know that?"

I feel my confidence trying to peel itself back up from the depths of my emotional ocean floor.

"I just want to help you."

She sighs, slumping back against the booth. "I know."

We're silent for a few heartbeats, each of us trying to read the other without speaking.

Does she hate this? Does she hate *me*?

"If you would consider doing this, but you don't want to do it with me, I can cast someone else," I say. "I just thought that it might make things easier for you, that you'd feel less nervous if you had me there to make it fun."

She grins. "You are the *king* of making things fun."

It's my turn to sip my drink, waiting for her to let me into her mind. Chloe has always been intentional with her words. She's not one to spill her guts or overshare, so I know I may have to be patient and wait until she's ready to express her carefully guarded feelings.

"Can I have some time?" she asks softly. "To think about this?"

I nod eagerly. "Of course. I'll send you the contract, and you can decide whether or not you want to sign it and send it back to me."

"Is there a deadline?"

"The label wants everything locked in by the end of next week. Let me know sooner rather than later so I can find someone else if you decide you don't want to do it."

Chloe exhales, her shoulders falling as the breath exits her lips. "Okay."

"If this doesn't feel right for you, I totally understand," I say. "But I want you to seriously think about it. You have no reason to be nervous. And someone very wise is always telling me that sometimes it's good to push yourself to try new things."

She swats at my arm. "Don't you dare use my own advice against me!"

"Why not? You give the best advice."

I can see her thoughts turning inward. Her golden-brown hair falls over her eyes as she drops her chin. I want to reach across the table and sweep those stray hairs back from her forehead.

She nods resolutely and meets my eyes for a moment. "Okay. I'll think about it."

I reach my hand across the table for her to shake. She hesitates a moment before slipping her small hand into mine. I give it a firm pump. "Pleasure doing business with you, ma'am."

"I haven't signed anything yet."

"I don't want to influence your decision," I say without thinking, "but I hope you'll give me a chance."

She looks at me quizzically. I realize that my statement is loaded with suggestion. That I not only want her to take this deal, but that I also want *her*.

I hadn't worked through all the details of what acting like Chloe's fake boyfriend on camera would look like, but just the thought of it now that I'm sitting across from her makes my mind fuzzy. We've never crossed the line of friendship in our real life. Could toying with the dynamic of our friendship, even if we're just acting, change anything between us?

I'd be lying if I didn't say I hoped it would. All my years spent wooing and charming women won't have been for nothing if I can try my hand at winning Chloe's heart. This shoot would be my chance to show her just how wanted she is by me.

Maybe it won't help that my attempts to win her will be watched by my camera crew and captured forever in a Connor

Cane music video. Chloe is so introverted and shy that having an audience—not to mention the opinions of strangers online after the video releases—could seriously stress her out.

I pause my train of thought. I try not to overthink things in my life, and this shoot with Chloe has to be treated the same way. No worrying, just trusting myself and my true intentions. She'll feel them. I'll make sure of it. I don't have the entire plan mapped out, but I'm good at going with the flow. And I have a feeling that if Chloe agrees to do this, things are going to *flow*.

"So how were your illustrious clients today?" I ask, trying to cut a path through the thick tension I've created between us.

"Oh…" Chloe brushes her forehead. "They were fine."

"No bridezillas?"

Chloe looks relieved at the change of topic. "No, thank goodness. They were all easygoing."

After a few minutes of me firing questions at Chloe with an energy I hope eases her stress, our conversation trips back into a normal pace.

I'm slowly polishing off the last cake pop, trying to savor each bite. "When I get married one day, I'm having these served at my wedding."

Chloe giggles. "What a masculine contribution to the wedding menu."

I point my now empty stick at her. "Hey, now. Ask anybody in this room. I guarantee you nobody would pass on a good cake pop."

"They'd be a crowd pleaser, that's for sure."

The rain is dumping now, no longer the delicate drizzle it was when I'd arrived.

"I should get going before this storm turns ugly," Chloe says, sliding to the edge of her seat. "Thanks for meeting up with me."

"How could I pass up on a chance to grab coffee with my favorite person in the entire world?" I say, flashing a smile her way as we stand together. "I'm buying next time."

"I'm a much cheaper date than you are," Chloe says. "I only require one baked good, not twenty."

We press through the crowd of people, Chloe's head barely reaching my chest as she shuffles toward the exit in front of me.

We step outside and immediately get pelted by the downpour.

"I'll call you!" I shout as we move in opposite directions to where our cars are parked.

"Bye, now!" Chloe waves before shielding her head with her arms and running. I watch her long sweater sway back and forth, her black platform boots kicking up water as she jogs through the puddles accumulating on the sidewalk. I could have walked her to her car, lending her my jacket to protect her from the rain.

"Man, you've gotten rusty," I mutter to myself as I watch Chloe reach her car. She waves back at me before slipping inside. I resolve to be more conscious of her, just like I would be if she was my girlfriend.

I want to be the one to take care of her, just as she always takes care of me. Chloe makes me want to be a better person, and I hope that I can show her I've changed. I'm not the same man I was before my dad passed away.

I'm striving to be a man worthy of Chloe. The kind of man she deserves.

Chapter 12

Chloe

"Darlene?" I call once I reach the top of the stairs leading to the main floor from my basement apartment.

When she doesn't answer right away, I assume she's already gone to bed. I pad into the kitchen and fill the electric kettle on the counter with water, setting it to boil. The cabinet creaks as I pull it open and select a chamomile tea from Darlene's box of assorted herbal teas.

I press the tea sachet to my nose, breathing in its fragrance and closing my eyes. Memories of happy summers spent at my grandmother's flood into my mind. She grew the cheerful flowers in her garden, drying them out around her house to make her own brews and remedies.

"Mind making me a cup, too?" I spin to the doorway where Darlene is shuffling through in her fluffy pink bathrobe—or "dressing gown" as she insists on calling it.

"You're still up?" I ask. "Late night for you."

"You know me." She waves a hand dismissively. "Once I start a good book, I can't go to sleep until I've finished it."

"Uh-oh," I tease. "What are you reading now?"

She pulls the book out from the pocket of her robe, and I stifle a laugh at the cover. It's what I'd call a bodice ripper, clearly a scandalous romance novel featuring a shirtless man hovering over a half-dressed woman.

"Judge me, and I'll evict you," Darlene says, pulling open her tea cabinet to grab her own tea bag.

I smile broadly, trying to hold back my laughter. "Never. What happens in the library stays in the library."

She winks at me, slipping a thin arm around my shoulders. We're about the same height now. Me because I swear I keep shrinking from my scoliosis, and her because she's losing height due to old age.

"How's your back today, sweetheart?" she asks, rubbing a knobby hand over my shoulder blades.

"It is just fine, like always. Don't even worry about me."

I break away from her, grabbing two mugs and bringing them to the counter. I reach out and take her tea bag, dropping both into our mugs before filling them with boiling water.

"How are *you* feeling?" I ask, giving her a pointed look. "How did your appointment go today?"

She gives me a sassy, one-shouldered shrug. "Fine."

I level her with my gaze. "You wanna play that game with me?"

"You give me nothing, I give you nothing in return."

I fiddle with the tea bag string hanging from my mug. "Alright, you wanna know how I'm feeling today? I'll tell you. But not because I'm trying to complain."

"Good. Nobody likes a complainer." Darlene purses her lips together.

"I'm only telling you this because I know you care about me," I say, sighing. I retrieve the honey from another cabinet and a spoon from a drawer. "My back is not feeling great these days."

Darlene nods, picking up her mug and gesturing to her kitchen table. Once we're seated, I start talking again. I tell her about yesterday's incident at the track with Hunter, and how I had a hard time sleeping last night because I couldn't get comfortable. A nerve in my lower back was still tweaked today, so I had a few moments where my right leg went numb, and I had to wait for the feeling to come back.

"Trying to apply mascara on a client without giving away the fact that I can't feel my toes is no easy feat."

She listens patiently, taking tiny sips of her tea and nodding. She's quiet for a moment once I'm through speaking.

"I know I've told you this before..." she says finally. "But you don't want to regret moving too quickly through this season of your life. It will be gone before you know it."

I stir my tea bag around in my cup. "I know."

"Chloe." Darlene's tone means business, so I meet her eyes. "You need to start saying no so you can rest when things like this happen. It's the only way your body can heal."

I nod slowly, stirring a generous spoonful of honey into my mug.

"Pushing through pain is noble, but not always necessary. You don't get a prize for being strong." She places a weathered hand over mine that's resting on the table. "It's ok to pause and take care of yourself. It's the only way you're going to make it to my age and not be wheelchair-bound or in constant pain."

I keep my gaze fixed on my tea. "You're right."

"Don't you want to be as spry as I am when you're old like me?"

"Absolutely. Your level of energy is inspiring!" I exclaim. "Tell me all your secrets."

"I'll give them to you," Darlene chuckles. "Number one...don't dye your hair. It makes it turn gray faster."

I snort. "They didn't teach me that in cosmetology school, but alright."

"Number two..." She leans over and pats my hand again. "Rest. Say no. Slow down before you're forced to."

Darlene's not one to force her advice onto someone. When she offers counsel, it comes from a place of love. Her advice always holds significant weight in my mind and on my heart. I know this is her way of telling me that she's mindful of my anxiety. I appreciate her loving concern more than she knows.

"I had an interesting offer come through today," I say, clearing my throat. "From Hunter, actually."

Darlene sits up, rigid in her chair. "Did that boy finally propose?"

I laugh. "What? Darlene, that's crazy talk."

She levels me with a stare. "No, it's not. If he would just pull his head out of his a—"

"Listen!" I interrupt her before she gets into the Hunter-and-Chloe tirade she loves to throw out every so often. "It's a job offer."

"Darn." She sets her mug on the table and crosses her arms. "Not nearly as fun as an offer of marriage. What's he trying to sign you up for?"

"He wants me to be the actress in his next music video. The label's offering to pay me quite a bit of money for it. Enough for me to pay off my hospital bill, maybe take some days off, and bring on a second makeup artist."

Darlene smiles broadly. "Well, that sounds wonderful! Exactly what you need."

I grimace. "Yes, but there's a plot twist that I didn't see coming."

"No surprises there. We always have to make trade-offs to get what we want."

I shift in my seat, the chair creaking beneath me. "I'm not sure if I'm willing to make this one."

She sips her tea and waits for me to elaborate.

"Hunter will be playing my love interest in the video." I can feel a hot blush climbing up my neck as I hear myself say the words out loud. "So, he and I would have to act like a couple on camera."

"Sounds like the easiest money you'll ever make in your life." Darlene chortles. "You two have more chemistry than you know what to do with."

I roll my eyes. "No, we don't. We're best friends, Darlene. This could be *so* awkward."

She considers me for a moment. "You're afraid, aren't you?"

Suddenly, my half-full mug of chamomile tea becomes the most fascinating object in the room.

"You care about him. Deeply. You're worried that pretending to love each other might result in someone getting hurt."

I slowly look up, nodding. "Yeah."

"Hmmm..." She tilts her head, her silver hair catching in the dim light coming from the pendant over the dining table. "This is a tricky one, then."

"I would love to earn that money. I just don't know if I can do this without having another..." I pause. "Mental breakdown. And I don't know if I can do this with Hunter."

"This isn't really about the money, sweetheart." Darlene places a warm hand over mine. "You have the most tender heart of anyone I know. I understand that you want to protect it, but if Hunter is offering to do this for you, I guarantee you it's not about the money for him either. This is a matter of the heart for both of you."

I don't want to let myself hope that Hunter is offering to act alongside me because he's interested in me: Chloe, the forever best friend. It's easier to assume that he's doing this out of friendship—because he cares and is concerned about me.

"What should I do?"

Darlene offers me a gentle smile. "That is up to you. If it were me, I wouldn't let a chance like this pass me by out of fear. There's always the possibility of getting hurt in a relationship, as you well know."

I know she's referencing my strained relationship with my parents. We barely speak, and when we do, I'm usually on the phone with my therapist or Hunter immediately afterward.

"Things might not work out with you and Hunter, at least not in the way you hope. But there's also a chance that it *will* work out. You just have to decide if you're willing to try."

I return her smile and give her soft hand a squeeze. "Thank you."

"You're a beautiful, brilliant woman," she says assertively. "And if he doesn't fall head-over-heels for you after you do this video together, he is a complete idiot."

I laugh. "You are too good to me, Miss Darlene."

"As you are to me." She gives my hand another pat before standing up and collecting her mug. "I'd better go finish this book before the sun starts rising." She winks and waves as she leaves the kitchen.

"Goodnight!" I call out after her.

I polish off the last of my tea, scraping the honey that had settled on the bottom of the mug into the sink before washing it out.

I stuff my hands into the front pocket of my favorite gray hoodie, making my way back down the stairs to the basement.

This hoodie carried a different scent with it when I first acquired it. When I'd first slipped it on, it smelled of laundry detergent and Hunter's cologne of choice as a seventeen-year-old. He'd given it to me at a football game one night in high school when I'd forgotten to bring a jacket, and I'd never given it back.

I include still fitting into this hoodie on my list of reasons I'm grateful I'd reached my peak height at fourteen years old. It's oversized and slouchy, worn and soft from years of wear. I've had it for so long that sometimes I forget that it originally belonged to my best friend.

It may not smell like Hunter anymore, but the feeling of having a piece of him with me when we're apart still remains. I'd even taken this hoodie with me on my trip to Paris the summer after I'd graduated from cosmetology school. Pretty sure I slept in it every night.

I flick on the light in my bedroom, settling atop the linen duvet tossed over my bed. I reach for the romance novel on my nightstand, but my hand finds my phone instead.

I swipe the screen to unlock it, scrolling through social media for a few minutes in an attempt to distract myself. It works for a while until I stop my scroll on a screenshot Hunter just posted from Connor Cane's shoot last weekend.

Double tap. Keep scrolling.

Don't think about Hunter. Don't think about Hunter. DO NOT THINK ABOUT—

I sigh, opening my email to read over the contract again.

If I sign this contract, I'm signing up for what could potentially be the most embarrassing, humiliating experience of my life. Not to mention the risk of getting my heart shattered if it turns out that Hunter doesn't share my feelings.

I mull over Darlene's words in my mind. I don't want to act out of fear. I can't let my anxiety rule my decisions. I don't want to regret anything by immediately dismissing this opportunity because I'm scared out of my mind.

Hunter doesn't struggle with this kind of indecisiveness and anxiety. He always says, "What would you do if you knew you couldn't fail?"

If I knew I was destined to succeed, guaranteed to get what I want, I would go for it. I would carefully do my makeup, get dressed up in something feminine and sexy, and stand in front of those cameras with confidence. I would carry myself with grace, knowing that if I make a mistake, Hunter will be there to help me through it. I would let myself get tangled up in him. I'd allow myself to taste what love with Hunter would be like, even if we are just acting.

I glance up at the ceiling and make my decision.

I'm going to do this.

With shaking hands, I type my name and initials into the designated boxes throughout the document. Each confirmation of my signature feels like a step closer to the edge of a cliff—one I'm not entirely sure I want to jump off of.

What if there are sharp rocks at the bottom? What if the water is shallow? What if Hunter isn't there to catch me like he says he is?

When was the last time Hunter let you down? a little voice speaks into my heart.

It's been a long, long time since he failed to keep his word. He's been steady, always kind. Always Hunter.

I reach the final signature and quickly type my name in. I get a notification that the contract is complete and has been sent off to the label and to Hunter.

I fling my phone onto my bed and flop back into my sea of pillows.

The deed has been done.

Chapter 13

Hunter

When I'd received Chloe's email containing her signed contract, I'd nearly fallen out of bed. Blindsided.

She hadn't texted or called me first to run her thoughts by me. She hadn't taken a week to contemplate her decision. She'd signed it and sent it over less than twenty-four hours after I'd pitched my proposal.

At first, I felt like I'd been given the key to the universe. The world was now my oyster (another food I wouldn't touch with a ten-foot pole). Chloe had agreed to my crazy, stupid idea. This means she trusts me enough to walk beside her through this experience. And the money will buy her the help and time she so desperately needs.

My elation is only a small piece of what keeps me awake half of the night. The other barrage of thoughts that prevents me from resting are around what we're going to have to do on camera for this music video.

For any other music video, I would have zero qualms about asking the lead actors to touch, to hold hands, to embrace. To kiss.

But here I am, donning my puffy comforter like a cloak over my head and shoulders, pacing back and forth until I've worn a path into the carpet as I try to conceptualize this video with Chloe and myself as the actors.

This feels wrong. Permissive. Like I'm indulging in fantasies with Chloe that should not be allowed to flow freely through my mind.

In the past, I would have stamped out thoughts of pulling her in for a kiss, tampering down the blaze to prevent it from growing into a full-blown vision that I'd be far too tempted to bring to life.

But for the sake of the video (Say it with me, kids: "*For the sake of the video...*"), I *have* to work through the details in my mind. It's part of my job. I have to nail down the angle at which the camera will move in, where our hands will be placed, how long we'll linger before letting our lips touch. This is me being professional. This is me doing my job.

At least...that's what I tell myself as I flop back into my bed, restless after envisioning kissing the girl who's been in my life since we were fifteen years old.

I feel like I've manipulated her into giving me something I've wanted for way too long. This isn't the way I hoped we'd draw closer to each other. On camera. Watched by a group of people in person, and then watched by even more people online when the video releases.

I'm filled with regret for a moment before I remember why I pulled this together in the first place. It wasn't to mess with Chloe's heart, to indulge in my deepest, most hidden desires. It was to help her, to offer her some relief from the constant grind she maintains with her work.

It wasn't supposed to be me in the music video. If I had just cast someone else and set my feelings for Chloe aside, I would have been truly selfless.

But as soon as I signed myself up to act alongside her, this video became about me. I'm suddenly disgusted with my own selfishness, my need to hold onto Chloe when she doesn't even truly belong to me. That wasn't my call to make. I should have talked with her first, run some other actors by her before inserting myself into this job.

She may have signed the contract, but I haven't yet.

There's still time for me to cast someone else before the end of the week.

I resolve to talk to Chloe when I meet her for our morning run at the track. She needs to know that my true intention was to help her, not entice her into making out with me for my own pleasure. I don't play dirty like that—at least not anymore.

We're finding our pace, easing into our second lap around the track when I decide to bring up the video. The handful of cereal I crammed into my mouth before leaving my apartment is threatening to come back up as I work up the nerve to tell Chloe what kept me up all night.

"I got your contract last night," I say.

Chloe stumbles, recovering quickly. I press my lips together, not wanting to embarrass her by acknowledging her near face-plant on the track.

"Oh, great!" she says brightly, her tone forced. "That's good."

"I'm glad you decided to go through with it," I say, glancing over at her. Her white tank top accentuates her toned shoulders and arms. And don't get me started on how defined her calves and thighs are when she's running beside me. I nearly take a tumble myself as we round the corner, momentarily distracted by the sleek movement of her fit, petite body.

"I talked to Darlene about it last night," Chloe says, seemingly unaware of the fact that my own nose nearly met the pavement because I was too busy checking her out to notice the bend in the track. "I decided that I don't want to make decisions out of fear."

"I'm still scared, of course," she continues. "But as Darlene told me, sometimes you've got to make trade-offs to get what you want."

I raise my eyes to the cool blue sky, growing brighter every minute as the sun rises.

"Chloe…" I say, finally earning a glance my way, her eyes full of questions. "I was thinking about all of this last night…a lot."

We take a few strides in silence as I try to form my next sentence in my mind before speaking—a skill I most definitely lack.

"I think I'm going to cast someone else in the video."

Chloe abruptly stops mid-stride. "What?" She looks at me incredulously. "Are you kidding me right now?"

I'm panting, hands on my hips, as I try to catch my breath.

"I barely signed the contract last night, and you're already trying to replace me?" I can see the anger building in her stiff stance.

"No…" I backpedal. "Not in your role. In mine."

Chloe's brown eyes blaze, her breathing labored as we face off in the middle of the track.

She clamps her jaw down, silent for a few breaths before speaking. "Why?"

I raise my hands and immediately drop them to my sides again. "I just don't want you to feel like I'm...using you."

She shakes her head, confused. "How would you be using me? I thought you were doing this to help me."

"I am."

I know what I want to say to Chloe, but I don't dare speak my true feelings out loud. It's too dangerous to bare my heart to her when there's no guarantee that she feels the same way.

It's just that holding you on screen might cheapen the moment when I reach for you when we're actually alone. Kissing you in front of other people might ruin the first real kiss we share, should I ever get the chance. Pretending to be your boyfriend when I know I can't have you might ruin me, Chloe.

"Hunter, the only reason I agreed to do this was because you promised you'd be there to help me. You said you'd make sure I was comfortable..." Her cheeks redden with frustration. "Now that I've already signed my life away, you want to back out and leave me hanging?"

"I'm not leaving you hanging," I insist. "I'm trying to make things easier for..."

"For who, Hunter?" Chloe fumes. "For you?"

I gaze skyward, anticipating the fallout that's going to come hurtling my way in about five seconds.

Four...

Three...

Two...

"This is about you, isn't it?" Chloe grinds the toe of her shoe into the track, but I feel it in my heart. "You can't bear to have your playboy image tarnished by being seen with another girl on screen. You don't want all the flocks of women hovering over your DMs to think that you're in a relationship."

My jaw slackens. "What? Chloe, that's ridiculous. I don't give a rat's a–"

She shushes me, interrupting my curse.

"I don't care," I amend, "what anyone else thinks about my relationship status."

"Ha!" Chloe scoffs. "What a lie. That's all you've ever cared about, Hunter. Your relationship status completely defines who you are."

Her words land in the dead center of my chest, piercing through flesh and bone and burning me right through. My greatest insecurities are pushing their way to the surface, writhing out of the hole she just blew through my emotions. *The fear of rejection. The fear of being disliked by other people.*

The fear of being alone.

She hit me right where it hurts, and she knows it. Right where I'm the most vulnerable. I glower down at her, ready to fight back, but she beats me to it.

"You've always wanted to have your cake and eat it, too," she says, her words coming out in a rush. "You always want a girlfriend, but you also want to be able to flirt and party and kiss whomever you want, whenever you want. You leave a string of broken hearts behind you everywhere you go."

She takes a step toward me, pressing a finger into my chest. My workout shirt wrinkles under the pressure of her fingertip.

"I've got news for you, Hunter. That's not how relationships work. One day you're going to have to grow up and realize that you can't play both sides. You can't truly love someone and long for *everyone else* at the same time."

I feel a muscle tick in my jaw as she drops her hand, stepping away from me.

The brief pause she gives is long enough for me to speak up.

"Oh, ok," I say, cracking my knuckles and closing the gap between us again. "How about you, Chloe? So terrified of getting your heart broken that you shut everyone out. As soon as someone starts to show an interest in you or wants to get to know you, you push them away."

"That's not true."

I raise my eyebrows at her. "Entirely true. I may have failed in my relationships, over and over, but at least I've had the courage to take the chance on other women and at least try to find love."

"How many women have you *tried* now? Remind me," Chloe says, tilting her head and narrowing her eyes at me. "You'd think after trying out all thirty-one flavors at the ice cream parlor, you would have found one you liked."

I can feel my face burning at her reminder of my many past relationships.

"You know what, Chloe? I'd rather try and fail than hide away from the world like you do. At least I have the courage to *try*."

I'm surprised to see tears gathering in the rims around her eyes. I sigh, raking a hand through my hair. All I wanted was to make Chloe happy, but instead, I've made her cry.

Perfect. She's right. All I'm good at is breaking hearts.

"I get it." Chloe sniffs, brushing the tip of her nose with the back of her hand. "This is about me. You don't want to do this because it's with me."

I shake my head. "No, Chloe. You don't get it. I can't do this *because* it's with you."

She scoffs, glancing out over the turf field. "That's exactly what I just said."

"You're misunderstanding me," I say, taking a slow step toward her, then another, until we're close enough for me to reach out and touch her. I wish I could wrap her up in my arms, press a kiss to her hair, and tell her all the things that are on my heart. "I'm taking myself out of the equation to make this easier for you."

I wince immediately after the words leave my mouth. Chloe's eyes are wide and watery as she looks up at me. "Oh, *WOW*," she rails. "You think if we do this video together, I'm going to fall for you, Hunter? You're trying to protect me from all of..."—she gestures to all of me—"this?"

I rub a hand over my forehead. "For the LOVE. I can't say anything right."

"I can't believe you." She pushes past me, stalking across the track. "You're so *arrogant*!" she calls back to me.

"And you're so stubborn," I shoot back. "You don't understand what I'm trying to do!"

She whirls around, walking backward. "Oh, I understand completely. Don't worry, Hunter. You can rest easy knowing that there is *zero* chance that I will *ever* fall for you."

I clench my hands into fists. I'm starting to think that the track at Ridgeview High is cursed. Both times we've come here to run together have ended in arguments.

Chloe and I fight. It's inevitable to sometimes disagree with someone you know as well as we know each other. But this argument feels different. I'm furious that she completely misunderstood me, twisted my words around to make it seem like I was trying to preserve my singlehood and needed to get her out of the picture to do so.

Little does she know that her ominous statement, her declaration that there is zero chance of her ever falling for me, ignites a fire inside my chest that is smoldering inside me all the way home.

I should feel defeated. My ego should be completely deflated, a limp balloon that's lost its helium. Instead, I feel incredibly motivated. On fire for Chloe. Burning to prove her wrong. To make her eat her words. I am deathly afraid of being disliked, and Chloe just triggered my desire to bust out the ol' Hunter skillset of earning the approval of others.

I've been single long enough now to know that my heart has changed. Chloe is wrong about me, wrong about what I want and who I am. I don't want to mess around anymore. I want her heart. And I want her to give it to me freely.

I'm not going to let some random actor step into the role of her love interest in this video. Her challenge fuels me to commit to the job.

As soon as I get home, I sign my copy of the Back Road music video contract.

I'm going to pour every ounce of my energy into proving Chloe wrong. I'm going to do my very best to help her *choose* to fall for me, starting with breaking down every single one of the defenses she's going to raise up in front of those cameras and all those people. If I can break Chloe in that setting, I know I have a fighting chance to win her over when I finally get her alone.

Chapter 14

Chloe

Twelve years earlier...

I take a bite of the Uncrustable Hunter pawned off on me at lunch at the Ridgeview High cafeteria. He's one of those people who refuses to eat an Uncrustable unless they're solidly *frozen*. Who knew someone could be so picky about their pre-packaged, perfectly portioned PB&J?

He's stuffing his face with chicken nuggets instead, dousing them in enough ketchup to make his plate look like a crime scene.

"Want thum?" he asks through a mouthful of nasty, re-heated nuggs.

I crinkle my nose. "I'll pass."

He shrugs, shoveling more food into his mouth.

"So, did you get your tie for the dance yet?" I ask.

A few weeks back, I'd gathered every ounce of courage I possessed to ask Hunter to the Preference dance. I agonized for days over just how to pop the question, how to channel everything I knew and loved about my best friend into a clever combo of a poster and food delivered on his porch.

I'd settled on a candy message *a la posterboard* (Hey, *SweeTARTS*, I know how much dancing makes you *Snickers*).

He'd answered by having a pizza delivered to my house, the pepperoni sloppily spelling out the word YES.

Did I eat that entire pizza by myself in celebratory fashion that night? Possibly.

I went shopping with some friends last weekend to find my dress. As soon as I'd tried it on, I knew it was the one. Floor length with a slit up one thigh. Tiffany blue. Cinched just below the bust so there'd be no skin-tight fabric bunching up around the curves of my ribcage and lumpy spine.

I'd felt beautiful in the dress and thrilled at the prospect of getting extra time out of my brace, to feel the silky lining of the bodice against my *actual* skin.

I'd texted him a picture of the dress so that he could find himself a matching tie. Not me wearing the dress, of course. Can't have the groom seeing the bride before Preference—or...something along those lines.

Speaking of lines, Hunter and I have been strictly friends for a whole two years now. We're no longer the fresh meat, the bottom of the student totem pole. We have been elevated to juniors, with clout to match.

"No, I haven't yet..." He wipes his mouth with a napkin and gives me a nervous look.

"That's alright. You've still got time before next weekend—"

"Hey, do you remember Nicole?" he cuts me off.

I nod. "The girl from our English class?"

"Yeah..." Hunter pulls at his neck nervously. "She actually asked me to Preference yesterday. And I know I already said I'd go with you, but I felt bad that she wouldn't have a date."

I can feel every ounce of the Uncrustable that's settled in my stomach becoming a dead weight as his words sink in.

Hunter had already said yes to me. To being my date. And now he's also said yes to another girl?

I'm shrinking, wishing I could slowly slide under the table and disappear. Feeling so small. Insignificant. Easily brushed aside by someone I care super deeply about.

"I talked to Charlie about it last night, and he would be beyond stoked to take my place as your date." Hunter's eyes are wary, betraying the easy way he's lounging in his chair.

"Charlie?" I say softly. "Like...the-kid-who-bleaches-his-hair Charlie?"

"He's had a crush on you forever, Chlo. This would literally be his dream come true."

I feel anger blooming in my stomach. *Oh. Oh, ok. So this is what it's all about. Making Charlie's dreams come true. What about MY feelings, Hunter?*

"It really won't be any different since we'll all be going together, right?" he says, his dark eyes pleading. "Are you cool if we all just go as a group?"

I should shove my Uncrustable in his face. Smear peanut butter and jelly across his tan nose and cheeks.

But instead, I bite my tongue and nod, not wanting to reveal just how gutted I feel. How truly devastated I am that he's choosing Nicole over me. I can't let my hurt show, or he'll feel obligated to go to the dance with me.

And that's the very last thing I want to be to Hunter—an obligation.

I can feel tears blurring the edge of my vision, so I look down and nod again. "Sure, yeah, that's totally fine." I stand, sweeping my bookbag over my shoulder. "I've gotta get to art. You know how Mrs. Binning is about being late."

Hunter sits up in his chair at my sudden departure, a flash of confusion flitting across his face. "Oh...ok. Well...see you at practice, then."

I give him a wave and hustle out of that cafeteria like I've really got somewhere important to be.

Like a French club meeting. Or detention. Or Horace Slughorn's coveted Slug Club.

Anywhere but the bathroom stall where I find myself crying until I hear the warning bell ring.

I try to swipe my tears away, willing the puffiness in my eyes to deflate before I have to face my classmates. I'd finally experienced what I'd only read about in books.

Heartbreak. Pure, cold, disillusioned heartbreak.

When I get home, I tell my mom about Hunter choosing to go with someone else to Preference.

"Listen to you talk like that. You should be grateful to even have someone who wants to take you to that dance," she says briskly. "Most girls in your grade will probably be sitting at home alone while you're out there dancing the night away. Quit complaining, and get your homework done."

I shut up then, not wanting to instigate my mom's fury as she bangs cabinet doors and mutters to herself about how *nobody helps with a single thing around here*.

But Hunter's rejection had stung. And I don't feel lucky to be going to the dance with someone else. I feel slighted and numb.

How our friendship is supposed to survive this, I don't know.

Chapter 15

Chloe

It takes everything in me to not immediately answer the phone when I see Hunter is calling.

It goes against my nature, everything I've been conditioned to do since I was a teenager. Ignoring his calls feels criminal. A heinous act of rebellion worthy of capital punishment.

It's been three days now since our fight at Ridgeview High, and I haven't caved.

But today is Saturday. And Saturday mornings are reserved for brunch with Hunter at Bud's Biscuits. A standing date that we almost never miss, depending on our work schedules. I'm usually getting wedding clients prepped in the early hours, but I will always, *always* still manage to squeeze in biscuits and jam with Hunter if I can.

I'm already dragging around a ball and chain, lead heavy with guilt over not speaking to him for as long as I have. Leaving him to brunch alone feels horrible. And yet, I don't know how I'm supposed to face him, sit across the table from him, trading compound butters and buttermilk syrup jars without smearing some across his face or dumping it over his Harry Styles hair.

I'm still angry. Rightfully so. I feel like I've been duped. Hoodwinked by my best friend. I'll be the first to acknowledge that I have trust issues. Mom and Dad are to thank for that. But I'm over here grappling with the fact that Hunter charmed me into signing that contract, convinced me that he'd be there by my side, and then immediately bailed on his side of the bargain.

And then—and THEN!—he reveals that the reason he wants to back out is so that he can continue to hoard his single-as-a-Pringle status. At least, that's what I gleaned from our mostly one-sided conversation.

I've replayed his words over and over in my mind. It's like that game where someone whispers something into someone's ear, and the message gets passed from person to person until it becomes something entirely different. The words I now remember Hunter saying are most certainly not the words he actually said. But when I try to recall his actual words, my mind fills in the blanks with hurtful words that cut me deep every time I think about it.

He didn't want to do the music video because he didn't want to have to *pretend* with me. Romance—even in the fake sense—and Chloe can't mix. I got his message loud and clear. He didn't want to do it with *me*. Too much history between us. It would be too awkward and painful for him to have to pretend with me, to touch me, to hold me, even on camera.

I feel like I've been rejected by Hunter all over again. Junior year, Preference style.

I remember how empty I'd felt that night at the dance, watching Nicole and Hunter laughing on the dance floor. And though I'd eventually gotten over Hunter's snub, I still refuse to respond to Nicole's occasional comments she leaves on my posts.

I thought I knew better than to try to cross that line ever again.

Fool me once, shame on you. Fool me twice...

How could I have been so foolish? I fell for Hunter's hand-holding at the coffee shop, his enticing proposal that made me feel special. Seen. Like he wasn't just playing me like he's played all those other women.

I flip my phone over as Hunter calls again, intent on spending my morning reading and running errands before my next appointment in the afternoon.

Not ten minutes later, I hear a knock at the door to my basement apartment.

Nobody *ever* knocks at my door. Nobody except...

I will my heart to quit rapping against my ribs as I pull the door open, intent on giving him a piece of my mind—a small sampling of the tornado of feelings that have been swirling around me these past few days.

Oh, heaven help me.

He's got his glasses on today. The wire-rimmed, gold ones that make him look like an ar-*TEEST*. Like the college boys I'd met while traveling in Paris. He peers down at me through the lenses, and I feel my resolve immediately start to crack.

"Hey." He holds out his hands, plastic bags hanging from his fingers. "I brought brunch."

I feel a surge of emotion that I have to fight to hold back. He doesn't deserve to just show up, filling up my doorway with his presence and attempting to fill my stomach with warm, buttery brunch food.

I'm about to slowly close the door in Hunter's face when he must read my mind. He presses a palm to the door, forcing me to keep it open.

"Can I come in?"

I can smell the biscuits as the bags shift in his hand. My stomach growls audibly.

I relent, swinging the door open for him to enter. Hunter grins like he just won the lottery, brushing by me as he enters the apartment.

"Heather just about bit my head off when I placed my order to-go." He sets the bags down on my tiny table set in the middle of my kitchenette, opening boxes, setting out cutlery, making himself right at home. "She asked where you were."

He pulls out a chair and sits down, looking up at me expectantly. I must still be wearing a look of displeasure, because insecurity flits across his features.

"I want to talk about what happened, I really do..." he says gently. "But I know how it is when you haven't eaten, so..."

He holds out a plastic fork and knife my way and gives me a timid smile.

I sigh, taking the cutlery from his hands and easing into a chair. I open my Styrofoam box and take in the smell of fresh, warm biscuits, dotted with ripe blueberries, drizzled with lemon curd, and topped with Heather's homemade whipped cream. He even remembered to order my side of strawberry jam. Hunter's already digging into his biscuits and gravy, a mound of colorless mush in his container.

With my first bite, I'm transported back to countless Saturdays spent at Bud's Biscuits. Conversations across the table with Hunter, shared plates of biscuits, crispy bacon, and dollops of fluffy whipped cream.

After I've got a whole biscuit under my belt, Hunter wipes his mouth with a napkin and sits back in his chair.

"How is it?"

"Really good. Thank you." I manage to get the words out, but I sound like Scarlett Johansson. Clipped. Lips barely moving. Guarding my teeth closely.

His eyes search mine. "Is it alright if we talk now?"

I set down my fork and take a sip of water before daring to meet Hunter's eyes again. My arms tuck in across my chest as I wait for him to speak.

"I'm sorry, Chloe," he says, and I wish I didn't feel the icy fortress around my heart start to melt. "I went about things entirely wrong the other day."

I shift in my seat. "Well, I wasn't exactly…pleasant toward you, either."

A hint of a smile ticks at his lips. "I mean, I wasn't going to say anything, but…"

I purse my lips to keep my own smile at bay. "Please continue. I like this whole apology thing."

Hunter smirks. "I know you do. And I'd like to think I'm becoming better at it. I truly believe it's not about the arguments between us. Those are bound to happen." He leans closer, settling his elbows on the table. "It's about the make up."

I roll my eyes. "Everything's about *the make up* in my world."

Hunter steels me with his gaze. "I signed the contract. I'm going to be playing your love interest in the music video."

Inhale. Exhale. Would Snoop let his emotions show right now? No, ma'am. I'm poised. Unreadable.

"What made you change your mind?"

Hunter fiddles with his plastic fork, keeping his gaze lowered. "I couldn't stand the thought of you with some other man—even if it was just acting."

I swallow, pressing my tongue against the backside of my teeth. "Why does that suddenly matter to you?"

When Hunter looks back at me, it's like he wants me to read every nuance of his expression. The way his eyes sweep over my face, adoring. Savoring. Softening. The shyness in his crooked grin.

"It's always mattered to me, Chloe."

Forget Oprah and her poise. I'm shattering from the inside out. The stained-glass depictions of Hunter and Chloe that live in my memories are breaking down. Melting. Rearranging into picturesque scenes of heart-wrenching romance.

"Hunter..." I manage to say. "You're not making any sense right now."

He rakes his hands through his hair. "I have been a complete idiot for as long as you've known me. For fifteen years, I've let you live in the wings of my life. Everything changed last year after my dad passed away." His eyes are sincere, pleading. "I can't do this anymore. I can't be your friend anymore, Chloe."

I'm speechless, the rhythm of my heartbeat pounding in my ears.

"I want to be..." Hunter's voice is low, intimate. "More than just your best friend. I want to prove to you that I've changed. That I see you, Chloe. That I've always seen you."

I had expected an apology from Hunter at some point. The biscuit delivery was an added bonus. But this? A declaration of feelings? A confession of Hunter's desire to move our relationship out of the friend-zone?

I'm shook.

This is what I've always wanted, isn't it? For him to essentially kneel before me and bleed out his feelings for me. To be the maiden desired.

But now that it's happening, I feel…numb. Uncertain. Unable to revel in his words, because, as of right now, that's all they are. Words.

Hunter stands from the table, extending his hand for me to take. I hesitantly brush my fingers across his palm. He tightens his grip around my hand, helping me to my feet.

He thumbs my knuckles, gazing at our joined hands as if they're a treasured sight.

"I couldn't keep all of this to myself any longer," he says. "But I understand if you don't feel the same way, if you're not interested in seeing where things could go with us. The last thing I'd ever want to do is make things awkward between us."

I snort. "Too late, sweetheart."

Hunter grimaces. "It's never too late." He threads his long fingers between mine, pressing our palms together. Slowly, he lifts our joined hands to his lips.

His eyes never leave mine as his warm lips meet the skin of my knuckles. My lips part as if he'd just pressed a lingering kiss right to my mouth.

It's The Hunter Effect, I tell myself. *This is what he's good at. Charming his way into the hearts of women everywhere.*

But it's more than that.

It's the depth in his eyes. The yearning in his kiss. The way his lips turn up into an easy smile as he absorbs my reaction. He's reading right through my attempts to appear unaffected by him. I'm right where he wants me.

And that's why I decide to pull my hand away and sit roughly back into my chair. To send a clear message that I will not be so easily persuaded after he'd unintentionally broken my heart a few days earlier.

But he's Hunter. And Hunter is undeterred by my attempts to put distance between us.

He places a large hand on the back of my chair, the other landing on the table in front of me. He's hovering over me, trapping me underneath him as he bends down so we're eye to eye.

"I'm going to do everything in my power to convince you to give me a chance," he says. I see a muscle in his jaw tick. We're close enough that I could lean forward a few inches and press my lips to that spot, feel the rake of his stubble brush across my bottom lip...

"But you can take all the time you need. I'm in no rush when it comes to you."

He leans forward, the neckline of his shirt gaping open. I take in the length of his collarbone, the cut lines of his chest. I smell his cologne—a whisper of earth, stone, and clear running water.

I feel his lips press against my hairline, and I can't help but close my eyes and savor his gentle caress. Golden longing. No longer hidden in the shadows, flickering across my skin where he breathes.

I feel him pull away and flutter my eyes open. He's gathering up his to-go box, his utensils. He stuffs them into the bag and gives me a smile that warms me right through.

"Sunday dinner, tomorrow night?"

I comb my fingertips through my hair, sweeping strands behind my ears and trying to get my bearings.

"Yeah..." I breathe. "Yeah, that works."

"Okay." Hunter strides to the door, turning the knob before I can even ease myself out of my chair. "I'll pick you up at six."

I allow him the indulgence of a brief smile, which I quickly tamper down with a sharp series of nods. "Sounds great."

"Alright." He steps outside. "See you tomorrow."

Just like that, he's gone.

And just like that, I'm utterly undone.

Chapter 16

Hunter

I'm hyperaware of Chloe, even more than usual, as we spend Sunday night together at my mom's house. I'm waiting for her to acknowledge my honesty, to maybe give me some insight into what she's thinking about me. About us.***

But in typical Chloe fashion, she's sweet. She's kind. She's utterly impossible to read.

"One more round?" I pop the tetherball up into the air and catch it again.

Chloe shoves the sleeves of her massive sweater up to her elbows. This grandpa sweater lands mid-thigh, almost covering up the hemline of her short corduroy skirt. I've been struggling to keep my head in the game when the length of her legs are so visible, even in the waning twilight.

"Let's do it," she says, gesturing for more. "Bring it on, hotshot."

Per usual, we're tied one for one. I've been sloppy tonight, while Chloe's clearly playing to win.

I'd slung my arm over the back of her chair during dinner, earning me a questioning look from both Luke and Lainey, and a saucy wink from my mother, which I'm ninety-nine percent sure Chloe witnessed. Their judgment did nothing but fuel my decision to try to maintain some form of physical contact at all times while Chloe was anywhere near my person. I have to. The urge to be connected to her is completely involuntary. She's magnetic, my own personal kryptonite.

I'm giving myself permission to test the waters, and so far, she hasn't shoved me away.

Her black platform boots nearly trip her up as I sling the tetherball around the pole to her side of the court. She recovers at the last second, popping the ball back my way.

We parry back and forth for a few minutes until a rogue glance down at her legs results in me getting clocked in the side of the face with the tetherball.

"HA-HA!" Chloe laughs, her hands tangling in the rope as she reels the ball back in. She lets out another wild laugh. "I'm sorry. It's so rude of me to laugh at you...but that was *impeccable*."

I rub my hand over my jaw. "You're ruthless."

"I didn't hit you on purpose! You were too busy staring at me to see the ball coming."

"I was trying to be subtle."

She rolls her eyes, swinging around the pole to join me on my side of the court. "You're about as subtle as a sledgehammer."

I'm looking down into her twinkling eyes when she slowly reaches a hand up to my cheek. Her fingertips graze along my jawline.

"Are you ok? You took a pretty good hit."

I catch her hand in mine, feeling her fingers soften against my face as I briefly hold her there.

"Yeah, I'm fine." I swallow. Her touch slowly drifts down past my jaw, skimming along the sensitive skin of my neck before landing on my shoulder. I let go, but her hand remains, dancing along the neckline of my sweater and sending adrenaline coursing through my veins.

My gaze cuts between her eyes and her full lips as she tilts her head up toward mine.

"I win, I think," she says softly, her eyes dropping down to my lips for the briefest of seconds. Long enough for me to know that she's feeling the same electric current flowing between us, filling in the spaces where we aren't yet touching.

"Only because your opponent was gravely injured."

I place my hands on her upper arms, guiding her until she's pressed flush against the tetherball pole. I can feel her uneven breathing, see her chest rising and falling in tempo with mine.

I hadn't planned on our first kiss happening here on the tetherball court, but my teenage self is currently losing his mind, pressuring me to make the daydream I'd envisioned since I was fifteen years old a reality.

I've thought about kissing Chloe at pretty much every place we frequent together. Rosie's. The Toasted Bean. Radnor Lake. Bud's Biscuits. In my Jeep Wrangler.

Somehow, hidden in the shadows of the trees surrounding the house that I grew up in, this feels right. Fitting for us.

I'm desperate to show Chloe just how much I want her to win at everything in life. To be the champion of every little thing she does.

"I'll concede this time," I say, sliding one hand around the back side of her neck and the other finding her hip. I duck my head down, tilting my head and drawing her face up to mine.

Chloe's lashes fan out across her cheek as her eyes close, and she breathes out a nearly inaudible sigh the second before I skim my lips across hers.

Her full bottom lip brushes against mine, and I resist tasting her immediately, wanting to draw out this moment we've waited to share for so long.

I let my lips brush hers again, our breath mingling together in the cold, intent on tantalizing her as long as she'll let me. But instead, I feel Chloe's hands climb up my chest, grabbing fistfuls of my sweater as she pulls me to her.

Our lips crush together, the force of her kiss upending my plans to take things slow and steady. I return the pressure of her lips with an answering kiss of intense need. We taste each other, deepening the kiss. She's sugar sweet and honey wild, the press of her lips against mine both gentle and firm, guiding.

I tangle my fingers in her short hair, gently taking a handful of it in my fist. Her hands find the dip of my lower back, trailing a line down my spine. I follow suit, letting my palms splay out across her back, firmly pulling her to me and tracing the S-shaped curve of her spine through the knit of her thick sweater—

She abruptly pulls away, fear flitting through her eyes as she blinks rapidly.

I can feel her trying to step away from me, so I relent, allowing her body to slide out of my grasp. The space between us feels like a chasm as she tucks her hair behind her ears, nervously avoiding my gaze.

"I can't even tell you how long I've wanted to kiss you like that, Chloe Paulson."

She presses her palms to her cheeks, and in the almost dark, I can still see her strawberry-pink blush. She sighs, bracing herself against the tetherball pole.

"It's so hard for me to believe..." She pauses, laughing bitterly. "That you want to kiss me...for me, Hunter. Not just for the sake of kissing someone."

Her words hit me in the gut. Turns out one kiss can't take away years of bad habits, years of unintentionally painting myself as a womanizer. A flirt. The kind of man I never wanted to be.

"I promise you..." I say, brushing a hair blowing across her forehead back behind her ear. "I kissed you because I have dreamed of doing just that since I was fifteen years old. I'm genuinely sorry that it took me so long to get my crap together."

She gives me a sad smile, crossing her arms and shivering.

"Hunter, I'm sorry," she says, her tone wounded. "You'll have to forgive me if it takes me a while to come around to the fact that you're a changed man. That you genuinely want me. And not just because you're lonely."

She places a hand on my arm. "I wish I could let myself fall for you, Hunter. I can't dive in headfirst the way you want me to."

"I'm not asking you to," I say. "But I *am* going to entice you to do so every second that we're together."

Chloe drops her gaze again, her cheeks coloring. "You almost had me convinced tonight."

"I'd say I did convince you. You kissed *me*, Chloe."

She shakes her head. "*I did not!*"

I raise my eyebrows incredulously. "I tried to take it slow, but you charged in and took over."

"Well, I figured if this was the only kiss we'd share together, I'd better show you how I like to be kissed."

I tsk. "Chloe Paulson. I fully intend to kiss you every chance I get."

She meets my eyes again, her gaze serious. "I'm not going to let you play with my heart, Hunter."

"I would never do that," I breathe. "I want your heart to be given to me—willingly. Freely."

"I want to believe you," she says. "I wish it was easy for me to believe you."

I take her hand in mind, tightly twining our fingers together. "You've always told me that talk is cheap, thanks to the example your parents set for you. And I plan to show you, rather than just tell you, how much you mean to me. We've got plenty of time to see where this road takes us."

"Do we?" She arches an eyebrow. "It's only a matter of days before you're onto the next actress in one of your music videos..."

I grin. "Precisely."

Chloe swallows. "Oh wait...that's me...isn't it?" She lets out a girlish giggle and then clears her throat.

Oh, I've got you, Chloe Paulson. I've got you exactly where I want you.

Her eyes cloud over as she withdraws into herself again. I can feel my hold on her fading.

"Where do I fall," Chloe asks, "on your naughty-and-nice list of all the girls you've kissed?"

I shift uncomfortably. Talking about the other women I've kissed in the past is probably the least romantic thing we could do right now.

"You're at the top. The only one that's ever mattered to me."

I must have said something right, because Chloe gives me a satisfied smirk.

"If that's true, if you've always wanted to kiss me, why didn't you ever try before?"

A brisk wind blows over us, causing Chloe to start shivering again. I pull her toward me, wrapping her into a tight hug. She relents after a moment, settling into my chest and wrapping her arms around my waist.

"Because up until now, I was never worthy of you," I say softly into her hair. The fragrant smell of her salon-grade shampoo sends me into the stratosphere it's so enticing. "Let's be honest, I'm still not worthy of you..." I can feel her shrug against me. "But I want to be."

She pulls away and looks up at me, keeping her arms around my waist. "Are you saying you're finally ready to grow up?"

I wince. "Well...not entirely. I don't think I can give up the copious amounts of sugar I require to function on a daily basis."

She gives me a soft smile. "I don't want you to change for me, Hunter. I've always accepted you for exactly who you are. At every stage and every moment."

"I know that," I say, my hands finding her hips. "And that's exactly why I want to change. You make me want to be better."

Her eyes glitter in the shadows. I press a gentle kiss to her forehead, hoping to convey the sincerity of my words and feelings in the simple gesture.

"Thank you," she says quietly.

We stand there, holding each other in the growing darkness until the cold forces us inside.

It's not until we're back in my Jeep that I work up the nerve to open up to her, to actually verbalize the heavy weight I've been carrying since the chocolate-chip-cookie ambush with Mom and Luke.

Sharing something as intimate as a kiss with my best friend has me feeling some type of way. Makes me want to bare my soul to her, to share more with her.

"I'm surprised nobody mentioned anything about it tonight," I say as we're pulling out of the driveway, "but Mom's going to sell the house."

Chloe gasps, her eyes widening in shock. "What?"

I nod, sighing. "Yeah. Says she's ready to downsize."

Chloe draws her knees up to her chest, balling up in the passenger seat. "This is the worst news ever."

"You're telling me."

We drive in silence for a few more minutes before she reaches over and lays a hand on my leg. The space underneath her palm warms me, and I immediately feel understood.

"I'm so sorry, Hunter. This has to be so hard for you. It's hard for me, and I didn't even grow up in that house."

I shoot her a half smile. "It sucks. Mom wants me to go through my room and clean everything out."

"Do you need help? I'm pretty good at decluttering," she says confidently.

"When was the last time you saw the inside of my bedroom?"

Chloe scowls at me. "Uh...never."

I give her a pointed look.

"Okay, fine." She rolls her eyes. "Remember when we used to play sardines with that big group of cross-country runners back in the day? I definitely snooped around then."

I raise my eyebrows even further.

She looks at me sheepishly. "Aaaaand maybe I snuck into your room a few times when you weren't home."

"Then you'll know that it is a disaster zone."

She grimaces. "We've got our work cut out for us, then, don't we?"

We? I like this casual mention of WE. Makes me feel a little less alone in my misery over losing the house.

"If you're willing to help me out, consider yourself hired."

"I do require payment for my services," Chloe says coyly, staring straight ahead out the windshield.

And what form of payment might that be? More kisses? Cuddles? Make-out session in your driveway in about five minutes?

"Rosie's." She shoots me a smile.

Ahh, yes! You, sir! The chap in the sweater. Were you under the impression that you were about to get a little more than a cordial 'goodnight' tonight? Well, JOKE'S ON YOU, SUCKER! You were sorely mistaken.

I reel in my hope that Chloe was about to let me in on her side of things, to let me see into her heart. My hope that maybe she wanted to kiss some more, to keep the party going. I can't help but feel a little disappointed, and yet I will happily honor her simple request.

"Double scoop. Waffle cone." I swallow. "Consider it done."

Chapter 17

Chloe

I gasp, nearly dropping my eye shadow brush. I'm currently working my makeup magic on Lainey's best friend and roommate, Ella Mae. We're at their shared townhome in Carriage Court, utilizing the natural light from the sliding glass back door in the kitchen while I work.

"Oh!" Ella Mae startles in her chair at my fumble. "You ok?"

I'd been *this close* to accidentally dusting a contour brush loaded with a cobalt-blue shadow over her eyelid.

"Yes!" I exclaim a little too enthusiastically. *I'm fine, you're fine, we're all fine.*

I busy myself with my palettes, finding the correct shade of amber I'd used on her other eye to finish off the look.

You wanted a bronze smokey eye? Because I was thinking more along the lines of Ariel on her first date with Prince Eric. "Under the Sea" vibes. Sebastian shimmer.

I fully blame Hunter for my almost fatal error.

I stumbled into my apartment last night with quaking legs reminiscent of a newborn giraffe. Did I sleep a wink after kissing the man I've loved since I was a teenager? Why, no. No, I did not.

SHOCKER.

And here I am, trying to chit chat with my budding singer-songwriter of a client-slash-friend before she plays a writer's round at a cafe in town, not thinking about how kissing Hunter felt like locking lips with a literary hero brought to life. The man knows what he's DOING. Though I hate the fact that he's a much more experienced kisser than I am, there was something so attractive about his complete confidence. No hesitation. No fumbling. No gnashing of teeth.

Just sweet, sweet adoration. I could feel it with every press of his lips against mine, every gentle movement of his hands on my body. Each kiss we shared told me everything I'd always wanted to hear.

But he *can't* know just how much I buckled under his tender affection. I have to continue to hide the fact that I'm well acquainted with The Hunter Effect. I don't want to be like every other girl he's charmed, seduced, and drawn into his well-crafted web of charisma.

Because I'm nothing like them. Unlike the easy, gorgeous women he usually goes for, I want to make him work for it.

Despite my insecurities (Exhibit A: ending the kiss when I felt his hands start to explore the twists of my crooked spine), I know that I'm well worth the effort. I'm not going to collapse into a fit of girlish giggles every time he smiles at me—at least...not outwardly.

"So, do you ever work with male clients?" Ella Mae asks. "I want all the details on which dude in country music wears the most makeup."

I laugh, thankful for a distraction from the constant replay of THE KISS in my mind.

"I do! Close your eyes for me again." I sweep an angled brush along her lash line. "Most guys want me to apply as little makeup as possible. Those down-home country boys are horrified by it."

"There's got to be someone who's a little high maintenance, though. Do tell!"

"Hmmm..." I hum. "I can't think of anybody who's needed more than a little concealer and powder...look up for me." I gently define her lower lash line. "Although, you wouldn't believe how much time I spend styling Connor Cane's hair. That man is *particular*."

Ella Mae's cheeks redden in the mirror. "That doesn't surprise me one bit. His hair always looks way too perfect."

I grin at her. "True. But you can't deny the fact that he is a beautiful human."

"You're right. I can't lie. The hair does it for me."

I offer a quick curtsy. "You're welcome."

"I actually knew him." She shifts in her seat. "Before he was a hotshot country star."

My jaw drops. "No way! How do you guys know each other?"

"He and my older brother Trent were buddies in college. They're still pretty close. Connor still goes out to visit Trent in Washington every summer for some quality man time. Hunting, fishing..."

"Oh, yes. Give me all the mountain men in their flannels, building their campfires..." I grin. "How did I not know this?" I ask. "Connor is the sweetest soul. So kind to everybody on set. He prides himself on remembering people's names after meeting them just once."

She nods. "Yeah, he was always sweet to me, too, even though I was his best friend's little sister. I feel like the media paints him as this hoity-toity playboy."

"Well, the media is always trying to bring people down when they're at the top. He's had his fair share of troubles, but I think he has a really good heart."

Ella Mae sighs. "You've confirmed it. Now I'll *never* get over him."

I chuckle. "Do you guys still talk? I'll have to ask him about you at his next shoot."

She sucks in a breath. "Oh, please don't. We haven't seen each other in years."

I shrug. "If you change your mind, I know Hunter would totally let me invite you on set."

As soon as the words leave my mouth, I'm wishing I could reel them back in. No way would I want somebody ELSE I know to watch me and Hunter awkwardly stumble around on camera.

"That's super nice of you, but like I said, it's been a long time since we've seen each other." Ella Mae's eyes widen. "Wait a second. Connor's working on new music? Have you heard any of his new songs?"

I'm well aware of the contracts I signed for 'Cry, Baby' and 'Make Up', but I am not as well versed in the fine print. How much am I allowed to share? Better err on the side of *not much*.

"I have, actually," I say, starting to apply mascara. "Do you want to do this part yourself? Sometimes people are funny when I try to do their lashes for them."

"Probably because they feel like they might lose an eyeball should you twitch," Ella Mae quips. She accepts the tube of mascara and leans closer to the mirror.

"You sure you don't want the falsies?" I hold up the strip of lash extensions I'd selected for her.

Ella Mae shakes her head. "Nah. How can you blink with your eyelids weighed down by those caterpillars?"

"Very slowly."

I'm all about a natural look, so I set aside the lashes.

"So, can I ask..." Ella Mae says conspiratorially. "What's Connor's next single about?"

I decide that sharing a vague synopsis of the song doesn't constitute a breach of contract.

"It's pretty sweet, actually," I say. "It's about what comes after an argument in a relationship. Whether you decide to let your disagreements or differences tear you apart or try to work things out and grow together."

Ella Mae swipes the mascara over her long, blonde lashes. "I love that."

I search for my highlighter palette. "Hunter always says it's not about the argument. It's about how you choose to handle it. What matters most is the make up."

Ella Mae points the mascara wand toward me and grins. "No pun intended."

"It's a really sweet song. I think people are going to love it."

"Can I hear it? A little sneak preview?"

I shake my head. "Sadly, no. I have to keep the details under wraps."

She hands the mascara back to me, her lashes looking full and voluminous. "I don't want to be a fangirl like the rest of America, swooning over Connor Cane, but I genuinely love his songwriting. His lyrics are always spot on. He used to play songs he was working on for my brother and me back in the day, and I could never get them out of my head."

"That's high praise coming from a songwriter as good as you."

She shudders. "Yikes. I forgot that I have a gig tonight. Way to go, Chlo. Reminding me."

"Stop that. You're going to kill it!"

"I might kill something. Like the neck of my guitar from gripping the thing too tightly while I play." She holds up a mirror to inspect her face. "Wow, you have transformed me, Chloe. You're a doll."

I quickly do some touch ups on the curls I'd spun into her hair before spritzing her with a finishing spray and sending her off to soundcheck.

As I'm packing up my kit, I hear my phone buzz on the kitchen island.

Hunter: *CHLOE! You free tonight? I wanna go over some ideas for the video with you. *praying hands emoji**

Why does my stomach swoop like I just twisted through a massive loop on a thrill ride at the theme park? He didn't even *imply* what my brain starts conjuring up.

A hands-on demonstration? Count me in.

Chloe: *I should be home around 7!*

Hunter: **Thumbs up emoji* Can I come over then?*

I bite my lip. After last night, the idea of Hunter and me alone in my very secluded, very quiet apartment with only Darlene's snores filtering down through the vents feels a little too risky. I'm already envisioning cuddling up with him on the couch, making him tea in one of my mugs, and subsequently never drinking out of another mug again for as long as we both shall live.

No ma'am. No tea-time tangles for you tonight. Don't you DARE play things easy.

Chloe: *How about we meet at Rosie's?*
Hunter: *NOW WE'RE TALKING.*
Hunter: *Kitchen sink round...twelve?*
Chloe: *NOOOOO *puking emoji**
Hunter: *I'm so down. But first...I might need your help with something else.*

Why does that text send my innards into a twist? I know he's not implying anything, and yet I shamelessly hope he is.

You need me to help relieve the desire you've had to kiss me again? Why, certainly. Much obliged.

Hunter: *Could you meet me at my mom's first to help me start packing up my crap? I could use your organizational skills.*
Hunter: *And your company.*

This can't be easy for him. Facing the fact that his mom is going to up and leave the house that holds all his happiest memories. Sorting through all the things he's held onto since childhood. Acknowledging the hole in his life where his dad should still be.

Chloe: *Of course. I'll meet you over there in 30 minutes.*
Hunter: *Sounds great.*
Hunter: *Would you judge me if I told you I'd already stopped for a soft serve at the drive-thru today?*
Chloe: **laughing crying emoji**

I've always known that Hunter is a man-child and probably always will be. A complete kid at heart. I can only imagine the kind of playful, happy father he will be someday...

I slam my phone down on the counter. No thinking about Hunter as a father. No stirring up yearnings in my uterus to bear children—ESPECIALLY not *his* children.

I'm not even sure what carrying a child would look like for someone like me. Someone with a deformed spine and shrunken torso. Probably like a squat little apple. An apple with legs.

The short-torso problems will NEVER cease for me. I accepted that a long time ago.

But knowing Hunter for as long as I have, I know he wants to be a father someday. I'm not entirely sold on the idea of kids, but I'm pretty sure he could sway me should the opportunity present itself.

I don't intend on being WITH CHILD anytime soon. If ever. So ENOUGH OF THIS NONSENSE.

I'm wrapping the cord around my curling iron when the door to the garage flies open.

"YOO-HOO!" Lainey calls out, sweeping into the house like a vintage vision from the '80s. Oversized striped sweater, high-waisted denim, massive gold hoop earrings, thick red hair flowing in waves down her back like a Disney princess. Her arms are laden with grocery bags, so I hustle to help her get them onto the counter.

"Hey, friend!" she says brightly. I swear, Lainey carries a glow with her that radiates from the inside out. That natural light has been magnified since she and Luke got together, but I'm certain it's always been there. It's part of who she is.

"Don't you look stunning!" I gesture to her gorgeous sweater. "Is this thrifted?"

She nods. "Some dear woman set it aside at the checkout the other day, so you best believe I snatched it up!"

"I'm coming with you next time."

Lainey gasps. "You have to! I've found an amazing secondhand spot."

I help her hoist her bags onto the counter. "Can I help you put this stuff away?"

She waves a hand dismissively. "No, ma'am! Sit yourself down. I need you to try this chocolate bar I found."

She rustles through her grocery bags until she finds the bar. She peels off the wrapper, handing me a dark square of chocolate topped with flaky sea salt. We take a bite at the same time, and Lainey closes her eyes passionately, raising her hand in the air in praise. I feel the rich chocolate melt on my tongue and appreciate the texture, the contrast of the salt with the sweet notes from the chocolate.

"Oh..." I say. "That is so good."

She slaps her hands on the counter. "Right?! Luke hates dark chocolate, so I know this would be completely wasted on him."

I snort. "The man who practically drinks his coffee black doesn't like bitter chocolate?"

She nods, taking another bite. "Preposterous."

"I couldn't *pay* Hunter to eat something like this. He would spit it out immediately like a toddler."

Lainey tosses her hair back and laughs. "Why does that not surprise me? Those Ward boys, I'll tell you what."

We share a warm smile, which I immediately try to suck back into my face. I'm behaving as if we have something in common, like we're both tied to these twin brothers in the same intimate way. While I may be Hunter's closest friend, I'm not his fiancée.

I'm certain the words I KISSED HUNTER are now appearing in a flowing script across my forehead. I feel my cheeks warming, so I send my gaze down to the chocolate bar on the counter. "What brand is this? I need to pick one up next time I'm at the store."

Lainey doesn't take the bait. "How are you and Hunter doing?"

"We're...good. The same. The usual."

I swear her eyebrow ticks up toward her forehead. "Glad to hear it."

I stuff the remaining chocolate into my mouth.

"I heard about the music video."

My chewing grinds to a halt, and I swallow loudly. "Oh...you did?"

She nods, her eyes sympathetic. "Hunter talked to Luke about it. I told him to stay out of it...but he's Team Hunter and Chloe, all the way. He's shipping y'all *hard*."

I nod, avoiding her gaze and feeling a blush creeping up my neck. I should have opted for something other than the massive sweater I've got on over my dress today, specifically for this moment in which I am sweating bullets.

"We both are," Lainey says. I swallow. Hard.

I finally get the guts to meet her eyes. Her brown eyes are sparkling. "But I swear..." She shakes a fist in the air. "If Hunter breaks your heart, I will literally break his face."

I snort. "Good to know."

"I'm serious. He'd better play nice, or his future sister-in-law is coming for him."

"I know how you like to play, too." I smirk, remembering the ridiculous pranks she and Luke had played on each other before they'd started dating. "He's definitely afraid of you, even if he doesn't show it."

"Good. He should be."

I sweep my bags into my arms. "I'd better head out. I've got to go meet..." My voice trails off, and I can't hide the guilt from my face.

"Hunter?" Lainey grins. "Give him my regards."

I sigh, not even attempting to lie about the fact that I'm about to spend time with him. "I will."

Lainey waves to me from the porch, a knowing smile on her face. She didn't ask about the kiss, but I'm certain she knows. Women just *know* these things about each other. When a girl's been kissed by a man she loves, she wears it well.

I wonder if I would glow the way Lainey does if Hunter was mine. The way someone does when they're *completely, perfectly, incandescently happy.*

Chapter 18

Hunter

"What..." Chloe says, "is *this*?"

We're currently seated side by side up in my little loft in my childhood bedroom, dumping years of childhood memorabilia into cardboard boxes.

I take the trophy from her outstretched hand. "Oh, now come on, Chloe. You don't remember this?"

She shakes her head, pulling her hair back into her clip.

"This was one of the greatest victories of my entire rodeo career."

"*What*?" she asks incredulously. "You wanted to be a *cowboy*? You've never told me about this particular career aspiration."

I clear my throat dramatically, sweeping a hand out in front of us. "Many moons ago, when I was five or six years old, I, Hunter Ward, was chosen to compete in a rodeo event designed just for kids."

Chloe leans in closer, eyebrows raised. "Pie-eating contest?"

"You know what?" I fish around through another stack of trophies. "That one is around here somewhere. But no, this beauty was awarded to me for winning a different event."

Chloe tosses her head back, cackling. "You WOULD win a pie-eating contest as a kid."

"I was bottomless, Chloe. I'm still bottomless." I grin, joining in with her infectious laughter. "But allow me to continue, if you will."

She steels her expression, biting her lip to keep from laughing. "Please, continue."

"My dad signed both Luke and me up for this event every year until we exceeded the weight limit. It's called mutton bustin'."

She busts out laughing again. "NO. Not a real thing."

"Stop it," I scold. "You're telling me you've never heard of mutton bustin'?"

"*Hunter*," she wheezes. "You're killing me."

"No, you don't understand. It was the sheep that almost killed *me*."

She's done. I've lost her. She's flopped back into a pile of my old sports jerseys, hands over her eyes, laughing so hard that it's inaudible.

"Let me set the scene for you," I begin in my best storytelling voice. "The arena is full. Energy is high. Sheep are just waiting to bust out of their pens, ready to wreak havoc on the children of Franklin."

"OHMYGOSHSTOP."

"My name is called. I'm hustled into a little pen, a helmet is placed on my head, and a vest is strapped to my chest." I lunge forward onto all fours. "They set me on top of a sheep. Fluffy little bugger. I wrap my arms around it...and then they open the pen and let it take me for a ride. I hold on for dear life. Squeeze with all of my might with my arms and legs."

"*And then what?*"

I drop back to my seat on the floor, crossing my legs. "And then...I fall off. The sheep tramples me a little bit. Then, a bunch of other kids take their turns. But in the end, your boy Hunter held onto his sheep friend the longest, making me the winner of this"—I hold up the sheep-adorned trophy—"illustrious award."

Chloe snorts, pushing herself up onto her elbows so she can look at me. Her eyes are bright with laughter. "This isn't real. This *can't* be real."

"This *is* for real, Chloe! How did you grow up here your whole life and never once go to the rodeo?"

Chloe's smile drops for a brief moment. "Guess my parents didn't take me to do the same kinds of things your parents did."

I suck in a breath. "Shoot, I didn't mean..."

"No, I know." She sits up and kneels. "You're lucky you have such happy childhood memories." She picks up a stack of posters that are leaned up against the wall, flipping through them absently. "Were these from your track meets?" A dusting of glitter flutters across her lap. "Man, your girlfriends must have spent hours hand-crafting these."

Her voice trails off as she reaches a simple white poster, a message written out in alternating green and blue marker with blanks where candy bars had once been.

She blinks rapidly. "You still have this?"

I swallow as the memories come rushing back to me.

Finding this poster on my front porch, realizing that my best friend was asking me to the Preference dance. Wanting more than anything to go with her. The pepperoni pizza I'd sent her back as my response.

Nicole, the girl in our English class, asking me to Preference a couple weeks later. Charlie pressuring me to accept Nicole's offer so he could swoop in and take Chloe.

Deciding it was best to not risk my friendship with Chloe by taking her to the dance. Hastily making the decision to go with Nicole. Regretting it forever and ever, Amen.

"Preference. Junior year?"

Chloe sighs. "Yeah. *Not* one of my favorite memories of ours."

I feel like an elephant is stepping on my chest. The weight of what I'd done to her, how I'd brushed her aside like she didn't matter, settles fully on my heart.

"Man. I was a complete idiot."

Chloe is silent, continuing to flip through the posters.

"Why did you stay friends with me after I ditched you like that?" I ask softly.

Chloe lets the posters fall back against the wall, shifting sideways off her knees and tugging her dress down to cover her legs. "I guess I just figured I had to if I wanted to keep you in my life."

I shake my head. "I'm so sorry, Chloe. You had every right to hate me."

She gives me an understanding smile. "You're impossible to hate, Hunter. You were my best friend. I just figured that was your way of telling me that that's all I was to you." She picks at the hem of her silky dress, dropping her gaze. "Your friend."

I place my beloved mutton bustin' trophy into the box with its companions, regret building inside me.

"Some best friend I was. You didn't deserve that." I lift my gaze to meet hers. "I wanted to go with you—I swear I did. But at the same time, I was scared."

"Was it the blue tie I was going to make you wear?" Chloe wrinkles her nose. "I thought blue was your color."

I snort. "It *is* my color. We would have looked great together." I sigh, rubbing a hand over the rough stubble of my chin. "I was nervous that if something happened between us, if we tried to date and then broke up, I'd lose you. I didn't want that. I couldn't do it."

Her expression neutralizes, and she clears her throat.

I immediately recognize this move. This is what Chloe does when she doesn't want me to know what she's thinking, when she's trying to ice me out, trying to hide her feelings.

"No, ma'am. Don't shut down on me, Chloe. We need to talk about this."

She gives me a one-shouldered shrug. "It was so long ago, Hunter. Water under the bridge."

I see right through her armor, realizing she looks exactly the same as she did that day in the cafeteria when I told her I was going to the Preference dance with Nicole.

She did care. She's always cared.

She cares now.

"Are you…" I pause, collecting my thoughts. "Are you afraid that if we get too close…" Her eyes dart up to meet mine. "That I'll leave you high and dry again? Is that why you've kept me at a distance for all these years?"

Chloe smoothes a hand over her hair. "Maybe. I don't know."

"Don't give me that crap." I furrow my eyebrows, leaning close enough to her that I can breathe in the subtle floral scent of her perfume. "Lay it on me, Chloe."

She grits her teeth together, narrowing her eyes. "Why are you pushing me to open up to you right now?"

"Because I need to know."

"Fine." Chloe levels me with her gaze. "Yes, Hunter. I'm...concerned."

"About what?"

"The same thing I've always worried about with you—that you'll mess around with me until you get bored and then move on to the next Nicole or Sarah who comes waltzing into your life."

Her words crush me, bury me under a pile of bricks labeled with the names of all the women I've "messed around" with in my life when I could have had Chloe.

She wanted me then.

Does she still want me now?

I've been walking a fine line the past year since losing my dad. Tasked with rebuilding the way I move through the world, the way I live and love and treat others. Trying to do things differently than I'd always done them. Growing up so I could be in a serious relationship, one built on mutual trust and respect.

Clearly, I haven't even gotten the foundation of trust poured when it comes to my relationship with Chloe. She doesn't trust me yet.

"I know that this is probably just lip service to you," I say, my words measured. "But I promise you, Chloe, I will never do that to you again. Everything changed after last year. Everything."

Her eyes soften a bit around the edges. Knowing. Understanding what I'm saying. The gravity of what my dad's passing did to me.

"I've changed." I lick my lips. "And I plan to prove it to you."

She swallows, her tough exterior cracking for a moment as her pupils widen, and she nods. "I want to believe you, Hunter. But it's like you said...actions speak louder than words."

I glance down at my watch. "Let's get moving, then, because Rosie's closes in thirty minutes, and I promised you an ice cream tonight."

"That's right, boy. You DID."

"And I keep my promises."

She tilts her head to the side, giving me a dramatic grimace. "If you say so."

"Starting now."

Chloe grins. "Right now?"

"Right now." I gesture down to the floor of my bedroom. "After you."

"Good plan." Chloe starts crawling toward the ladder to make the descent down from the loft. "Can't have you looking up my dress."

"On second thought, get out of the way." I grin. "I'll go first."

Chapter 19

Hunter

"Can I sample the cotton candy flavor?"

Chloe snorts, giving me a look that lands on the judgmental end of the scale.

"Hey"—I point a finger at her threateningly—"watch yourself."

"What are you, *four*?" she snickers, taking a spoonful of her go-to flavor: salted caramel. I take issue with this. No dessert should be salted.

"You're such a hypocrite." I swipe the sample spoon from the employee behind the counter at Rosie's. "Sometimes you've just gotta switch things up, ok?"

Chloe raises both her eyebrows at me. "By resorting to the most nuclear, artificially flavored and colored ice cream in this establishment? Seems a little desperate."

Chloe's right. The cotton candy flavor tastes a lotta bit like soap.

"On second thought..." I tap the tiny spoon against my chin. "I'll take a medium waffle cone with cookies and cream and..." I glance at Chloe, waiting for the eye roll. "Birthday cake."

Chloe smirks. "So much for branching out."

"It tasted like crap," I whisper into her hair.

"So does a freshly pressed green juice, and yet, somehow, we all power through."

I accept my generously loaded, handcrafted waffle cone. After our ice creams are paid for, we settle into our usual booth by the window.

"Who eats ice cream that's purposefully flavored to taste like an entirely different dessert?"

I shake my head. "Please shut up, and let me enjoy my birthday cake ice cream in peace."

She smiles around a mouthful. "Sorry."

We eat in silence for a moment. I steal another glance over at Chloe when she's not looking my way, drinking in her straight hair effortlessly swept back into a clip, the thick cream sweater she's wearing over a floral slip dress. She looks like she's stepped right out of a Parisian Pinterest board. Chic and classy.

"I want you to dress yourself for the music video," I say. "I love your look tonight."

Her cheeks color slightly. "Are you trying to save a few bucks by denying me a stylist?"

I roll my eyes. "Yeah. Your outrageously expensive taste doesn't fit in the budget for this one."

I pull my phone out of my jacket pocket, opening the notes I've been compiling for the shoot on Friday.

"I'll email you more details tonight, but I wanted to throw some ideas at you about the music video to see what you think."

She nods, and I can see the nerves dancing behind her eyes and in the way the hand gripping her spoon slightly shakes.

I try not to smile in response to her reaction. She doesn't want me knowing that I affect her the way I do, but I'm reveling in it, enjoying every second she's over there squirming because of me.

Correction: because of her *feelings* for me.

I know I'm not just imagining things. I felt the depth of her desire, her attraction to me in the kiss we'd shared the other night and again tonight as we worked together on packing up my things at Mom's house. Chloe's heart is precious, and I feel privileged to even have a chance to make it beat a little faster, to earn myself a permanent position there.

Not every man Chloe meets gets to move in closer, to see the real Chloe. But here I am, across the table from her, about to tell her my plans for the video.

My plans to get her to fall in love with me.

"So..." I scroll through my notes. "Day one of the shoot takes place at the art museum downtown."

"Wait..." she says, her mouth full. "Did we go on a field trip there once?"

"Yes, ma'am, we did. They're letting us shoot early, before the museum opens. It will just be us there..." I take another bite of ice cream. "And Jax, of course. And Sean will be shooting."

She nods. "Didn't want to bring the full crew?"

"I want it to feel intimate."

Just you and me, Chlo.

My plan is to help her forget that anyone else is there at the museum with us. To make the world around us disappear.

"I'm heading over to the museum tomorrow to plan out the shots with Jax if you want to come and get a feel for it."

Chloe frowns. "I wish I could, but tomorrow's crazy for me. I'll just have to see it on Friday."

"That's great." I give her another onceover. "You should wear this outfit."

She tugs at her sweater. "For real? I have much nicer things in my closet. This is my *grandma* sweater."

I tilt my head to the side, dropping my eyes down to her dress. "I like it."

Chloe's full-on blushing now. "Maybe I'll send you some pictures of some other options, and you can choose."

I shrug, trying to not show the thrill that races through me at the prospect of a private Chloe fashion show sent directly to my phone.

Prime-time programming, right there. I'll DVR that ish.

"If you want to."

"What's the plan for day two?"

"I haven't worked through all the details yet, but we'll be shooting at the old historic theater downtown. That's where Connor's going to be doing his performance stuff."

"Cute."

No, no, Madam. You are mistaken. Cute is reserved for cuddly puppies and teenage flings. This will fall into the irresistibly romantic category.

"I'm envisioning the storyline being about the start of the relationship, showing the memories the couple created together, and then showing similar shots in the same locations again with just me there. Alone."

Chloe grimaces. "Sad for you."

"But then..." I raise a finger. "There's a happy ending. A make up. We can't leave Connor's fans heartbroken."

Chloe swirls her spoon through her ice cream. "Where's that going to take place?"

"I found a really cool old house we're going to shoot at on day one, in the evening. Jax and I were working all day today on getting it decorated so it looks like we live there." I swallow. "And by we...I mean...the fictional couple in the video."

"I'm looking forward to seeing your taste in home decor. Hope it's improved since your teenage years."

I wince. I went through a hunter-green phase in high school, turning literally everything in my childhood bedroom to a nice shade of dark green. It had been super cool at the time, but now it just feels like a monochromatic cave. "Thankfully, Jax has an eye for those kinds of things. Everything I put in the cart got vetoed by him—immediately."

"He's so opinionated about the most random things," she says.

"I, for one, am grateful for that. He doesn't do anything halfway."

She eyes me from across the table. "Neither do you."

That's right, girl. No half-a** efforts from this guy.

"You know what? I think it may surprise you how much you enjoy being my co-star." I settle back into my seat, sending a grin her way.

"Right," she scoffs. "Because who doesn't love prancing around public places, pretending to be someone you're not?"

"I, for one, *do* love it." I smirk. "And I prance publicly. Daily."

She sighs. "I just want to get through it."

"Why are you acting like you're getting a root canal or a spinal tap?" I ask. "This is supposed to be fun, Chloe. You'd better come to work with a good attitude. At least make the effort to enjoy yourself."

She shoots me a glare. "So glad this is *your* idea of a good time."

"You're so determined to hate it, but you haven't even experienced it yet. You may just switch careers after this shoot. You'll be in high demand as soon as the music video community sees your irresistible beauty on screen."

Chloe coughs, her eyes growing watery. "Or it will be so painful to watch I'll be banned from acting in anything ever again. My name will be blackened in this town forever."

I shake my head. "I won't let that happen. I'll make sure to only use shots featuring your good side."

She gasps. "I have a *good side*?"

"Every side is your good side," I mutter.

She narrows her eyes at me and swipes her spoon through my cookies and cream, stealing a bite. She grimaces dramatically. "Ugh...it was tainted by your nasty birthday cake."

We finish our desserts and talk through a few more ideas as we leave Rosie's together.

Leaves are skittering down the sidewalk and through the parking lot outside, the chilly autumn wind gusting around us. Chloe's hair whips around her face, and she laughs, making me want to brush her hair out of her eyes and give her a windswept kiss.

"Thanks for helping me tonight," I say. "I needed that."

"Me, too."

We share a look for a beat, and my eyes naturally drop down to her lips. Before I can even consider making some kind of move, she clears her throat and puts some distance between us.

"See you tomorrow?" she asks, stepping off the curb. She gasps as her foot splashes right into a puddle, spraying muddy water up her bare leg and onto her gorgeous dress.

"NOT THE DRESS!" I scoop her up into my arms and walk purposefully to where her car is parked next to mine.

"HUNTER! PUT ME DOWN!" she yells, clutching her keys and phone to her chest as she bounces in my arms.

"I will NOT have you soiling this outfit before the shoot this weekend!"

Chloe tosses her head back and laughs. I can't help but join in, the sound is so contagious. My chest warms as if I've taken a swig of hot coffee or a bite of a warm biscuit. I carefully adjust her body in my arms so she's hopefully in a more comfortable position.

I stop once we reach her car, glancing down at her face. We're nearly nose to nose for a breath, and it takes everything in me to not sweep my lips over hers. She's trapped in my arms. She couldn't fight me off if she tried.

But I don't want to push her too fast, too soon. I can't afford to lose the ground we've gained tonight. So, instead, I carefully help her to the ground.

"That was utterly unnecessary," she scolds, but there's laughter still lingering in her eyes.

"What kind of a co-star would I be if I allowed you to slosh around in puddles, wearing your perfectly styled outfit?"

She rolls her eyes, unlocking her car with her keys. "Well, thank you for your valiant effort. I'll send over a variety of significantly better options tonight."

I give her a salute as she slides into the driver's seat of her car. "Sounds like a plan."

She waves, giving me a shy smile that tugs at my heartstrings the way Puss in Boots did the first time I saw *Shrek 2*.

I've got my headphones on, listening to "Make Up" for the umpteenth time. My eyes are closed, allowing me to be fully in the zone. I'm visualizing each shot of the music video and how they'll align with the lyrics. I've even got the lighting in each location locked down in my mind.

My phone vibrates in my pocket, breaking my concentration. I pause the song and slide out my phone, my pulse quickening as I see that it's a text from Chloe.

I tap open my messages and nearly fall out of my chair as I click on the first picture she's sent me. It's a selfie taken in the full-length mirror in her bedroom.

She's wearing a red, floral wrap dress with sleeves that end at her elbows. The heels she's got on elongate her muscular legs, and I feel a lump growing in my throat as I zoom in on her cut calves...

My perusal of Chloe's legs is cut short as another photo comes through. This time, she's wearing white on white, a knit top tucked into high-waisted, wide-leg pants that remind me of the female movie stars of the 1960s. She's drop-dead gorgeous.

I'm fully unprepared for her third photo, and when I open it, I smile so big that my cheeks hurt and my headphones are nearly displaced from my head.

She's wearing my sweatshirt, the one I gave her in high school, paired with baggy pajama pants. It's a good thing I'm not physically in her presence, because seeing her in an article of clothing I'd given her all those years ago is doing funny things to my heart rate. If I was there in her room right now, I would literally tackle her to the ground and kiss her until she begged for mercy. It would be completely involuntary.

A text from Chloe comes through next:

CHLOE: *Pick number three, milord!*
HUNTER: *You still have that old thing?!*
CHLOE: *Still my favorite sweatshirt! Comfy as ever.*
HUNTER: *In that case, I want it back.*
CHLOE: *What do you think about the outfits?*
HUNTER: *Love them all. Bring them all.*
CHLOE: *Done.*
CHLOE: *You'd better get your beauty rest, Mr. Director Man. Can't have you dozing off on the job.*

I pause before typing out my response. What I want to say is, *how am I supposed to sleep when all I want to do is stare at these glorious photos of you?*

HUNTER: *I'd encourage you to get your beauty rest, too, but clearly you don't need it. Night, Chlo.*

Chapter 20

Chloe

Please don't fall apart. Please don't fall apart.
I'm repeating this mantra to myself more than I am to my dress, but the missing button I hadn't discovered until I'd entered the art museum is causing me an unexpected amount of distress.

Now is NOT the time to have a Janet Jackson wardrobe malfunction—not in front of my best friend and his pared down filming crew.

I've been fully in my head this morning, replaying the moments Hunter and I have shared over the past couple of weeks.

I thought we were comfortable in our respective roles we'd been playing since high school. Friends of the intimate nature. The kind who call each other on the daily, who send each other posts we see on social media with zero context or explanation and still know exactly why that particular post reminded us of the other. The kind of friends who work together with unspoken ease, who can be laughing hysterically one minute and then contemplating something deep the next.

The kind of friends who kiss on a tetherball court?

Now, I'm no friendship expert, but I'm ninety-nine percent confident that friends DON'T do that.

Nor do they share lingering hugs, gentle touches, and gazes loaded with a whole lotta something that feels way, way bigger than just LIKE.

Jax, Hunter, and Sean are huddled together in front of a display of black-and-white photographs, a white wall punctuated by pieces of art of various sizes. I'm pretending to examine the art display, stealing glances over at Hunter every 6.5 seconds or so.

Hunter is nodding now, arms folded across his chest. He looks unbearably handsome in a simple linen shirt, unbuttoned at the top, and black pants. His hair has that signature wavy flow to it, slightly undone. He's wearing a stack of leather bracelets on one wrist to keep him from looking too dressed up. Hunter always errs slightly on the side of rugged, so I'm not surprised that he's topped off his outfit with his favorite worn black leather boots.

I chose to wear the red dress today, topping off the look with side-swept hair, reminiscent of Marilyn Monroe and Ava Gardner, and a simple red lip.

Hunter had stared at me when I'd walked into the museum, the warm brown of his eyes deepening as they met mine. I'd nearly broken out in hives being locked under his gaze. He didn't say a word, but the look on his face spoke volumes.

He liked what he saw. And he wasn't afraid to let me know it.

He catches me watching him, throwing me a crooked grin.

I keep telling myself to stop getting my hopes up. To remember that the charged moments we've shared might appear to be larger than life to me because I'm *willing* them to be. Because this is what I've always wanted, what my heart has yearned for.

Jax suddenly claps his hands together and says, "Let's get rolling, kiddos."

And now my mouth is dry, my palms are starting to sweat, and my dress gaps open at my chest where the rogue button has been lost.

I try to adjust the dress so my neckline doesn't drop quite so low, but it's a lost cause.

I feel Hunter towering over me, his shadow falling across my line of vision.

"You ready?" he asks, his voice low like he's telling me a secret.

I take a deep breath and nod. Slowly, my eyes travel up to the tiny triangle of exposed chest where his shirt is unbuttoned at the top, his smooth neck, and finally up to his quirked smile. I don't have the guts to fully meet his gaze, so I settle on his mouth.

Heavens.

A very recent memory floods me. A memory that includes feeling those full lips moving with mine, burning through all my friendship fences until I was pulling him into me like I needed him more than I needed air.

ROOKIE MISTAKE, CHLOE. Lips are a no-go.

"Mmmhmm," I hum, yanking my dress down in the back in the hopes that he hasn't already seen right down the front of my dress from his higher vantage point—*hashtag short people problems.*

"Great." He tilts his head, and I see his smile widen, still not daring to look him in the eye for fear of completely losing my nerve.

"For this first shot, you're going to stand here..." He shuffles over a few paces, showing me my mark. "And I'll be right here."

"Okay." I step over to my mark. Hunter steps back a couple feet and assesses the lighting, running his tongue over his teeth.

"Yeah, that will work." He turns back to Sean and Jax. "Is this right, gents?"

Sean's wearing a heavy-duty camera on a rig strapped to his chest. "Looks great."

"You done mutilating your dress there, Chloe?" Jax asks, his pale-blond eyebrows raised to the heavens. "You look great, honey, but that poor dress of yours is going to be in tatters if you don't stop yanking it around."

"Sorry," I breathe, forcing myself to stop adjusting my dress and hoping the gap at my neckline stays appropriately *closed*.

"Ready when you kids are," Jax says, giving me a pointed look.

"I'm good now," I respond.

My heart rate starts to do a wild dance inside my chest. I can feel my lungs tightening, my breath growing thinner. "Wait, what exactly are we doing?"

Hunter joins me back on his mark.

"Hey..." he says, placing a hand on my lower back. "Don't stress out on me already. We haven't even started shooting yet."

I huff out a breath. "You haven't given me any instructions!"

He takes a step closer, his fingers pressing gently into my back. "I was thinking this shot would represent when we first meet, so we'll first stand side by side, taking in this beautiful wall of art..." He gestures widely, making a rainbow motion with his outstretched hand. "We'll steal a couple glances at each other before I work up the courage to talk to you."

I hold out a hand expectantly.

He slaps it and then offers me a fist bump, which I naturally ignore.

"What?" he chuckles.

"Where's my script?" I ask, raising my eyebrows. "If there's going to be talking in this shoot, I'm going to need my lines to be spoonfed to me."

Hunter snorts. "No script here, sweetheart. We're going to improvise."

I shift from foot to foot. "I'm no good at improv, Hunter."

He turns me to face him, ducking his head down so I'm forced to meet his gaze. His eyes crinkle at the edges as he offers me a kind smile. "Chloe. We can do this. Just follow my lead and try to act like all of this is totally natural. None of the audio is going to be used in the video, so we literally can talk about our favorite cold cereal of choice, and nobody will know."

I bite my lip and nod, feeling my heart rate slow down a little, my breath coming a little more easily. "Cold cereal. I can work with that."

He slides his hand off my back and steps a pace away. "Let's just roll with it. We're good, boys." He gives them a thumbs up.

"Camera speed," Jax says.

"Rolling," Sean responds.

"Just pretend we've never met," Hunter says. "Like we're two strangers seeing each other for the first time."

I'm grateful that this first shot is from behind, because I'm certain the camera would be picking up on my wild heart that's fixing to burst clean out of my dress right now.

I inhale deeply through my nose and exhale through my mouth, willing a sense of calm to come over me. Once my mind feels a little less panicked and a little more clear, I settle into my heels in a stance that I hope looks confident. I gaze up at the artwork, my eyes traveling along the sharp lines of architecture captured in the photographs.

Remember why you're doing this. For the leg up in your career. For the massage therapy and chiropractor appointments you haven't prioritized for far too long. For future you who does not want to be in a wheelchair.

For yourself.

For Hunter.

If I want this to be believable, I need to allow myself to fall into this fantasy, completely get swept up in the magic of what it would be like if we were meeting for the first time, here in this museum. I need to let myself believe that my best friend I've loved since I was fifteen years old is someone I don't know, someone I could see myself falling for.

The last thing I want is to embarrass or disappoint Hunter by appearing stiff or uncomfortable on camera. So, I close my eyes briefly, dropping into a forbidden place I've stuffed deep, deep down into the recesses of my soul. The place where Hunter and I are a real possibility. Where I want him, and I'm not afraid to let him know it.

I open my eyes, feeling a growing confidence start to blossom in my chest, and that's what leads me to look over at Hunter.

I imagine that I've never seen him before, that he's someone I've never met. It's totally okay for me to let myself take him in, to appreciate his tall, lean body. His tangle of dark hair, the bump in the bridge of his nose, the way his muscles fill out his white shirt.

I don't want to be afraid anymore. I want to believe that I'm worthy of being loved by someone like Hunter, just the way I am.

His eyes cut to me, and I see his lips twitch in a shy smile. I quickly look back at the wall, not wanting him to think I've been staring for too long.

I tilt my head, taking a step closer to one of the photographs, as if it's the most interesting thing I have ever laid eyes upon.

The back of my neck prickles with the knowledge that Hunter's watching me unabashedly—just the way I've always wished he would.

I glance back over at him and am surprised to find that he's already moved closer. As we lock eyes, he takes a few slow steps toward me. He stops about two feet away, staring at the same photograph I've chosen to admire.

After a beat, Hunter shakes his head. "This one's not my favorite."

I raise an eyebrow up at him. "Oh? Why's that?"

He points to the bottom corner of the image. "Every time I look at this spot, all I see is a unicorn. Looking at said unicorn immediately makes me hungry, reminds me of what I'd consider to be the greatest cereal of all time." He pauses for a beat. "Lucky Charms."

"What an abstract interpretation of this piece," I say, pressing my lips together to hide my smile.

"What about you?" Hunter gestures to the photo. "What do you see?"

I purse my lips, scanning over the image. "My eye is naturally drawn to this part of the photo..." I trace a circle around the area I'm talking about. "Simply because it looks just like a piece of toast. Which could be a subtle tribute by the artist to what I would deem to be the truly most iconic cereal of all time: Cinnamon Toast Crunch."

Hunter squints. "Ah. Yes. I see it."

We share a hesitant smile, my heart doing a backflip as Hunter extends a hand to me.

"Hunter."

I take his hand in mine, giving it a squeeze and slow shake. "Chloe."

"Chloe," he says softly, his eyes dropping down to my lips. "I know this is forward of me, and we've only just met, but I would regret letting this opportunity pass me by."

For a second, I swear he's going to slip his hands around my waist and press his lips to mine, and I don't think I'd have the willpower to fight it.

Instead, he drops my hand and asks, "Would you like to partake in a meal of cold cereal with me sometime?"

I can't help myself. A laugh escapes my lips, and I clasp my hands in front of my body.

"It wouldn't even have to be for breakfast," he clarifies. "We could throw caution to the wind and eat cereal any time of day. My schedule is pretty open."

I glance down at my heels and chuckle before meeting his eyes again. They're bright, full of the laughter we've always shared so effortlessly.

"I'd like that."

"Great."

I hear a snort break out from behind us. "Cut!"

The spell is broken, and suddenly, I'm not the Chloe who just got picked up by the most charming man she's ever met while looking at an art exhibit.

I'm just *me* Chloe. The girl whose dress is gaping in the front and whose stomach is audibly growling simply at the mention of cereal.

Hunter rubs his hands together, smiling gleefully. "You liked that, Jax?"

"It's a good thing you're both hot, because that dialogue was tragic." Jax shakes his head.

Sean shrugs. "I thought you were pretty smooth, myself."

Hunter nods, pressing his palms together in gratitude. "Thank you, Sean."

I'm silently thanking Jax and Sean for not asking for my opinion on Hunter's attempt to hit on me. Was I utterly charmed by his boyish wit? Absolutely. But *never will I ever* tell anyone that my knees are slightly weak at the moment, and it has nothing to do with the fact that I only ate three meager pieces of clementine for breakfast.

I cross one leg over the other and place my hands on my hips, drawing in a deep breath.

One take down, and my walls are already crumbling. Hunter is going to break me down, one shot at a time. I don't know how I'm supposed to make it out of the shoot with all the pieces of my heart still intact.

Chapter 21

Chloe

"Just hold me," Hunter says firmly.
"*I can't.*"
He sighs.

My chin trembles, and I duck my head with embarrassment.

My anxiety is making this unexpectedly difficult for the both of us. He's been trying to persuade me to go along with his directions for a few minutes now, but I need more time. I've got to ease into things. The nerves have been building all afternoon, and now the panic is starting to set in.

Shooting at the museum this morning had been a piece of cake. I'd felt relatively at ease, not at all uncomfortable with acting out the meet-cute on camera.

After we'd shot a few scenes together, Hunter had a quick wardrobe change before re-shooting the same scenes by himself. I'd stood off to the side, observing quietly like I always do so well.

But now that we're skipping ahead on the fictional timeline to the scene that's supposed to take place at the old house we'd found in Franklin, I'm digging in my heels. Stressed to the max. On the verge of a breakdown.

"This is supposed to be the most romantic scene of the video, Chlo," Hunter says softly. I cross my arms over my chest and stare out toward the quiet road in front of the house.

"Is there a problem, children?" Jax asks. "Because I'm happy to play mediator if we need to sit down for a little kumbaya sesh."

"Nope, we're good." Hunter shoots him a reassuring smile.

I continue to glare up at him from the doorway. He runs a hand through his hair in frustration.

I'm getting the vibe that Hunter hopes that this scene will go just as easily as this morning had. I'm not trying to be high maintenance, but I refuse to jump from flirting to kissing on camera in the space of a couple of hours.

Hunter explained to me that his character is supposed to show up on the doorstep of what is supposed to be my home. We have a conversation for a moment before he takes me into his arms for a kiss, sweeping me up and into the house.

This is meant to be the one kiss to rule them all. A kiss that signifies a turning point in our on-screen relationship. This is where the make up begins. Where this character acknowledges where he was wrong, how he took her for granted, and then starts fighting to get her back.

But I'm currently refusing to even *hug* Hunter back, so I know getting a good kiss on camera is probably starting to feel like a distant fantasy for him.

"Do you want me to lay out what's happening between these characters for you?" he asks, successfully keeping his tone patient and steady despite my stubbornness. "Would that help you feel more comfortable?"

I huff, feeling my neck flush. "It's just hard for me to go from first meeting you a couple of hours ago to suddenly being...all over each other. We skipped all the meat of this relationship."

He presses his lips together to keep himself from smiling. "This is how filming works, Chloe. All movies are shot out of order. Some actors have to kiss each other or...you know...their very first day on set."

I roughly tuck the front of my white top into my wide-leg, cropped pants. "I get that. It's just easier said than done."

"Give us just one minute, gents," Hunter says to Jax and Sean, who shrug back. He prods me into the house and lets the screen door shut behind us.

"How can I help you feel okay with this?"

I let my angry face take a breather and allow the nerves I'm feeling to briefly show in my expression now that I'm away from the pressure of the crew.

"I don't know...I've just never done this before."

"False. We spent hours this morning shooting together, and you were a complete natural."

I suddenly dart down the narrow hallway to ensure that nobody can hear our conversation, giving Hunter no choice but to follow. He ducks under the low door frame that leads to the kitchen as I turn to face him.

Soft light is pouring in through the window over the sink, and I'm reminded that the clock is ticking. This golden light streaming into the house as the sun sets off to the west is prime for shooting this scene. But if we don't start rolling soon, we are going to lose our lighting window. The anxiety is building in my chest over trying to do all of this within such a tight window.

"Tell me what you're worried about," Hunter says calmly.

I look up at him in frustration, a hot blush coloring my cheeks that definitely matches my cherry-red lips.

"I just..." I lean back against the kitchen sink, wanting to curl into myself in a panic, to make myself small. "I just feel so embarrassed doing this in front of people, Hunter."

He cocks his head to the side. "Doing what? I haven't done anything yet but knock on the door."

"You know what I'm talking about." I give him a death glare from beneath my lashes.

"Kissing me? Is that what's got your knickers in a twist?"

"YES!" I exclaim. "I don't know how we're supposed to do *that* in front of *them*."

I know my eyes are wide with fear, my cheeks flushed with nervousness. But Hunter seems to be able to see past my nerves, past my anxiety. Like I'm the most beautiful woman he has ever laid eyes upon.

Like he'll be gutted if he doesn't get to kiss me tonight.

Is there a slight chance that he feels these nerves too? Maybe he's just better at hiding his feelings underneath a cloak of cool confidence. He's got that signature Hunter smile hitching up on one side of his face.

"Chloe..." He takes a cautious step toward me, like he's trying not to frighten me away. "I'm nervous, too. You realize that, right?"

I frown at him. "No, you're not. You're Hunter."

Another step brings him closer. "FYI, Hunter is human, too. I'm not thrilled about sharing a sweet, intimate moment with you in front of other people. I get it."

One more step, and he closes the gap between us.

"But I'd be lying if I said I didn't want to kiss you, Chloe."

I suck in a sharp breath, craning my neck so I can look up at him.

"At this point, I don't even care if we kiss on camera, but I'm going to kiss you right now because I want to. Because I want you."

Before I can dart away, Hunter picks me up, and I squeak in shock. Gently, he sets me down on the kitchen counter, planting his hands on either side of my body. We're face to face now, and I can see the scatter of freckles on his nose and cheeks, the curve of his lips, the stubble on his jawline, and the smooth lines of his collarbone.

He tilts his head and looks directly into my eyes, placing his hands on my knees. He's about to go in for the kill when I bite my lip in hesitation.

"Full disclosure: I'm wearing bright-red lipstick, Hunter," I say softly, unable to hide the smile that grows as I envision the damage this shade of lipstick is going to do to his face. "The boys will know we've been kissing. I'm going to have to reapply your makeup, too."

"So be it."

I feel a surge of nerves as he gently squeezes my knees with his fingers, then he presses a gentle kiss to my lips. I can tell he wants to follow my lead, to slowly warm things up.

But the moment our lips meet, it's like the clouds part, and my nerves start to melt away. Kissing Hunter feels like slipping into my favorite sweatshirt or sliding into freshly laundered sheets on a fluffy bed—the most natural, comforting, simple thing in the world.

He kisses me again, slowly, intentionally dragging out each soft press of his lips to mine. It takes me a minute to realize that my pulse is racing for an entirely different reason now, one that fills me up and makes me feel present, alive in this single moment.

I eventually respond by threading one hand through his hair at the back of his neck. The warm light pouring in from the kitchen window is golden behind my closed lids, and all I can smell and feel is Hunter. His steady warmth, his sweetness, the depth of our friendship. He's surrounding me, consuming me.

He has no idea what kind of hold he has—he's always had—on me.

I'm not in any rush to deepen this kiss, but we reach a natural point where we taste each other. I have to steady myself at the flood of feelings that wash over me as we lose ourselves in this kiss. Hunter grips my knees tighter, and I wrap my arms around his broad shoulders to embrace him, to pull him closer.

I feel like every moment I'm sharing here in this kitchen with Hunter is a gift. A treasured memory I will recall for the rest of my life.

As the kiss slows, I feel lightheaded, like I'm going to need a minute to collect myself before opening my eyes and re-entering reality.

I pull my lips away from his and then carefully place my palms on his cheeks. I run a thumb over Hunter's bottom lip, gently at first, and then back and forth roughly.

"This stain is never going to come off," I grumble. "This is a *long-wear* lipstick."

"Couldn't care less." A slow smile spreads across Hunter's cherry-stained lips.

"What are you going to tell them?"

He shrugs, sliding his hands up my thighs and around my lower back. "That we had to rehearse the kiss first."

I bark out a laugh. "I'm not kissing you like *that* out there."

"We'll see."

He drops a kiss to my forehead, making my breath hitch in my throat. This tenderness, this gentleness...it's everything to me right now.

After a few minutes of vigorous scrubbing with a wipe from my makeup kit, I deem Hunter's lips to be nearly lipstick free.

I'm going to have to hide the fact that my hands are slightly shaky, and my knees feel a little unsteady after our kiss.

We return to the porch, and Jax and Sean immediately give us obnoxious winks and thumbs up. I watch Hunter cut his hand back and forth across his throat and mouth, "BE COOL." But the smile on his face tells all. He's proud of the fact that they're rooting for him. For us.

"You ready?" Jax asks, quirking an eyebrow at us.

"Ready," I say, flashing Hunter a shy grin as I close the door from the inside.

"I want a wide shot first, and then we can shoot a few close-ups," Hunter says to Sean. The boys turn to walk down the porch steps to get in position for the shot, but their voices carry through the opening in the screen door.

"So how was it?" Sean asks.

"How was what?" Hunter answers.

"Did you break anything in there? You know we'll have to pay for damages, right?"

"Trust me, the only thing that could break tonight is my heart if Chloe turns me away."

I can't keep the grin from spreading across my face as I shut the door, preventing me from hearing the rest of their hushed conversation.

A few moments later, Jax calls out, "Action!"

I picture Hunter strolling up the walkway, trying to embody the defeated yet determined man Connor Cane described in his country song.

I hear his steps outside, and he pauses a moment before laying a knock on the front door. I wait a beat before allowing the door to swing open.

I look up at Hunter with what I hope comes across as a serious expression of distrust. I hope that the disdain and hurt in my eyes breaks his heart wide open. I want him to *want* to comfort me, to tell me he's sorry for everything he's done. To do whatever he needs to do to make things right.

"Hunter?" I say softly, holding the door open.

"Chloe," Hunter says meekly. "I know I don't deserve even a minute of your time, but I came here to apologize to you. To make things right. To own up to what I've done."

I lean up against the doorframe, my lips pressed into a thin line. "I didn't think I'd ever see you again."

He takes a step closer. "I need to apologize."

"Yes, you do."

"First...I'm sorry for what I did to your impeccable, perfect lipstick earlier this evening."

I feel my cheek twitch, but I don't smile. "Oh?"

"I shouldn't have done it. You'd probably spent an hour perfecting your lips, and in just a few moments, I completely, utterly destroyed them."

I look down and swallow as if I'm seriously contemplating his apology.

After a beat, I glance back up at him from underneath my lashes.

"I'm glad you kissed me." My voice comes out barely louder than a whisper. I just spoke the truth. Put it out into the world.

Let Hunter see that he's getting under my skin, that I like where things are going between us.

We share a smile.

"Can I come in?"

I hesitate a moment before opening the door wide enough for Hunter to pass through.

"CUT!" Jax calls out from behind us in the yard. We both look over in his direction. "We need some tight shots of you lovebirds before you break character. These eyes you're giving each other...PHEW. Got me SWEATIN'!"

I take a few deep breaths as we reset for the close-up shots.

"You gonna be okay to do this?" he asks, concern in his eyes.

I give him a confident nod. "I think we're good now."

Although the tightness in my chest is still present, it's not consuming. It's manageable. A distant pull of feelings that I'm sure will ebb and flow but aren't strong enough to pull me under.

I'm going to be okay. We're going to be okay.

I have Hunter to thank for that.

Chapter 22

Chloe

I'm three rows from the back of the historic theater downtown, watching Connor Cane shoot his performance for the "Make Up" music video.

He was uncharacteristically nervous this morning when I styled his hair and touched up his skin before the shoot started—barely spoke three words to me the whole time he was in the chair.

Connor's halfway through his last pass of the song, and the boys are shooting the last round of close-ups. I can still hear Connor's clear, soulful voice from the back of the auditorium. He's singing along to every word with the same commitment he would if we were shooting a live performance.

I've got the whole song memorized by now. But for some reason, hearing this one on repeat doesn't grate on me like "Cry, Baby" did.

Maybe because I'm spending half of the song trying to visualize how Hunter is going to piece together the story shots of the two of us in between these gorgeous performance shots.

The lighting onstage is dramatic, stark and full of contrast. Connor is dressed in a simple white t-shirt and jeans, ensuring that the focus is fully on his face while he's singing.

I shift in my chair, feeling a pinch in my lower back as I move. Yikes. May need to emerge from my perch on this chair *veerrry* slowly when the time comes.

I feel a little dip in my stomach as my eyes find Hunter. We'll dive right into shooting our next scene as a couple as soon as Connor's wrapped things up.

He's got his arms crossed over his chest, bobbing his head along to the beat as he watches the shot on the monitor Jax has set up near the front row of seats. I study his profile, the way the shadows darken the hollows under his cheekbones. Even from back here, I can see the smile on his lips. He is loving every minute of this shoot—unlike me.

Thou shalt not lie, Chloe dearest.

Alright, alright. Was it surprisingly enjoyable to spend so much time with Hunter yesterday shooting at the museum? Absolutely. Did I crumble like a shortbread cookie when he kissed me in the kitchen at the house last night? And then proceed to fully disintegrate and blow away like dust on the wind when we'd kissed again…and again…and again on camera? One hundred percent.

Each kiss had been sweeter than the last, like Hunter was pouring more and more of himself into each one. I shamelessly drank him in, somehow able to tune out the fact that our kisses were being watched by two onlookers and recorded for the world to see.

He'd kept his word. So far, none of this had felt too far out of my wheelhouse or impossibly uncomfortable. In fact, I'm feeling more settled today than I have in a long time, knowing that my only job is to look and act like I'm in love with Hunter.

Which shouldn't be too hard, considering these are my TRUE FEELINGS HERE. Totally revealed. Bared to him and everyone else who will see this video.

Hunter suddenly turns, grinning as he registers the fact that I'm already looking his way. It's like he felt my eyes on him.

I give him an awkward thumbs up. *Great job, pal. Way to go, tiger.*

He scrunches his nose at me.

My first take on his telepathic message: *Get over here, you beautiful creature, and let me show you what a* real *make up looks like.*

Realistic reading: *Almost done, Chlo. You doing alright?*

Connor strums through the final chorus, his guitar blending in perfectly with the recording playing over the speakers. He plays on his own records, which I admire. Most of the artists we work with are singers, not musicians. Connor really is the total package. I'm not even a massive country music fan, but his songs are growing on me.

We all break out into applause as the song ends, and Sean cuts the camera.

"NICE!" Hunter says enthusiastically. "You killed that last take. Cinematic gold."

Connor nods humbly, rising from his stool and running a hand through his hair. "Felt good, man. Felt like the shows I used to play when I first moved out to Nashville." He gestures to the back of the theater where I'm seated and grins. "Just me onstage with an acoustic guitar, playing to an audience of one—usually my mom."

A smile breaks across my face. "So proud of you, son!" I call out.

"Get over here, Mama," Jax replies to me. "You're up."

Sean starts switching out the lens on his camera to set up the next shot. Jax is fussing with my dress and hair, and I feel my heart rate start to pick up.

"I'll send you a cut of this by the end of the week," Hunter calls out to Connor.

He gives us all a wave and disappears out the double doors on one side of the theater.

I feel a hand on my lower back. "How are you holding up?"

Hunter's thumb digs into the right side of my lower back, where the muscles bunch and tighten around my twisted lumbar curve.

"Oof," I breathe as he finds a knot in my back so tight that an Eagle Scout couldn't untangle it.

"Would you relax a little, Chloe?" Hunter drops his voice down, speaking into my ear. "Quit being so uptight."

"That's got nothing to do with being uptight," I hiss as his thumb presses in right where the nerves that run down my spine never seem to get any relief. "And everything to do with the fact that I ran at Ridgeview this morning."

I turn to face him. Hunter drops his hand, a flicker of hurt in his eyes. "You went running without me?"

"I figured we didn't need to get into a fight today, so it was probably best for me to fly solo this time."

He nods, puckering out his lips into a pout. "I guess you're right. Can't afford to be in a tiff when we're supposed to be in love."

I swallow. *Yeah, some of us have already crossed that metaphorical threshold. Made themselves real comfortable in the land of love. Speaking the native tongue as if it's second nature.*

"Hunter?" Sean calls out, making us both turn.

"Yessir?"

"Do you want to shoot the interior first? Or set up outside while we still have light?"

Hunter strides over to Sean to talk details, giving me a chance to catch my breath. I feel like I should be fanning myself, exhaling dramatically with chipmunk cheeks puffed out. But instead, I take a deep, slow breath in through my nose and let it out. *Cool, calm, and collected. That's what we are today, ma'am. Unruffled.*

"You doing ok, honey?" Jax asks from beside me, making me jump.

"Yeah, yeah," I say, waving a hand through the air. "All good. Can I help with anything?"

Jax's pale eyebrows are raised so high they nearly meet his hairline. "Yeah, could you do me a favor?"

I nod, waiting expectantly.

"Could you stop giving Hunter those sexy eyes when the cameras aren't even rolling? You're going to tire them out."

I roll my eyes, chuckling. "Oh, my. Shut up."

He bumps me with his shoulder. "But seriously. You two are so hot together you're going to burn this place down. And that would be nothing short of a legal nightmare for me."

I feel a blush crawling up my neck, and I cross my arms, as if that will somehow help me draw all my obvious feelings back inside my body where they belong.

"Don't fret, gorgeous." Jax ducks his head so I'm forced to meet his eyes. "Your *not-so-secret* secret is safe with me."

I clear my throat. "Riddle me this. Am I easier to work with than the usual girls Hunter casts?"

Jax barks out a laugh. "You, honey, are in an entirely different league. A breath of fresh air for everyone here on set."

I lift a shoulder and coyly bat my lashes. "You flatter me, darling."

"No, truly," Jax says, turning away from me briefly as Sean calls out his name. "I want you in every video. Everyone could use a little more of *your* legs in *that* dress." He gives me a sassy wink and starts walking toward Sean. "This better be important, or I'm going to be incredibly peeved."

I pull the hem of my black dress down farther. Leave it to Jax-with-no-filter to comment on the length of my dress. I'm kicking myself for not wearing something longer for this scene. I hadn't had much say in the matter. Hunter had insisted that this tied in perfectly with the look he was going for.

I'm still tugging and shifting the dress around on my body when Hunter rejoins me on the side of the stage.

"What are you doing?"

I force myself to keep my hands rigidly at my sides. *Nutcracker Chloe, at your service.* "Just trying to make myself more modest. Jax made a comment about my dress."

I definitely don't feel my heart squeeze at the lingering glance Hunter gives my legs. Nor do I suddenly feel a burning in my belly that sends my heart into a frenzy as he gives me an appreciative look, direct and confident.

"You're stunning, Chloe," he says, his voice low. "You'll be breaking hearts all across America in that dress."

Well, now you've gone and done it, Hunter Ward.

Whatever was left of my reserve of willpower is disappearing by the second. He's saying all the right things, giving me all the right cues.

I'm reminded as we take our marks and set up for the shot that I'm currently under the influence of The Hunter Effect. I've seen the man in action. Watched him work the room. Witnessed countless women fawn over him and practically swoon in his presence.

And now that the full force of his charm is being worked on me, I can't drudge up the grit to resist him. How could *anyone* resist him?

"Alright, Mr. Director Man," I say, "what exactly are we doing in this scene?"

He presses his palms together thoughtfully. "This is supposed to take place in the middle of the video, when our relationship is still blissfully new."

My chest tightens at the word *our*.

This isn't real. This isn't real. This isn't real.

But here's the kicker, folks. To me, this feels very, very real. Not what's playing out on camera, but what I'm feeling and living in real time with this man standing beside me.

"Most of what I want to shoot here is kind of abstract. Silhouettes. Shadows."

I nod, loving the way his creative mind works.

"So, are we shooting onstage first?"

"Yeah, so you'll stand here..." Hunter takes my hand in his and leads me to a spot dead center onstage.

Under the heat of the lights, with the warmth of Hunter's hand in mine, I feel a little lightheaded—and lighthearted. Like we're back in high school in theater class, young kids again.

Except—thank the heavens above—I've had a major glow-up, and Hunter is still, well...Hunter.

He's still got that perfectly swooped dark hair and wire-rimmed glasses that have always invited fantasies of kissing him in a library or bookstore—ones where he's got me pressed up against a bookshelf and proceeds to kiss me into oblivion.

Hi, everyone, my name is Chloe ("Hiiii, Chloe."), and I'm a self-diagnosed book nerd.

"We're going to light the shot mostly from behind," Hunter explains, drawing me back into the present. "It will mostly be us just...you know..."

I arch an eyebrow at him. "More kissing?"

He smirks. "I was going to say dancing. But we can easily throw in some kissing if you're into it."

Oh, she's into it. She's way into it. Way more into it than she should be.

"You know, I'm starting to think you've got an agenda with this video," I say.

Easy, girl. Think before you speak.

Almost-thirty-flirty-and-thriving Chloe is dying to make her grand entrance now that she's claimed the spotlight.

"Oh?" Hunter starts rolling up the sleeves on his button-down shirt. "And what might that be?"

I can't think of a single sexy thing to say in response to his question. I can hear the jeers of my inner bully loud and clear. *Smooth one, Chloe. Where's your confidence now?*

So, naturally, I settle on something neutral. Something the jury can't use against me should they hear me claiming that I do not and have never had feelings for *this man*.

"This is as close as you're ever going to get to performing onstage."

Hunter shakes his head, his smile widening as he tries to hold back his laughter.

"Listen, Chlo. This is my big break."

"Oh, I know," I say, grinning. "The record labels are going to be banging down your door, wanting to hear your demos as soon as they witness your indomitable stage presence."

Hunter rolls his eyes. "Okay, now you're just being mean. You know I'll never get to live out that dream."

"Now's your chance." I prod him in the ribs. "Ask Jax for a mic."

Hunter snorts. "Fat chance he'd ever let me sing anything."

Suddenly, the lights go out, leaving us in near darkness for a moment before lights start to illuminate behind us across the stage. One by one, single Edison bulbs appear, seemingly floating at different heights around us. The sight takes my breath away.

"Wow," I breathe.

I'm swept up in the beauty of the set, my eyes roaming over the lights before landing back on Hunter's face.

His expression disarms me. His eyes are filled with wonder, a golden brown in the glow of the lights. He's wearing a completely unguarded, crooked, close-lipped smile. But his eyes aren't trained on our stunning surroundings.

They're trained on *me*.

"We ready up there?" Jax yells from somewhere in the middle of the darkened theater.

Hunter gives him a thumbs up. "Throw on some music, baby."

Chapter 23

Hunter

Whose idea was it to spend a couple of hours slow dancing with Chloe on this terribly romantic stage? OH! Ha ha. Right. This was *my* idea.
Oh, the cleverness of me.

I've had my arms wrapped around her for a few minutes now, slowly swaying back and forth to the music. I've breathed in the smell of her light, floral perfume, felt the ridges of her protruding spine and ribs through the silky fabric of her black dress. It's almost as if we're completely alone up here since the rest of the crew is bathed in darkness throughout the theater.

Chloe had been stiff as a board as we'd danced through the first take, but now that we've gotten the flow of the song down on the second pass, her tense shoulders have dropped. Her whole body has softened in my arms. I think I could stay here with Chloe for the rest of the night and never get tired of those shy looks she keeps giving me from way down there at her hobbit height.

Granted, the top of her head almost reaches my chin in the heels she's wearing, which will probably look better on camera anyway.

The final chords of the song end, and Jax starts whooping and clapping obnoxiously from offstage.

Chloe slithers from my grasp, pulling on the hem of her dress nervously, as if that will somehow cover up her toned legs.

"Okay, homecoming king and queen. Let's tighten things up a little bit," he yells out.

Sean starts making his way onto the stage while Jax starts moving the monitor toward the theater seats where he'll watch the next shot.

"What does that mean?" Chloe asks.

"Tight shots. Close-ups."

"How's my lipstick?" she asks, smoothing a piece of hair back into her low bun.

She's giving me full permission to assess the current state of her enticing berry-red lipstick? Christmas just came early.

I duck my head down, moving closer. If I'm going to do this job, I'm going to do it well. Her lips part slightly as I take inventory of her mouth.

"Your lips are perfect, Chloe," I say. "Maybe I should kiss you, though, just to test the durability of your lipstick."

I'm rewarded with a signature Chloe eye roll.

But then, she gives me a half smile, her rich berry lips tantalizing me as she presses them together.

"Is this the same color you were wearing the other night?"

She scoffs. "Hunter Ward. Have I taught you nothing?"

I shrug innocently.

"I was wearing a scarlet-red lip yesterday, with more orange undertones," she explains, hands on her hips. "This color is more on the purple end of the red spectrum."

"But...it's still red."

"Well, yeah, but..."

"So, what you're telling me," I say, "is that the color of your *red* lips is not, in fact, red."

"Oh my word!" she laughs. "You're an artist, Hunter. You know just as well as I do that the shades and hues that exist within each color are endless."

"Got it," I pretend to be jotting down notes on the palm of my hand with an imaginary pencil. "Never comment on the color of a woman's lipstick unless you want to be made to feel like an idiot."

She shakes her head, laughing, and I can't help but smile with satisfaction. Making Chloe laugh is now my greatest ambition. It's infectious, captivating. A rare gift bestowed on those she truly finds funny.

It's a personal triumph when I make the list. I'm right up there with Jack Black as Nacho Libre. She's never been able to handle that movie.

"Talk to me," Jax claps his hands together.

I exhale as I collect my thoughts and bring to mind my vision for these shots, running a hand through my hair. Chloe tsks, immediately standing on her tiptoes in an attempt to fix whatever I've just done to my hair. I hope it's not too far off from what it looked like when she'd styled it first thing this morning.

Not gonna lie, having Chloe dab powder on my face earlier might have made me feel like less of a man. She insisted that nobody would notice, that it was purely so I didn't look like a vampire on camera. I squirmed in my chair as her fluffy makeup brushes dusted at random parts of my face and held back countless sneezes in an effort to be a well-behaved client.

I'm brought back to the present as Chloe rakes her finger gently through my hair, then steps back to assess her work. "That's better."

"How's my lipstick?" she asks, turning to Jax.

He squints down at her lips. "It wouldn't hurt to add a little more since this next shot is going to be a close-up."

She gestures to Jax as he hands her a compact mirror and her lipstick from his fanny pack. "See, Hunter? How hard is it to be honest when I ask you a question?"

I shrug. "I apologize for being entirely unhelpful."

Jax snorts. "More like useless."

"Okay, okay," I laugh. "Let me paint you a picture for this next shot."

Chloe reapplies her lipstick while I explain my ideas to Jax. He nods, understanding the direction I'm hoping to go in.

Sean joins Chloe and me onstage, his hefty camera rig strapped to his chest.

"Just remember," he says, "your movements need to be smaller so I can capture them. No leaping about the stage."

Chloe looks at me sternly. "Hunter."

"Hmm?"

"You heard the man. No leaping."

I nod briskly. "Got it."

Sean starts pressing buttons on the camera, and I take that opportunity to slowly bring Chloe back into my arms. She resists at first, like she always does, but I press one hand firmly on her lower back, the other finding her fingers and intertwining them with mine. I pull her to me, and she relents as I pull our intertwined hands up to rest on my chest.

I drop my lips down to her ear. "This will be all about subtlety, capturing the nuances of the dynamic between us."

Chloe nods, swallowing.

"I want you to just do whatever feels natural." I feel my heart rate start to pick up as she looks up at me. There's a flicker in her brown eyes that tells me she's unnerved being this close to me, but the way her eyes briefly drop down to my lips tells me that she likes it—hopefully just as much as I relish being this close to her.

"Camera speed," Jax says from his seat in the front row, the monitor set up in front of him.

"Rolling."

The song starts playing over the speakers again, for the umpteenth time today. But I'm not bothered by it at all. As far as I'm concerned, this is *our* song. Our moment to share together.

We start to sway again in rhythm to the music, but this time, I keep one of Chloe's hands tight to my chest. Her eyes remain locked firmly on my shirt collar through the first verse and pre-chorus, so I decide to be the one to make the first move.

I lower my lips to her forehead, feeling her soft hair and skin as my lips make contact. I feel her draw in a breath as I press a gentle kiss to her hairline, closing my eyes and savoring the smell of her elegant perfume.

We both exhale at the same time, and I slowly let my nose trail down her forehead, then follow the delicate line of her nose so that she's forced to move, to acknowledge me.

I nudge the tip of her nose with mine, lost in the music, in the moment. The chorus kicks in, and her lashes flutter as she brushes her nose against mine again.

We start tantalizing the other with the tiniest movements of our bodies, the most subtle shifts in our points of contact.

Her free hand slowly skates all the way up my arm to my shoulder, across my traps, and behind my neck. Her fingers lace into my hair, tugging gently. I follow suit, letting my hand wander to the side of her neck where I carefully trail a finger down the soft skin there.

Her eyes close, and her lips part. She allows her full bottom lip to catch on mine, and I can feel her breath on my lips.

Oooh, she's good.

I press my fingertips more firmly into the back of her neck, tilting my head so our lips brush again, featherlight.

Our hands are still flush with my chest, so I know she can feel my pulse racing through my shirt. And I'm fine with that. I want her to know, to feel, just how much she affects me.

We reach the breakdown of the bridge, right before the last chorus kicks in, and I'm done fighting her, completely worn out from trying to resist this woman I'm completely in love with.

I release her hand from where it's been resting on my chest, taking both sides of her face in my hands. I tenderly brush my thumbs over her cheekbones, and she finally meets my eyes.

The look she is giving me breaks my heart in the best kind of way. I can see fear, desire, and hope all swirling together in her expression, heightened in this vulnerable moment.

We've always been good at reading each other, and right now, there's no mistaking the unguarded feelings I'm seeing in her eyes. She's asking me to show her that this is real, that I'm not just acting.

You asked for it.

I slowly tilt her head up with my hands and lower my lips to hers.

When our lips meet, I swear I can feel her start to break down. She doesn't sigh audibly, but her body settles, stills. She's entirely present in this beautiful moment, just like I am.

I press another kiss to her lips, willing her to understand the message I'm trying to convey.

You don't need to be afraid.

We breathe together, our lips still connected.

You'll be safe with me.

Our lips momentarily part before we immediately dive into another lingering, savoring, sweet kiss.

I wish I could read her mind, that she'd open up to me in a way that would allow me to see all of her fears, her worries and desires. I want to know everything. I want her to let me in.

This shoot is so much more than just a job we're both working. This is part of our story, and I'm hoping that this moment can be part of the catalyst that helps draw us closer. That Chloe will have the courage to trust me, to know that I've changed. That I will be true to her and love her the way she deserves to be loved.

I'm barely aware of the song winding down as Chloe settles back onto her heels, looking up at me with an unreadable expression on her face.

Not even five seconds after the song ends, she's closed herself off from me again.

"Nice," Sean says from behind the camera. "That was beautiful, guys."

Chloe slips her hands out from mine, clasping her hands together in front of her body. Her eyes dart around nervously, as if she's just remembered there are other people in the room.

"Thanks, man," I say, smiling at Chloe. She gives me a quick, fake smile back.

"Is it ok if I step out for a few minutes?" she asks quietly.

I nod. "Of course. You okay?"

"Mmhmm," she says with unnatural brightness. "Yeah, I think I just need a little fresh air."

Before I even have the chance to respond, she's walking briskly away from me across the stage, her heels echoing throughout the empty theater with each step.

I run a hand through my hair and let out a long breath as I watch her disappear into the darkness.

A light slices through the theater as she reaches the back doors and escapes out onto the street.

Sean turns to me, gesturing to the door as it swings shut.

"You gonna go after her, man?"

"She said she needed a break."

Sean shakes his head. "When my wife says things like that, I've learned that it means that she and I probably need to talk."

I nod, taking off in a jog across the stage, down the stairs, and down the aisle until I reach the back door.

Chapter 24

Chloe

I'm facing the street, my back to the theater, when I hear the door creak open. I know it's Hunter without even having to turn around.

A steady stream of cars passes by—Franklin's version of rush hour. The sky is still a brilliant blue, soon to be streaked with the warm hues of the sunset.

"Hey."

I swallow and raise my eyes skyward until they reach the rooftops of the historic buildings downtown. I follow the lines of the rooftops, trying to keep the emotion I'm holding back from spilling over and ruining my makeup.

Hunter joins me at the curb. I don't dare look his way.

"You okay?"

I take a deep breath in through my nose, then let it out slowly. There are no words for what I'm feeling right now. Conflicted. Hurt. Known. Seen.

Loved.

Afraid.

"Did I do something wrong?"

I sniff.

I sigh. "No, Hunter. You're doing everything right."

And that's what's got me coming completely undone.

He reaches for my hand, lightly brushing his fingertips down the inside of my wrist before lacing his fingers through mine.

I finally look up at him, and there's no way he's going to miss the mist gathering in the corners of my eyes. He gives my hand a squeeze, concern written across his features. His easy smile is gone—a rare sight.

I stare down at our shoes. The soft black leather of his boots. The thin straps of my black heels laced across my feet.

He's always been patient. I know he'll wait as long as he needs to for me to speak. He never pushes me to share my feelings, to open up. He waits until I feel comfortable, and then he listens.

Always listens.

I drag my eyes back up to meet his again, feeling my heart knocking against my chest as I work up the courage to speak my feelings out loud. To tell him why half of my heart is overflowing with happiness, while the other half is still hiding in the shadows.

"I'm scared, Hunter."

He stiffens.

"I'm scared of getting my heart broken." I pause. He waits in silence, watching me steadily. "I don't want to be a rebound, or someone you can just toy with."

He nods.

"The past couple of days have been nothing short of wonderful."

Really? That's the confession that gives the tears permission to start flowing?

I swipe at my cheeks, not used to showing emotion so openly. Embarrassment reddens my cheeks and neck.

"But..." I choke down the growing knot in my throat. "I'm not faking this."

Hunter gently swipes a thumb over the back of my hand. "And you think I am?"

I shrug, unable to focus on Hunter's blurry face behind the sudden onslaught of emotional precipitation I'm caught up in.

He waits a few more beats to see if I'm going to continue speaking, and when I don't fill the silence, he clears his throat.

"We've got to start somewhere, you know?" Hunter says. "This part of our story may be playing out on camera, but I promise you I'm *not* acting, Chloe."

I feel like my chest is closing in on itself. I want so badly to believe Hunter, to trust him. But even after hearing the words I'd hoped to hear, some part of me still doubts him.

We've got to start somewhere.

Maybe the reason I'm still so afraid is that I don't truly believe I'm worthy of being loved, completely and totally. There are still some lingering, shadowy doubts about my self-worth that were planted when I was thirteen years old—when I was diagnosed with my scoliosis.

I've tried to consciously love and accept myself, flaws and all, but for some reason, it feels so much harder to believe that someone else, someone like Hunter, could accept those parts of me that are a little twisted, a little crooked, a little uneven.

But don't I love and appreciate those parts of him? The quirks, the flaws, the things that make him unique?

I take a steadying breath.

"Maybe I've gone about all of this completely wrong." Hunter runs a hand through his hair, making it even more voluminous. "Maybe I should have tried to pursue you five years ago. Ten years ago. When we were fifteen. I don't know."

"I honestly wasn't ready for you, Chloe. Not until now. I've had a lot of growing up to do."

I sniffle. "You *still* have a lot of growing up to do."

Hunter snorts. "I know, I know." My hand feels warm in his. Safe.

"I don't think it's too late for us," he says softly. The whir of the cars going by fills the temporary quiet between us. A breeze lifts my hair, dances through his. His lips lift in a gentle, adoring smile. I remember what it feels like to have that smile pressed to mine. My insides quiver at the memory.

"I did all this just to have a fighting chance with you, Chlo." Hunter's eyebrows lower over his eyes thoughtfully. "I would have just asked you out to brunch, but we already do that. Every Saturday."

I let out a soft laugh. "True."

"Couldn't take you on an ice cream date, either, now could I?"

I shake my head.

"I didn't want to mess with our friendship. I didn't want to ruin the beautiful thing we already have."

His gaze steels on mine, and I swear my stomach drops into my toes.

"But if we both want to move forward together, to try this thing out, we have to change things. It's uncomfortable. It's scary. But we have to have faith that we're doing the right thing."

"This is more than just uncomfortable for me, you know?" I say thickly. "You're all I've got, Hunter. I can't lose you."

His jaw ticks, and he presses his lips together before drawing me into his arms. I press my cheek to his chest, feel his steady heartbeat in my ear. His breathing is even, comforting. I breathe in the leathery smell of his cologne, close my eyes, and try to match my breath to his.

We stand there, holding each other for a long while. My arms are wrapped around his waist, his arms are enclosing me in a cocoon against his chest.

"I'm going to call it," Hunter finally says, his voice rumbling in my ear. "The shoot."

I pull back, looking up at his chin. "No, don't do that. I can pull myself together, and we can go back—"

He shakes his head, letting his hands trace lines down my arms until our hands are intertwined. "We've got plenty of footage to work with."

"No, I'm serious. I'm good to go. We can shoot some more. I don't want to be the reason this video doesn't live up to your standard of perfection."

Hunter scoffs. "You're in it. That automatically qualifies it as perfect."

He gazes across the street thoughtfully before looking back at me, a cheeky grin on his face.

"Oh, no," I breathe. "What wild idea are you cooking up in that little head of yours?"

He bites his lip briefly before speaking. "Tell you what. Why don't you just head back to your house, get yourself changed into something comfy, and I'll come pick you up in a couple of hours?"

I scrunch up my nose. "For what?"

"That's for me to know and for you to find out."

I place my hands on my hips. "Hunter Ward. You know how I feel about surprises."

He shrugs. "And?"

I carefully use my fingers to wipe away the rogue mascara that has dripped down under my lash line. "I don't want to seem unprofessional. Or like I'm running away."

"You won't. The guys will understand. We'll pack up and get out of here, and then I'll text you."

"My makeup kit is still in there."

"I'll grab it for you. Anything else?"

I try to push past him to re-enter the theater. "I don't trust you to not leave something valuable behind."

"You have to start trusting me, Chloe," Hunter says, gently holding me back by placing his large, strong hands on my shoulders. "I can be trusted to collect your effects. And if I somehow forget something, I will personally replace it. Scout's honor."

"You were never a scout!" I scoff.

"Doesn't matter. It's the honor part that counts for something, right?" He darts to the theater door. "Be right back."

In a flash, he's back, my purse and makeup kit in his hands.

"Your things, my lady."

"Thank you."

He starts walking briskly down the sidewalk.

"Where are you going?"

"Your car!"

I have to hustle to keep up with him and his long legs.

He reaches into my purse and draws out my keys, unlocking my car door as soon as it's in sight.

"I am perfectly capable of unlocking my own vehicle, thank you very much!"

"I am well aware."

He pops my trunk and starts loading my kit into the trunk. I try to help, but he tuts and fusses every time I draw near.

He closes the trunk, turning to face me. "Please, let me take care of things here. I need you to go home and take some time to wind down. I'll call you when I'm on my way to pick you up."

I squint up at him, a sudden burst of wind whipping pieces of hair out of my bun and into my eyes. Goosebumps appear on my legs, and I shiver.

"Get out of here before it starts storming or something." Hunter looks behind him, grimacing as he notices the perfectly clear-blue sky. Fat chance of that happening.

"Are you sure? One hundred percent?"

"Yes, now go. Please. I'm asking you nicely."

I shake my head, wrapping my arms around my chest as the wind picks up again. "Alright. I don't know why I'm listening to you right now."

"Because this is what you need. I know you, Chloe." He points to himself. "Best friend, remember?"

I can't help but smile. He opens my driver's side door for me before dropping my keys into my outstretched hand.

"Drive safe. You're carrying precious cargo."

"You're telling me," I reply. "That kit back there is probably worth more than this car."

"I was talking about you, love."

My cheeks warm at the mere mention of the L word. Even if it was just used as a term of endearment, hearing that word on his lips has sent my nervous system into hyperdrive.

He closes my door and pats my car door twice. Then, he waves before heading back into the theater.

I start my car, cranking up the heat immediately. The seats are slick and cold on the back of my bare legs.

When I pull into the driveway of Darlene's house, I take my usual parking spot on the right side. It takes me a minute to lug all the pieces of my kit back to my apartment. On my second trip back to my car, I'm surprised to see Darlene's car waiting in the driveway, headlights beaming onto the stark-white garage door.

She rolls her window down and waves to me. "Well, don't you look gorgeous!"

I give her a curtsy. "Where are you off to?"

She waves a hand dismissively through the air. "Just thought I'd take a little drive and enjoy the scenery."

I glance around at the autumn leaves littering the street, the golden light streaming through the branches of the trees. "It is a gorgeous night."

"And what about you? Are you coming or going?"

"Just getting back from the shoot."

Her brown eyes widen. "THE shoot?"

I nod. "Yeah."

"You mean Hunter saw you all dressed up like that and didn't beg to come home with you?"

I gasp in mock offense. "Miss Darlene! I'm not that kind of woman!"

She barks out a laugh. "Well, I am. I guarantee you that man will be showing up here tonight whether you want him to or not. I say let him in."

I chuckle. "He *did* say he'd come pick me up in a little bit."

Darlene presses a hand to her chest. "What did I tell you? He's a smitten kitten."

I press my lips into a tight smile. "I don't know about that."

"I do." Darlene gives me a wink. "Have fun tonight. Don't do anything I wouldn't do."

"That leaves a whole lot of room for interpretation." I shake my head and laugh as she rolls her window up and pulls out of the driveway.

Chapter 25

Chloe

Twelve years earlier...

We're five minutes into the movie, and I'm already holding back tears.

And no, it's not because I get misty every time that song starts playing during the opening credits of *Remember the Titans*. Although, admittedly, sometimes I do have to swallow real hard while watching this movie. It tugs at my heartstrings.

"Popcorn?" Hunter whisper-yells obnoxiously into my ear.

I flinch, nearly falling off the edge of the couch where I'm currently squashed, scooted to the end of the sofa after a long line of tall teenage boys decided to sit down, one by one. And so I remain the only girl who was apparently invited to this movie night at Hunter's house.

"Oh, sure."

Hunter tosses the pillow he's been holding onto his twin brother, Luke's, lap.

Luke scoots over, taking Hunter's seat and stretching out his long limbs so I'm crunched up at the end of the couch.

"You can sit over here, if you'd like." He grins. "By Charlie."

He's a total tease, trying to force me to be sandwiched between him and Charlie-with-the-frosted-tips. He knows how much I dislike Charlie and is just trying to get a rise out of me.

"What was that, Hunter?" I say loudly. "You need my help?" I dart up onto my feet and practically book it after Hunter to the kitchen.

He's standing near the microwave, two unwrapped bags of popcorn in his hands.

"Shall we go with Orville?" he asks. "Or could I perhaps interest you in a little..."—he whips the other bag out in front of him like he's showcasing a prized possession—"BUTTER LOVER'S?"

I can't help but snicker at his nonsense. "You *know* the boys are going to want extra butter."

"Right you are." He quickly turns around and places the bag in the microwave.

Normally, I'd be quick to do a subtle scan of my best friend whilst he's facing away from me, but tonight, even my attraction for all things Hunter feels like it's been destroyed, along with—not to be melodramatic or anything—my hope in *all* men.

I settle back against the kitchen counter near the sink, my eyes sweeping over the spacious, spotless room.

Does Hunter even know how lucky he is to live in a home where he's loved? Where his parents don't argue every single time they're in each other's presence? Does he know how blessed he is to have a mother who doesn't disappear for days on end when things get really bad, leaving him alone to fend for himself?

I cast my gaze up to the sconces hanging over the island, letting the light blur as tears build again in my eyes.

"So, I was thinking that, for Halloween this year, we could dress up together. Go trick-or-treating in a group or something." Hunter cracks his knuckles and faces me, his back leaning against the edge of the kitchen island.

Before I can hide my feelings like I usually do, a traitorous tear slides down my nose. I quickly swipe the back of my sleeve across my nose and sniffle.

"Whoa, Chlo..." Hunter says, bringing his hands to my upper arms. "You okay?"

I sniffle again, trying to suck back the emotion that I've been holding inside me all day. "Yeah, yeah, I'm fine."

Hunter squeezes my arms, ducking his head so I'm forced to look at him. "You sure? You wanna talk about it?" He glances over at the microwave. "We've still got two minutes and thirty seconds on this bag, and then three more minutes for the next bag. That's, like, five minutes of talk time."

I give him a watery smile, and more tears start slipping down my cheeks.

His brown eyes are filled with concern, and he grabs me a paper towel and starts dabbing at my cheeks.

"Is it your mom again?"

I nod, my lip quivering. "And my dad."

Hunter sighs, rubbing my arm with his big, strong hand.

"Are they..." He winces. "Is it official?"

I nod, letting the tears silently flow now that I'm not the only person carrying the burden of my parents' impending divorce.

"Oh, no. I'm so, so sorry," Hunter says, sweeping me into a hug. He presses my head to his chest, resting his cheek on my hair. One hand wraps around my shoulders while the other rubs the back of my head rhythmically.

The gesture surprises me. Hunter has given me quick hugs, side embraces, but he's never held me like this. I haven't been hugged or held by anyone in ages, and I feel myself settling against his strong and steady presence like it's my lifeline. I wrap my arms around his waist and hold him back tightly.

I cry into his sweatshirt, and he gently rubs my hair. We're standing there in that position long after the timer for the popcorn goes off before I speak again.

"He's staying in Alabama." I swallow. "To be with his *other* family."

Hunter stays silent, giving me the space to speak if I want to. I never talk about these kinds of things with anyone else. I know that whatever I tell Hunter stays with Hunter. He doesn't spread rumors or participate in petty gossip. He's the safest person I have right now.

"Are you going to go live with him?"

I shake my head. "Absolutely not. The whole thing is so messed up. And I want to finish high school here."

"Good."

Hunter gives me a tight squeeze, and I swear I feel his warm mouth brush the top of my head before he pulls away.

He swipes at my wet cheeks again and smiles at me. "Well, if you ever need a place to crash or a shoulder to cry on, I'm here for you, Chlo. You know that, right?"

I feel like melting into the wood floor at his kindness. I muster up a nod and sniff again.

"Do you want me to drive you home?"

I shake my head. "No, I can't handle being there tonight. My mom drove off this afternoon after she got the call from Dad's lawyer. I have no idea when she'll be back."

Hunter presses his lips together. "Then you can stay here tonight. Let me go talk to my mom."

"Thank you." I nod gratefully, feeling totally understood and cared for in a way that almost makes up for my parents' lack of care and sensitivity toward me.

"THINK FAST." Hunter tosses the second bag of popcorn at me, and I catch it. "Do you mind popping that while I go find Mom real quick?"

"I'll try not to burn it."

Hunter grins and backs out of the kitchen. "Be right back."

I place the popcorn in the microwave, dry my tears, and take a few deep breaths.

Later that night, after all the boys have left and Maggie settles me into one of their guest bedrooms, I get a text that fills my heart with hope—a hope that I'd thought was lost along with my parents' marriage.

HUNTER: *Everything is going to be okay, Chloe. There are so many people who love you and will take care of you through this. We've got you.*

I feel the tears threatening to flow again, but this time, they're tears of gratitude.

I type out a reply before letting my head hit the pillow.

CHLOE: *Thank you, Hunter. You're the greatest friend a girl could ever ask for.*

Chapter 26

Hunter

Thirty seconds...twenty seconds...fifteen seconds...

I fling open the microwave door as the distance between popping kernels slows. I may not be a gourmet chef, but I do not intend to burn our Butter Lovers popcorn. Not tonight.

Chloe is settled in the tiny living room of my apartment, snuggled under a makeshift canopy of spare sheets. I can see her glowing under the string of lights I hung across the top of the tent, all rosy cheeks and bright eyes.

I'd nearly choked when she'd walked out of her basement apartment wearing the sweatshirt I'd given her in high school and a pair of black joggers. Every time I look her way, my chest constricts, tightens. It's like we've traveled back in time to when we were sixteen and running cross country together. But this time, we get to rewrite our story and spice it up in all the right ways.

I pour the warm popcorn into my favorite Harry Potter limited edition bucket I'd bought at the theater when the last movie came out. Hermoine Granger's face and Ron Weasley's red mop might be a little faded, but Harry himself is just as visible as the day I'd brought the thing home. Ageless.

Chloe laughs as I crouch down and join her in the tent. "You still have that *heirloom*?"

I nod pointedly at her sweatshirt. "Right back atcha."

She grabs a handful of popcorn and tosses it at my face. She's lounging back on a stack of pillows, half covered by a fluffy blanket I borrowed from my mom's house on the way home.

"So, which feature film will we be enjoying this evening?"

"PLEASE HOLD." I dart to my feet, nearly knocking over the popcorn and tearing down the tent. I take hold of the blanket I've got covering my flat screen TV mounted to the wall and give it a flick.

The blanket settles to the ground, and I unmute the TV with the remote, filling the room with the glorious strains of Hedwig's theme.

Chloe gasps. "No way. Are we doing this? We're actually doing this?"

I offer her a regal bow. "Tonight's showing of *Harry Potter and the Prisoner of Azkaban* is brought to you by our sponsor." I whip out a package of slightly crushed peanut M&Ms from my pocket. "Mars, Incorporated."

"You didn't!"

I take my place under the tent and push play on the remote before handing Chloe her favorite candy. "I did."

She clutches them to her chest and breathes out a sigh. "This is my dream. I must be dreaming."

I can't help but grin as she eagerly dumps her M&Ms out into the popcorn bucket and settles back on her pillow fortress as the movie begins.

Chloe could probably quote this entire movie. She and I bonded over this particular book in the series in high school, and we used to watch this movie every year around Halloween. I always tried to campaign for us to watch all of the films in order, but Chloe would somehow get her way, and we'd end up watching this film first and never finding time to enjoy the other seven.

It dawned on me as we were shooting in the theater that Chloe and I haven't done our Harry Potter movie night since high school. I wanted to bring back that tradition for her tonight, to provide her with a chance to relax and enjoy a few of the simple things she loves most: Harry Potter, peanut M&Ms, and popcorn.

I glance over at her and squint. She's nudging her nose with her sleeve.

"Are you...crying?"

She pouts, sniffling. "No."

I chuckle. "Here we go. Two minutes into the movie, and we're already in need of tissues."

"Oh, don't worry. I've cried into the sleeves of this sweatshirt more times than I can count."

My gut drops. *Because of me?*

"Hold up," I say. "My sweatshirt doubles as your hankie?"

She shifts in her seat. "No, no. This is just my favorite sweatshirt. My go-to when I feel sad."

I nod, tossing a handful of popcorn into my mouth. "I get it. I feel the same way about my Speedo."

Chloe tosses her head back, laughing. Her light-brown hair fans out across the pillow, her eyes disappearing as she giggles.

I force myself to look back at the screen, but even my favorite volume of the Harry Potter saga can't compete with Chloe tonight.

We watch a few more minutes of the movie, enjoying our snacks before Chloe starts showing off her ability to quote even the most obscure lines from one of her favorite flicks.

"*Excellent nosh, Petunia.*"

My eyes widen. "Your English accent is spot on."

"I owe the entirety of my ability to sound like a stuffy English woman to Aunt Marge."

"What a horrible woman."

"She's deliciously horrible. Like Umbridge."

We settle into silence, and I'm suddenly self-conscious of how loudly I'm chomping on my popcorn. *Settle down, sonny.*

It's like I can visibly see Chloe stilling, settling. Slowing down. She sinks comfortably back into her pillow throne, smiling and laughing effortlessly as we watch the movie together. Seeing her glow with happiness because of something I've done for her tastes like gold.

I will make this sheet fort a permanent fixture in my living room for Chloe to disappear under every night if she wants to. I'll set aside my watch list and watch whatever her heart desires. *Pride and Prejudice*? Throw it on. *How to Lose a Guy in Ten Days*? SEEN IT. LOVED IT.

This has to be what was missing in every other relationship I've been in. This pure desire to see Chloe happy, even at the expense of my own happiness. Because her happiness multiplies mine tenfold.

Once our popcorn is finished, I set aside the bucket and rest back on my own stack of pillows, arms behind my head, elbows out wide.

Chloe is inches from me on her side of the fort. If she rolled over to her right side, she'd fit right under my arm. Though, if she did move so much as a centimeter toward me, I'd be sure to swoop her up, and this movie night would meet its abrupt end.

We're about an hour into the movie when Chloe slowly drags herself into an upright position.

"What do you need? A libation? A refill on the M&Ms?"

"A *libation*?!" Chloe cackles. "STOP."

"Your wish is my command."

She rolls her shoulders back and crosses her legs in front of her, tilting her neck from side to side.

"Your back ok?"

"It's alright." She twists from side to side. "Just need to sit up for a bit."

She sighs, arching her back. I can tell she's trying to hide the fact that she's in pain, and that knowledge pains me.

"Why do you try to act like nothing's wrong when you're clearly hurting?" I ask.

She narrows her eyes at me. "Pipe down, would you? I'm fine."

"No." I shift on my arms so that I'm in a seated position behind Chloe. "Let me help you."

I straddle my legs around either side of her, positioning myself so I can press my hands into her back. She stiffens as I reach for her, but she doesn't try to stop me as I start rolling my knuckles down the sides of her spine.

She shifts and breathes deeply when my hands reach knotted, sore muscles, giving me the cue to slow down and tend to those places. I use my thumbs to press into the taut muscles and tendons that constantly compensate for her scoliosis. I look down, noting the way one side of her ribs protrudes out while the other caves in, the way her spine twists and curves down into her waistline.

"Do you still have your brace?" I ask into her ear.

She nods. "I think I do have it, actually. In a box somewhere."

"I remember when you showed it to me for the first time," I say. "I couldn't believe your doctors subjected you to such an acute form of torture."

She shrugs. "I didn't really have a choice."

I move my hands up to her shoulders but find it's hard to apply good pressure when the hood of her sweatshirt keeps getting in the way.

"This okay?"

"Mmmhmm."

"Want me to work your shoulders?"

"Sure."

"Then could you…" I pause, not wanting to sound like I'm gunning for anything other than a chance to be helpful. "It would be easier if you took off your hoodie."

"Oh, yeah." Chloe scoots forward, reaching for the hem of her sweatshirt. Because she's seated and trapped underneath the tent of sheets, she struggles to pull it off. So, I oblige, helping her ease it over her head and arms.

She's wearing a fitted tank top underneath, giving me the chance to press my thumbs into her warm skin.

"Remember when you'd help me carry my bookbag senior year?"

I grin. "I was your pack mule. Your jacka—"

"I didn't ask you to be!"

"I wanted to. Your bag weighed, like, fifty pounds with all those books."

"And my locker was in Timbuktu."

"That's right," I laugh. "I'd forgotten about that."

She's quiet for a moment before she speaks again. "You've always been so sweet to me."

I can feel her start to relax against me as I patiently and gently tend to her back. I'm running my thumbs slowly up and down her neck when she reaches around and grabs one of my hands.

"Thank you," she says, her voice breathy. "That felt amazing."

"Happy to help."

I skate my other thumb over the soft skin of her neck, leaning down to press a gentle kiss into the place where her neck meets her shoulder.

She exhales slowly, and I let my lips linger on her skin, feeling the warmth of her body as she leans back into my lap.

I nuzzle my nose into her neck, wrapping my arms around her. She reaches up, holding my forearms tightly in her hands. I breathe her in, closing my eyes as I feel her relax against me.

"If I'd asked you out when we'd first met," I say into her shoulder, "would you have gone out with me?"

She lets out a little laugh through her nose. "That depends."

"On what?"

"On whether or not you'd have shared your Uncrustables with me."

I suck in a breath. "Ooooh...that's a tough one."

Chloe sits up, turning sideways so she can look at me. "Are you serious? You wouldn't have?"

I grimace. "You know how much I love my Uncrustables."

She rolls her eyes, pursing her lips to keep from smiling.

I'd love nothing more than to slide my hand behind her neck, to pull her to me, and to kiss her right about now.

"What time is it? Do you know?" she asks.

My hopeful kiss bubble bursts. Violently.

"Uh..." I lean back and squint at the clock on the microwave. "I don't have my glasses on, so it looks like either some form of ancient hieroglyphics or a series of Roman numerals."

Chloe fishes around in her pocket and pulls out her phone. "Shoot. It's later than I thought."

She looks at me, pleading. "I'm so sorry to you and Harry, but I have a wedding early tomorrow morning. Can we take a rain check on finishing this another time?"

I nod, trying not to show my disappointment. "For sure. I'll take you home."

We get pelted with rain as we exit my apartment, so I ensure that Chloe's hood is securely fastened around her head, strings pulled tight.

"Oh my GOSH," she gasps. "You used to do this to me all the time. So annoying!"

"You're welcome," I say. Thunder rumbles overhead, so I compensate by increasing my volume obnoxiously. "YOUR HAIR WILL THANK ME LATER."

I usher her out to my Jeep, getting drenched without a hood to cover myself. As soon as I've backed out of my parking spot, I reach across the console, gripping Chloe's hand in mine the entire drive back to her house.

We pull into her driveway, and I put the Jeep in park.

Chloe reaches for the door handle, and I feel a warmth course through my chest. "Dang, girl. You're going to just leave me like that, wet and cold?"

She considers me for a moment, letting her hand linger on the handle without opening the door.

"Thank you for tonight," she says softly. "That meant more to me than you'll ever know."

I tighten my grip on her hand. "You're welcome. I know how much you love Draco Malfoy."

In a moment, she swivels in her seat to face me. She lets go of the door, reaching up to let her fingertips graze my cheek. My breathing grows uneven as she leans in, her cold fingertips making goosebumps break out where she touches my neck.

Our lips meet briefly, warm and sweet. I'm ready to drag her onto my lap, to kiss her in the passenger seat of my Jeep the way I've always wanted to.

But she pulls away all too quickly. "Night, Hunter."

"Sweet dreams, Chlo."

I tap the steering wheel as she slips out into the rain, running around the side of the house and out of sight.

Chapter 27

Hunter

I've got my headphones on, Mountain Dew resting on a coaster, and my Adobe Premiere program pulled up on my laptop.

I feel like a kid on Christmas as I download the files from the "Make Up" shoot to my external hard drive, eager to dive into the footage Sean sent over. As I drag and drop the clips into the video-editing software, the thumbnails alone do funny things to my pulse.

Chloe.

So many shades and smiles and glimpses of her that make me want to chug my entire Dew right here, right now, and slam the can brusquely back down on the desk.

I open the first file and am greeted with a wide shot of Chloe and me in the museum. I let the clip play through, my eyes drawn to Chloe in that red dress. She's got her fingers twisted together behind her back, her head tilted as she gazes up at the artwork on the wall.

Me, on the other hand...

I've got my eyes locked on her, my stance casual, but anybody watching this video would instantly be able to tell that I'm drawn to Chloe like a moth to a flame.

I quickly scroll down through my imports, unable to resist opening a clip of Chloe and me, nose to nose, about to kiss on the stage of the historic theater.

Sean had shot these close-ups at a higher frame rate, so I adjust my timeline settings and play the clip as it was meant to be seen—in slow motion.

The kiss is *epic*.

Fireworks. Sweet and spicy. Gets me all hot and bothered. I tug at the neck of my sweater and clear my throat, resisting the urge to put that moment where I kissed the girl of my dreams on loop for an hour while I slowly sip my drink.

I grin like a fool as I continue to watch bits and pieces of the clips before importing Connor's song to begin my edits.

Headphones on, I drag Adobe Premiere over to the larger monitor on the right side of my desk. If I'm going to spend my day watching Chloe and me fall in love on camera, might as well be on the big screen.

Several hours and several Mountain Dews later, I've got a first cut ready to share with the team.

I feel my chest swell with pride as I think about the people who helped make this vision of mine a reality. Connor. Jax. Sean.

Chloe.

Chapter 28

Chloe

Hunter: *First cut of the video DONE!*
Chloe: **Puke emoji* I'm so nervous.*
Hunter: *It's gorgeous. Connor's gorgeous. You're gorgeous.*
Chloe: *You gonna send me a link?*
Hunter: *Just emailed you the unlisted vid.*

My half-eaten apple strudel is suddenly NOT sittin' pretty. I burrow into my seat at the cafe where I'd stopped for lunch and lift the neck of my sweater up to cover my mouth. I tuck my headphones into my ears so I don't give the neighboring tables a sneak preview of Connor's unreleased song without his permission. With shaking hands, I find Hunter's email and click on the link to the video.

I'm breathing through the knit of my sweater like it's a brown paper bag, trying to keep my stomach from rolling as the opening shot appears on my phone screen.

I've heard that watching yourself on camera is like hearing your voice played back on a recording for the first time—slightly unnerving and extremely uncomfortable. This has got to be the reason some actors refuse to watch the films they act in.

But as the opening chords to the song fill my ears, I'm swept up in a gorgeous slow-motion montage of shots that Hunter has pieced together masterfully. Connor Cane onstage, the edges of the single spotlight hazy and smoky around him. Hunter and me gazing at each other from across the art exhibit hall. A tight shot of our silhouettes, noses brushing, lips parted.

My heart squeezes in my chest as I watch the rest of the video. I don't know why I expected this project to be any different from Hunter's other videos. It's artfully shot and edited, by far Connor's most beautiful video yet.

As the final shot of Connor onstage fades to black, a strange sense of pride rises in my chest, an acknowledgment that I got to play a part in telling his story of second chances, of redemption. A story about what it takes to humbly apologize and the miracle of starting over.

This is bigger than just Hunter and me, and I can see that now. Connor's song has been given visual life through this video, and it honestly tugged at my heartstrings in a way I wasn't expecting it to.

I immediately swipe back to the start of the video and watch it again, this time appreciating the golden light sweeping over the old house we'd shot at. The warmth in Hunter's eyes when he looks at me. The honest vulnerability we share together as we dance, wrapped in each other's arms.

The smile is growing on my face with each shot I watch, and so is the sense that I've accomplished something big in saying yes to this project. I said yes to the unknown, to leaping out of my comfort zone. Hunter had extended a hand and guided me into the dark, but I'd been the one to take one hesitant step forward at a time. And now, here we are, on the other side of fear, and I feel stronger and better for it.

Proud of myself. Proud of Hunter and his team. Proud to have been a part of this act of creation.

I squirm a little bit as I watch us kiss on screen. Our kisses feel loaded with so much depth and history, it's almost like I'm watching a—dare I say it—*wedding video*.

A text banner drops down over the top of my screen.

Hunter: *It's just the first cut. We'll tighten it up a lot more after we get Back Road's feedback.*

I pause the video and click over to my texts.

Chloe: *Hunter, I don't have any words.*

Hunter: **grimacing face emoji* Uh-oh...*

Chloe: *This video is stunning. So beautiful. I'm honored to have been a part of it.*

Hunter: *YOU HAVE NO IDEA HOW RELIEVED I AM TO HEAR THIS!!!*

Hunter: *I was terrified that you were going to hate it.*

Chloe: **crying laughing emoji* I could never hate anything you create, Hunter! You're amazing.*

Chloe: *We need to celebrate.*

I set my phone down on the table and reach for my spiced cider, smiling as I take a sip and glance out the window. Golden light is filtering through the fluttering leaves on the trees outside, casting everything in a warm glow. I feel that glow growing inside me, too. An answering sign that, right now, I feel truly happy. I take a bite of the apple strudel I'd abandoned, appreciating the crisp, buttery layers of pastry. Perfectly spiced filling. Sweetness of the fresh apples in their prime of this autumn season.

I want more of this. More saying yes to the things that make me happy. More slowing down and feeling the warm sun on my skin, watching the way the shadows play on the sidewalk. More pastries and coffee and smiles and laughter. More time to just *be*.

Maybe this pace I've been keeping in my life has been my way of staying safe. When I'm busy, I don't have time to think about the things that may not be going right in my life. If I keep running, I don't have to acknowledge the twinges of pain that are signals from my body that I need to slow down.

I'm tired...more tired than I realized. I've needed this chance to reassess more than I knew. I can feel it in my body, in my soul. *This* is what Chloe needs more of right now.

Also...more Hunter.

I couldn't get over his thoughtfulness last night, the way he remembered the simple things that make me smile. And that he put in the effort and time to create that moment for us. It was sweet. Sweeter than sweet.

It was *loving*.

I've known what it's like to love Hunter, to care for him and listen to him, to be there to lift him when he's down. But I haven't truly experienced the reciprocation of that love. At least, not until now.

He hasn't said the words, but I feel how much he cares for me in every small gesture. The way he'd carefully, gently kneaded my sore, stiff back. His stupid, self-satisfied grin when he succeeds in making me laugh. The way he observes me, intuitively discerning exactly what I need and when I need it.

I'm in *deep*. Just like Darlene said I would be.

I want to show him my gratitude for all that he's done for me, for his kindness and attentiveness. So, I polish off my pastry and send him another text.

Chloe: *Do you have plans Friday night? I'm slammed until then.*

Hunter: *Yes. I have a bundle of sheets that need to be scoured clean. They're thoroughly soiled with butter from SOMEONE'S popcorn. *butter emoji**

Chloe: *Well, perhaps you could squeeze in some time with me between loads of laundry?*

Hunter: *Absolutely. You just tell me when and where, and I will bring my washing board to-go.*

Chloe: *I'll let you know by tomorrow. Proud of you, Hunter. Connor and everyone at Back Road is going to love the video.*

Hunter: *It wouldn't be what it is without you.*

I turn my face to the window again, biting back a grin. Gratitude fills my heart for Hunter. For all that he's taught me. For the gift of having this part of our story captured, frozen in time forever.

It's past noon, and I've got another job booked on the other side of town at one. A local boutique is shooting their winter collection, and I got hired as the makeup artist for their models.

Stepping outside, I breathe in the cool, autumn air. Everything feels warm, painted golden by the sun.

Is this what love feels like? Because if so, I'd like to bottle it up and carry it with me always.

Chapter 29

Hunter

I've been raking Mom's yard for what feels like hours, collecting enough leaves to mound them into a tall pile.

I step back and swipe an arm across my sweaty forehead, heavily debating tossing my rake aside and diving into the leaf pile like we did when we were kids.

Except, back then, Dad would do all the work, carefully pulling leaves into the center of the yard, methodically raking them into a pile, and then calling us boys out back to come play in them. He'd jump right into the leaves with us, tossing handfuls of them our way and tackling us into the pile until we'd all but smashed it down flat. Even the smell of the dying grass, the crunch of the dry leaves under my feet takes me back to those moments we'd shared here.

I turn my head up to the sky and am greeted by wispy clouds moving quickly, and I notice heavier, gray clouds gathering along the far treeline. The rain is coming, so I've got to make quick work of getting these leaves into bags before they're sopping wet.

"You there!" a voice calls from the back porch, making me turn. Luke is stalking across the yard toward me, hands full of heavy, black trash bags. "Put your back into it!"

I lean against my rake, raising a hand in greeting as he closes the gap between us.

He looks at the magnitude of my pile, and his eyes widen. "Dude, I'm genuinely impressed by this. How long have you been at it?"

"A while. Nice of you to show up."

Luke flings a trash bag out in front of him, opening it up. "Better late than never."

I grab another bag, and we start shoveling leaves into the bags as quickly as we can.

"Work stuff?"

"Nah, wedding stuff, actually."

"Ah, yes. Wedding stuff." I chuck a handful of leaves at him. "Speaking of weddings, I hate to make things awkward, but you realize that you haven't popped the question yet, right?"

Luke squints at me like I'm a moron. "Yes, I have. Lainey literally has a ring on her finger."

"No, brother," I say theatrically. "Not that question. The *other* question."

Luke rolls his eyes, impatient with my teasing. "And what might that be?"

I clear my throat, standing tall and leaning on the handle of my rake. "Dearest brother, wilt thou stand by me as I enter into the sacred union of matrimony..."—I pause—"as my best man?"

Luke laughs, tossing a few leaves my way. "Oh, right. *That* question."

We work silently for a few moments.

"I'm WAITING," I hiss.

"You are so annoying." Luke sighs, standing upright. "Hunter…"

"My dearly beloved."

"Hunter…" Luke grins. "Will you do me the honor of being my best man at my wedding?"

"I THOUGHT YOU'D NEVER ASK!" I slap him on the back. "The answer is YES."

"There are conditions, though, Hunter. You have to promise to behave yourself." He gives me a stern look. "And not embarrass me at the wedding."

"I can't promise that."

"Then I rescind my offer."

"Fine." I tie up a full bag of leaves. "I'll behave." I smirk. "But as the best man, I get to give a speech."

"Keep it kosher."

"Completely kosher. And I get to be the one who decorates your getaway car."

"Absolutely not." Luke shakes his head. "You are forbidden from touching my Porsche. I refuse to drive around with obscene drawings or inappropriate words on those windows."

I laugh, my chest filling with a lightness that only comes from being with my family—and Chloe. Who I'd like to make a permanent part of the family, if things go the way I hope they will.

"Calm down, good sir," I say. "Chloe will ensure that I don't draw anything *obscene* on your beloved Porsche."

"Oh, will she?"

I occupy myself with stuffing a third bag of leaves. Luke does the same.

"How'd the shoot go this week?"

"Best shoot of my career."

Luke sucks in a loud breath. "No way. No freaking way."

I tie up the bag and try to hide my grin from my twin.

"You *finally* kissed her?"

The smile breaks free. I can't help it. "We aren't talking about me right now. We are talking about your wedding. You guys have a date yet?"

"Where were you at Sunday dinner last week?" Luke gives me a shove. "We literally announced it at the dinner table."

I squint up at the treeline. "No recollection of that whatsoever."

"You were too busy staring at Chloe."

Thunder rumbles overhead, pushing us to work faster.

"April something?" I venture a guess. "Right?"

"Ahh, so he was listening."

"Partially."

"So how was it?"

"How was what?"

Luke gives me a measured stare. "The kiss, you fool."

I shake my head, leaning against my rake as thunder cuts through the air. The humidity is building, and the wind is picking up, sending rogue leaves spinning out of my pile.

"Best kiss of my life," I say. "All twenty-three of them."

Luke smiles at me, his white teeth nearly blinding me. The man rarely smiles full on, but when he does, it's brilliant and sincere.

"This is epic." He claps a hand on my shoulder. "So, now what?"

"That is the question of the hour."

The question that's been on my mind for weeks now—and even more so since the shoot wrapped. Chloe and I have shared way too many intimate moments and conversations for this all to turn to nothing. We're on the right track, moving forward toward the happiness we both deserve. It's taking everything in me not to move at hyper-speed, to get on the fast track to making her mine in the most official ways possible.

"I don't want to scare her off by trying to move too quickly," I say. "But I know what I feel. And I know she feels it, too."

The first drops of the storm hit my forehead and nose in quick succession.

"You guys have known each other so long that it really doesn't matter how quickly things move," Luke says, his perfectly coiffed hair getting tousled by the wind. "You should just marry the girl."

It's not like I haven't thought about marrying Chloe, which is *wild*. Who does that? Who jumps from being best friends straight to marriage? Nobody I know.

"I don't know, man. I want to date her properly, give her time to figure out if she wants it, too."

As the rain starts to come down heavily, Luke and I each collect as many garbage bags as we can carry and book it to the garage.

We run back to get the rest of the bags, getting soaked in the sudden downpour on our second sprint back to the house.

"Dang," I say, shaking water from my hair, my t-shirt soaked through. "We *almost* raked up all the leaves."

"The wind will blow the rest away. I'm sure Mom will appreciate our valiant effort."

Mom's white Lexus hadn't been parked in the garage when I'd gotten to the house, but it's there now.

"I say," Luke says, slicking his wet hair back with one hand, "if you know she's the one for you, you should just tell her.

That's what I did with Lainey." Luke sniffs, swiping at a rogue raindrop dripping down his nose. We're both looking out at the rain dumping just outside the open garage door. "I told her that I was one hundred percent certain that I wanted to be with her, and that whenever she was ready, we could move forward and get married."

I smirk. "Didn't take you long."

He shrugs. "When you know, you know."

When you know, you know.

Luke sniffs again, wiping water droplets from his face. "I'm going to go tell Mom about you and Chloe." He turns abruptly, taking a couple long strides that lead him to the door.

"No, come on, man!" I hustle after him. "She'll go getting all kinds of ideas. We can't tell her. Not yet."

Luke throws open the door. "Mama, you close by? Hunter's got some news to share with you."

I sigh, pausing in the open doorway and contemplating running back out into the rain to avoid this conversation with my mother.

Luke gives me a cheeky grin and crosses his arms across his built chest. I make a mental note to start doing more chest workouts so mine can rival his.

"It's in regards to a certain young woman," he yells, putting the final nail into my coffin.

"Now you've done it," I mutter.

"Oh, I already know, sweetheart," Mama says as she rounds the corner into the mudroom. "Chloe called me earlier today."

"She...*what*?"

"She called just to see how I was doing." Mama tries and fails to hide her guilty expression. "And I may have asked a few strategic questions..."

"You didn't."

"I did." She beams at me. "Now shut that door behind you before you catch a chill."

I'm working on cleaning out the rest of my bedroom upstairs. Mom's seated on the bed, waxing poetic about each bookmark, faded rubber wristband, and handwritten note I pull out of the relic that is my nightstand.

Amongst all the other random oddities, I find an old paper towel, folded into quarters. I unfold it, immediately recognizing Dad's tiny chicken scratch.

"You got a magnifying glass?" I squint down at the note. "This one's from Dad."

Mom chuckles. "I never understood how he could write things so incredibly small."

Hunter,

So proud of you and the good you put out into the world. Have a great day today, and don't stress about the meet. You're going to kill it. We'll be there, cheering you on.

Love,

Dad

"I'd forgotten about these." I hand the paper towel over to Mom. "He used to write us notes on napkins or whatever he could find and leave them on the kitchen counter for us to read before we left for school."

"He was the most thoughtful man." Mom gives me a nostalgic smile, glancing up from the paper towel note. "He always wanted you boys to know how loved you were. How proud he was of you."

I settle next to my mom on the bed, the full-size mattress creaking as I sit. "That's all I want now. To make him proud."

I feel Mom's hand land on my shoulder. "He is, Hunter. Don't you doubt that for a minute."

I take a steadying breath. "Sometimes, I wish I would have done things differently, taken things more seriously, like he always encouraged me to do."

Mom slowly moves her hand back and forth across my upper back, a comforting gesture she's performed since I was a little boy.

"Remember that we tried to always remind you that you'll have the rest of your life to be serious. Your joie de vivre is one of the things I love most about you."

I glance over at Mom, noticing the wrinkles around her eyes have deepened slightly, the white roots of her blonde hair standing out a little more sharply. Her smile lines appear as her lips lift. "It's never too late to become the man you want to be. But it's not going to happen all at once or overnight."

I snort. "Don't I know it."

"Chloe adores you, Hunter," she says softly. "And I adore you both. What the two of you have is really something, and you're moving in the right direction. One step at a time. You don't have to have everything figured out all at once."

I glance down at the paper towel note before carefully folding it back up and adding it to my stack of notes to keep.

When you know, you know.

"I just want to be worthy of her."

Mom tilts her head, looking at me lovingly. She's wearing that expression that mothers somehow can pull out even when you've pissed them off or disappointed them.

"You've always been worthy of love, Hunter. Now's just the right time for you to prove that to the woman *you* love."

We share a smile, and I glance down at my phone. "It's getting late. Let me finish up here, and I'll get out of your hair so you can get your sleep."

She eases off the bed. "Take your time. I love having you here."

"Love you, Mama."

She kisses the top of my hair before leaving the room.

Chapter 30

Chloe

This.

This is by far the most attractive version of Hunter I've ever set eyes upon. And not just because he's wearing a flannel shirt, rolled up so his forearms and the leather bracelets on his wrists are exposed.

I'm also swooning over him because he's got little ol' Darlene on his arm, bending down so that he can hear her when she speaks. I pull out my phone and snap a photo of the two of them, arm in arm as they pass under the *pumpkin patch* sign. I can't help myself. I grab a wagon and follow them into the adorable farm, the embodiment of autumn charm.

Hunter glances back at me over his shoulder, giving me his signature nose scrunch before getting dragged toward a towering mountain of pumpkins by Darlene.

"So what are we looking for?" he asks Darlene as she extricates herself from his arm, insisting that she can walk perfectly fine by herself. "Just point to the perfect pumpkins and I'll load them up for you."

"These are nice," she says, giving a solid, deep orange pumpkin a pat. "I want a variety of sizes to line up the porch steps so it looks inviting."

"You always do a beautiful job of that," I say, running my fingertips over the ridges of a squat, white pumpkin. "The kids are never afraid to come trick-or-treat at your house."

"I heard," Hunter leans in towards us, lowering his voice to a whisper. "That you give out full size candy bars. Is that just a rumor?"

Darlene presses a knobbly finger to her lips. "Shh...only to my favorites."

Hunter draws back, pretending to be offended. "I know for a fact that I did not get a full size candy bar when I came by your house last Halloween."

"Well that's because you're not a child, my dear." Darlene chuckles. "That one." She points to a massive pumpkin.

"An excellent choice." Hunter hefts the pumpkin into the wagon. "And for the record, I'm a child at heart. Plus, I know I'm at the top of your list of favorites, Darlene. So I'll be looking forward to the Twix bar you're saving to give especially to me on Halloween night."

Darlene swats at Hunter, shaking her head.

It's been our standing tradition to venture out to the local farm every October to pick out pumpkins for the front porch ever since I moved in with Darlene a few years back. It had been her idea to invite Hunter along for the activity this year. I swear her eyes sparkle more when he's around, and I wonder if that same sparkle can be seen all over my face when I'm in his presence, too.

We wander between the hay bales, sifting through everything from gnarled orange and green pumpkins to pristine white mini ones. We round a corner and I'm stopped in my tracks by a massive display of the most romantic gourds of them all.

"The cinderella pumpkin," I breathe, running a hand over the smooth surface of the dusty blue, picturesque pumpkins.

"Those are perfect for soup and pie, you know," Darlene says, picking up a smaller one to inspect.

"They'd look beautiful on the porch, too." I select one that's not too tall, not too flat. "Let's get this one."

Hunter pretends to heave the wagon behind him as we make our way to the marketplace. "Don't worry about me." he breathes heavily. "Just getting my workout in for the day."

"Oh, hush," Darlene scolds. "Chloe, do you remember the flavor of jam we bought last year? It was so delicious."

I follow Darlene into the covered market, where the shelves are filled with fresh, local preserves.

"Oh my goodness." I peer at the labels on the jars of jam, trying to remember which one we'd slathered on our pancakes and biscuits last fall and finished off in a matter of days. "I wanna say it was this one." I pull a jar of apricot preserves off the shelf.

"Let's buy two this time," Darlene says, grabbing herself a jar, too. "Do you remember when your grandmother and I would make jam every August? She grew plums and I'd buy flats of strawberries…"

"And I'd eat as many as I possibly could before either of you noticed."

Darlene smiles at me, her eyes bright as ever behind her glasses. "Oh, honey, we always noticed. We'd let you eat and eat until we thought you couldn't possibly eat any more. For such a small thing, you always had such an appetite."

I grab a third jar of jam off the shelf–raspberry this time. "Still do."

"That makes two of you." Darlene gestures to where Hunter is swooning over the biggest jars of peaches I've ever seen.

He looks over at us longingly, mouth slightly agape. "Can I...can we..."

"Throw them in the wagon," I say, grinning at his childlike excitement as he lifts the peaches off the shelf and gingerly wedges the jar between two pumpkins in the wagon.

"You *would* pick the most sugary fruit of them all," I tease.

Hunter shrugs, the corners of his lips lifting as he leans close enough to brush them against my hair. "If I can't have your mouth, then I guess I'll have to settle for peaches."

"Hunter!" I scold in a sharp whisper, my eyes darting to Darlene, who seems to suddenly be very occupied with the baskets overflowing with apples. The apples closest to me are no longer the only pink ladies in the house tonight.

"What?" His breath skitters across my skin, warming my cheeks. "A man can't compare his lover's lips to his favorite fruit?"

I stare, wide eyed, up at him. The cut of his cheekbones, the swoop of his hair over his brow. I'd love nothing more than to slip my hand down into that open collar of his flannel, to run my fingertips over his collarbones and smooth chest. I feel the warmth of my blushing face spreading down my neck.

"What did you just call me?" I ask coyly, toying with one of the buttons on his shirt.

"Lover." he says softly, his lips slanting into a smile. I'm full on burning now, set alight from the inside out.

"To be honest," I counter. "I'd prefer you to refer to me as your highness, or perhaps goddess divine."

"I'll call you whatever you want, as long as I get to call you mine."

I'm lost, tumbling down into the rabbit hole that leads to whatever this place is called. This place where Hunter belongs to me, and I'm *his*.

He grabs my hand, stopping my fiddling with his shirt and laces his fingers into mine. He brings our joined hands to his mouth, warming them with the most tender, slow kiss across my knuckles.

Someone's going to have to peel the remains of my melted soul from off the dusty dirt floor.

"Should we go pay for these before I do any more damage?" Darlene says, her arms loaded with a bag of apples.

"Allow me," Hunter lets go of my hand to help Darlene take her purchases to the checkout, dragging our wagon behind him with his other hand.

I'm suddenly surprised by the prickle of tears that I can feel gathering in the corners of my eyes. Hunter and Darlene blur, and the market lights strung overhead turn into streaks of gold.

I trust him.

The realization settles over me in a wash of pure clarity.

I watch Hunter smile and greet the teenager working at the checkout counter, lighting up the entire room with who he is. Who he always has been.

I thought it would take months, maybe years, to work through the doubts and fears that have weighed on my heart. But at this moment, I feel feather-light. Lighter than I've felt in a long, long time.

My back still twinges as I help load the pumpkins up onto the counter. My lips still tremble as I work to hide the emotion building in my chest. But that tightness, that gripping fear that

I've carried for so long is no longer pressing on me like it used to.

The need to hustle, to constantly keep moving so that I wouldn't have to *feel*...

I'm feeling it now. Slowing down means accepting the lows as well as the highs. Feeling everything, even when it's uncomfortable for me to do so.

And when Hunter subtly pays for Darlene's harvest haul while she's still fishing around in her purse, it takes everything in me not to grab him by his flannel and plant a kiss right on his mouth.

He catches my eye as he turns to grab the wagon handle. I must be wearing my heart on my sleeve like I'm always trying *not* to do, because a smile breaks out across his face that warms me right through.

He knows.

He knows how much I love him, that I've always loved him.

He knows that I want him just as much as he wants me.

And I'm finally okay with it.

About an hour later, all of the pumpkins have been strategically placed, spilling aesthetically down Darlene's porch steps.

"Where are the cobwebs? Plastic tarantulas?" Hunter asks, leaning over the porch railing. "I'll help you throw them up."

Darlene gives him a withering look. "We're aiming to be *inviting*, here, Hunter. Not *haunting*."

"Right, right. Got it." He winks at me. "Nothing creepy for Miss Darlene."

I adjust one of the tiny white pumpkins, drawing it closer to the edge of the step it's resting on.

"I think it looks perfect." I say, tilting my head and walking backwards down the front walk to get a view of the whole scene. "You'll be the most popular house on the block."

"I hope the two of you will stay for a bit to help me hand out candy," she replies. "Crowd control."

Hunter nods emphatically. "We accept cash or check, and occasionally candy as forms of payment."

Darlene chuckles

"I'll go make us some tea. Come in when you're ready so you can show me that video I've heard so much about."

Hunter lopes down the steps to join me near the sidewalk. Darlene gives us a wave from the porch.

Once Darlene's safely inside her house, Hunter wraps an arm around my shoulders from behind, locking me against his warm body. His embrace feels like an invitation to settle in, to stay a while, to make myself right at home.

Don't mind if I do.

"Speaking of checks..." Hunter says into my hair. "Did you get yours yet?"

I nod. "It hit my bank account yesterday."

He gives me a little squeeze. "Good."

When I'd seen the money from the "Make Up" shoot had arrived, I hadn't wasted any time posting on my social media accounts that I was looking to hire an assistant.

The response had blown me away. So many talented artists in the Nashville area were excited about the opportunity to work with me, making me feel a sense of gratitude that I'm still carrying in my heart. The real challenge was going to be choosing just one out of the many incredible artists who'd responded to my posts.

I'd also made an appointment for later this week with Darlene's favorite chiropractor, who she's been trying to get me to see for years—run by none other than Charlie-with-the-frosted-tips' beloved father. His practice is still going strong, with Charlie himself working as the latest orthopedic specialist.

"Thank you, Hunter," I breathe. "So many good things have happened to me because of you."

"You're everything to me, Chloe," he presses a kiss to the top of my head. "Just let me know when you're ready for round two and I'll get you booked on your next video shoot."

I snort. "Fat chance. Never signing up for that again."

"Not even if I'm your co-star?"

"Hmmm..." I tilt my head thoughtfully. "I suppose I would have to take that minor detail into consideration."

I drop my head back against his solid chest and hold onto his arm with both hands. We breathe together for a moment, the rise and fall of our lungs in sync. My eyes flutter closed and I let myself rest against him, feeling entirely relaxed for the first time in a long, long time.

I give myself permission to just be still, to be present in what it feels like to be held by the man I love.

It's better than anything I've ever felt before. In Hunter's arms, I'm settled, grounded, and safe.

Home.

Chapter 31

Hunter

"Is it weird," I ask, "that I'm still attracted to you, even with a beard?"

Chloe strokes her long, fake beard—the cherry on top of her Hagrid costume. "Hagrid takes great pride in his facial hair, so no. Not at all."

Another gaggle of trick-or-treaters clusters at the door, interrupting our conversation. The sun has set, the stars are starting to appear, and the air has turned frosty outside.

"Look at you!" Chloe says to a sparkling princess as she takes some candy from the bowl. "I love your dress."

The girl peers up at Chloe suspiciously. "Thanks. I like your…uh…beard?" She wrinkles her nose in a forced smile before dashing off Darlene's front porch. Chloe shuffles back inside in her heavy boots.

She holds up the now empty bowl. "That's the last of your candy, Darlene!"

Darlene's head appears from around the doorway to the kitchen. "Oh, good. Glad to be rid of it."

"Don't lie," I tease as we join her in the kitchen, and Chloe starts washing out the bowl at the sink. "You have a secret stash hidden somewhere. I know it."

"You'll never get it out of me," Darlene says, her back to me as she opens the fridge.

Chloe points to a cabinet to the left of the sink, widening her eyes and mouthing the words, *top shelf*.

"You're too short to be Hagrid," I'd laughed when she'd answered the door. "Gimli, maybe?"

She'd simply grunted and hustled me inside so we could be ready when the trick-or-treaters arrived.

I tap my wand against my leg. Jax had lent me his Slytherin robes and green tie, and I'd found a greasy blond wig to top off my Draco Malfoy look. Chloe was supposed to dress up as a fellow Hogwarts student but had pulled a fast one on me by scrounging up a rugged Hagrid costume instead. I bite back a laugh at her, five-foot-nothing, frizzy hair and beard, the rest of her hidden under a bulky coat.

"I did make something special for you two today." Darlene pulls a dish out of the fridge and sets it on the table.

Chloe gasps, whirling around so fast that her beard slides sideways, exposing half of her face. "You didn't!"

Darlene winks up at me. "Don't be too impressed. I used canned pumpkin."

I tsk. "You're telling me that this pumpkin pie does not, in fact, contain one of the many pumpkins we painstakingly chose for this very purpose?"

She moves swiftly toward the cabinet to the left of the sink, pulling plates down for us. I catch a glimpse of a basket on the top shelf filled to the brim with shiny wrappers. *Candy stash located.*

"Darlene! When did you have time to do this?" Chloe helps set out forks and finds a knife to cut the pie. "You know this pie is my absolute favorite."

"I practically have the recipe memorized. Don't go thinking I slaved away for hours on this for you." She gives me a wink.

"So sweet of you," I add.

She dishes up slices of pie for each of us, and we take our seats at the table.

"Oh!" Darlene suddenly stands, startling Chloe and making her drop her fork. "The whipped cream!"

"Now we're talking." I clap my hands together.

Chloe gives me a stern look. "Don't even think about it, Hunter."

"What?"

She drops her voice to a whisper, leaning over toward me so that her beard drags across her pie. "No eating whipped cream straight out of the can."

"Why ever not?" I ask innocently.

"I will buy you another can that you can feast upon to your heart's content." Her eyes are pleading now. "Don't you dare do it in front of Darlene."

"Your beard is in your pie."

Chloe peels off her beard, unhooking the loops from her ears and setting it on her lap. Even with her overly drawn-on eyebrows, she's as stunning as ever.

"Whipped cream, Hunter?" Darlene offers.

"Of course, thank you," I say with the utmost decorum, my eyes locked with Chloe's as Darlene gives me a generous swirl on top of my pie.

Chloe stares me down, eyebrow arched menacingly like I'm a toddler testing the etiquette limits at the family dinner table.

"Chloe?"

"Yes, please."

Once our pies are properly peaked with luscious mounds of whipped cream, we dig in. Chloe was right: Darlene's pie is divine. It takes everything in me to not literally lick the remains of it off my plate.

"Have another piece, Hunter," Darlene insists, scooping more pie onto my plate. "It's made mostly of vegetables."

"Well, when you put it that way…"

I load up my pie with whipped cream, wanting so badly to tip that can back and swirl it into my mouth. But I resist. I'm a new man. I've got to behave sometimes if I want to keep Chloe around.

And I do. I want her—Hagrid beard and all.

"Darlene, this was so good," I say. "Thank you for always taking such good care of us."

She bustles around the kitchen, dishing up generous slices of pie onto a paper plate. "Take some to your mother, will you?"

Chloe eyes me again, and I know she's telepathically telling me that those slices of pie had better make it to my mom's house. No secretly stuffing my face on the car ride over.

Dang it.

"I'm not backing down just because you're a wizard."

"You were expelled from Hogwarts, you great oaf," I taunt, winding up the tetherball before knocking it over to Chloe's side of the pole. "You're no match for the evil Draco Malfoy."

She jumps valiantly as the ball comes her way, her beard flopping with the effort. Her fingertips barely graze the ball, and it swings back over to my side of the tetherball court. I palm it high over her head, and the game is over within a few seconds as soon as the ball smacks against layers of wound-up rope.

She curses, fussing with the buttons of her overcoat. "This coat is killing my vibe."

"Take it off!" I chant. "Take it off!"

Chloe rolls her eyes, shrugging out of the coat. I grab the tetherball as it unwinds so it doesn't knock her over.

I'm not prepared for the sight of her in a fitted gray sweater layered over a white collared shirt. Her short plaid skirt matches her tie, both in signature Gryffindor scarlet and gold.

"What's this?" I say as she pulls off her beard and tosses it on top of her discarded coat. "A costume change? How very dramatic."

She fluffs out her curly hair. "Hermoine Granger. Pleasure." Her accent is spot on.

I drop the ball and cross over to her side of the tetherball court. "Hermoine and Draco? How scandalous."

She grabs my tie, pulling me closer.

"Terribly scandalous."

I wrap my arms around her, loving the feel of her body against mine. She tilts her head back, her palms pressed flat against my chest. I splay my hands out across her back, noting the fact that I can fully feel the curves of her spine, her protruding ribs, and she's not pushing me away.

"I've always wondered," she says, her voice low, "what it would be like to kiss Draco."

A slow smile spreads across my face. "Have you, now?"

"I feel like, out of everyone at Hogwarts, he'd be the best kisser, by far."

"Well, well, well. I'll let you be the judge of that."

I lower my head, finding her lips effortlessly. Our mouths meet, and it's like all the stars align in the sky above us. We move together, holding each other and deepening the kiss. When I can feel that she's about to pull away, I gently take her full bottom lip in my teeth. Chloe laughs as I release her, her hands digging into my robes.

"He's a Slytherin, ok?" I say against her mouth before kissing her again. "You know he plays dirty."

She takes the sides of my jaw in her hands, planting the softest of kisses on each of my cheekbones. The tip of my nose. Across my lips.

"And Hermoine would play nice."

"What about Hagrid?" I ask. "How well does that dude kiss?"

Chloe throws her head back and lets out a joyful laugh. "Want me to put the beard back on?"

"You kids done out there?" Lainey's voice carries down the porch from her position at the open back door. "Movie is about to start!"

Before Chloe can protest, I sweep her up into my arms and carry her back up the porch steps.

"Wait!" She struggles against me. "We didn't finish the game!"

I shrug. "Call it a draw."

"Heck no." She tries again to push against me. "I want to WIN."

"We'll miss the beginning of the movie," I say into her hair. "Besides...I brought you peanut M&Ms."

She immediately stills, brushing a kiss across my jawline. "All is forgiven. As long as you run back outside immediately and retrieve my Hagrid costume."

"As you wish."

I duck into the open doorway where Lainey's waiting for us, bowl of popcorn in hand. I set Chloe down, and she straightens her skirt, grinning up at me like I've just given her the world.

I haven't done that quite yet, but I plan to—if she'll let me.

Chapter 32

Chloe

"Chloe?" Darlene calls from upstairs. "Delivery for you!"

I set my eye shadow palette down and make my way to the main level of Darlene's house. She's got a black garment bag stretched between her hands.

"Happy birthday, darlin'." She presses a kiss to my cheek as I take the garment bag from her.

"Thank you, ma'am." I hold the bag up as high as I can by the hanger, but it still drags on the floor. "What on earth is this?"

Darlene clasps her wrinkled hands together, her eyes shimmering behind her glasses. "Someone special must be thinking about you on your birthday."

My parents are in the send-a-quick-text-before-midnight birthday camp, so that rules them out.

"If you don't open it, I'll do it for you."

"Impatient, are we?" I tease, pulling the zipper down to reveal the contents of the garment bag.

I catch a glimpse of silky fabric. Tiffany blue. I pull the sides of the bag open and take in the thin straps, the cinch just below the waist.

My breath catches in my throat. This dress looks almost identical to the one I wore to the Preference dance senior year.

The dance I had asked Hunter to. A wave of anxiety washes over me at the memory of being rejected by him.

"There's a note." Darlene pulls an envelope from the hanger. I trade her the dress for the letter, slipping my shaking finger under the seal.

I slide a thick card out of the envelope, the gold foil of the text shimmering in the morning light filtering in from the open screen door.

Your presence is requested at seven o'clock in the evening on November sixteenth at Ridgeview High School. Formal attire required.

I flip the card over and find an addition to the invitation written in a distinct scrawl.

Can't wait to see you in this dress tonight. - Hunter

I clutch the card to my chest, meeting Darlene's expectant eyes. "Well?" she breathes.

I hand her the card, still unable to find my voice.

She draws in a sharp breath as she flips the card over. "Oh, sweetheart. He's pulling out all the stops for you tonight, isn't he?"

I feel like I'm coming out of an insane, twisty loop on a rollercoaster. What is this alternate reality I'm currently living in? Because I think it's about time I start making myself at home here. Here in this space where Hunter and I are together, committed completely to each other.

This world where he surprises me with a Tiffany-blue dress, an invitation, and a clear attempt to recreate a part of our story that hadn't gone the way either of us had hoped it would.

"Aren't you going to try it on?" Darlene pushes the dress back into my hands. "Get yourself into that dress."

I walk back down to my basement apartment in a daze, my heart feeling both heavy and light at the same time.

I carefully pull the dress out of the garment bag, hanging it up so I can really take it in.

How Hunter found a dress so similar to the one I'd chosen as a teenager is beyond me. I'd wager he got a little help from Lainey or Jax.

I shed my pajama set and unzip the dress, easing it over my head. I can still remember the cool sweep of the fabric across the skin of my back and stomach when I tried on the original dress in high school, free from the confines of my back brace for a night.

The dress reaches the floor, a subtle slit opening up just above my right knee. It's more form-fitting than the one I'd worn as a teen, hugging my curves without feeling restrictive. I stand in front of my full-length mirror, twirling back and forth and feeling like that hopeful seventeen-year-old again.

I sweep my hair back off my neck, deciding that the gorgeous bustline of this dress needs to be featured tonight. Thank goodness I'm *slightly* bustier than I was in high school.

I'm already picturing the natural, youthful, dewy look I want to create tonight. Exactly how my hair should be styled, the shades of shadow that can be layered to highlight the color of my eyes, even in dim lighting.

"Oh, Chloe," Darlene says from the open doorway. "I'm sorry. I couldn't wait for you to come back upstairs."

I work the catwalk back and forth across my bedroom floor. "What do you think?"

"Hunter is going to drop dead at the sight of you," she says, her eyes growing misty as they sweep over me. "He is one lucky man to get to have you. I hope you know that."

"I do. At least, now I do."

I feel emotion rising in my own throat, and I can't help but wrap Darlene into an embrace. I breathe in, inhaling the scent of lavender and citrus she always wears.

"I'm lucky, too," I say softly, pulling back and meeting her eyes. "He is a good man."

Darlene nods. "He'd better be. Or he'll have me to answer to."

I brush my hands down the front of my dress, feeling the nerves gathering in my chest.

"Come up, and have some breakfast when you're ready." Darlene pats my hand. "Take your time."

She leaves me, and I sit down on the edge of my bed. My closet door is open, giving me a view of my rows of dresses, sweaters, skirts, and shoes. My eyes land on the stack of clear plastic bins I've shoved into a corner, and I immediately hop back off the bed.

I clear some room between hanging items of clothing and heft out the top box, dropping it on my bed. I remove the lid, rummaging through its contents.

Most of the box is occupied by my prosthetic brace. I pull it out, knocking on the hefty, plastic contraption before setting it aside. I feel an unexpected sense of gratitude for all that my scoliosis has taught me, especially now that I'm moving through life at a much slower pace, grateful to be loved in spite of my imperfections.

And grateful to be seen as so much more than just the girl with the twisted spine.

I return back to the box, pulling out my graduation cap and gown, a portfolio of all of the artwork I'd created, and a couple bracelets and trinkets that, at some point, I'd decided were worth keeping.

And finally, wrapped up in my old cross-country sweatpants, I find them.

A slightly faded Tiffany-blue, knee-length dress and a pair of strappy silver shoes—the same pair I'd worn to the Preference dance.

The style is outdated, and the sharp heels themselves are tinted a little brown. But there are perks to having reached your full height at fourteen—my shoe size hasn't changed, and I'm easily able to slip them on. I fasten the buckles at my ankles, feeling a bit like Cinderella about to attend a re-do of the ball where she met her prince.

There will be no fleeing or losing of shoes tonight, I can guarantee that. I intend to allow myself to be swept up in this fairy tale that Hunter is creating for me, to let my happiness bubble over the way I'd hoped it would all those years ago.

When I pull into the parking lot at Ridgeview High, it's empty except for a few straggler cars. I spot Hunter's Jeep parked near the entrance to the football field. I take a steadying breath as I turn off my car.

Deep breaths, Chloe. Long, slow breaths.

I've felt nerves before, but not like this. This is next-level twitterpation, a youthful eagerness that leaves me a little shaky and unsteady on my feet as I shut my car door behind me.

Thankfully, it's unseasonably warm tonight, or I'd be shivering in my thin dress. I gather my skirt in one hand so it doesn't drag on the pavement, holding my clutch in the other hand.

Iceberg cool. Snoop Dogg calm.

I make my way to the gate that leads out to the track where Hunter and I come to run. The gate creaks as I pass through it, and that's when I hear the strains of music coming from the football field. I look out to where the sound is coming from and nearly crumple into a heap right there on the starting line.

There's a small, wooden platform set up on the field, covered by a white canopy. Warm lights are strung across the entryway, and there, on the edge of the platform, stands the most dapper man I've ever seen.

Hunter is my teenage dream brought to life, dressed in a well-cut, navy-blue suit. His hands are in his pockets, and as he steps off the platform toward me, my eyes drop to his tie—Tiffany blue.

We draw toward each other slowly, and I'm burning up already under the way his dark eyes roam over me and the brilliant smile that stretches across his face.

We're a foot away from each other when Hunter reaches out a hand for me to take. I let my dress down, freeing my hand so I can slip it into his. He's warm, so inviting, and irresistibly handsome in his suit.

"I was getting worried, there," he says, smirking. "Thought you might stand me up as payback."

"Water under the bridge."

His eyes drag down over my dress, and I don't miss how his gaze lingers on the slit where my leg is exposed. His eyes cut back up to mine, and I'm certain the vulnerability, the affection, and appreciation held there are a reflection of my own. I swallow, feeling the shift in air pressure, the slight increase of my pulse as he intertwines his fingers with mine and gives my hand a squeeze.

"You look absolutely stunning tonight, Chlo."

I give a subtle curtsy. "I suppose I owe that to you." He runs his thumb over the silky fabric at my waistline, and I feel the warmth of his touch all the way down to my toes. "Where did you find this dress?"

"Lainey," he explains. "She is a wizard."

"I figured you had some help."

He scoffs. "Are you saying I couldn't have done this myself?"

"No, of course not," I insist. "This was just so specific, so personal to us. I don't know how she found something so similar to the one..." My voice trails off as Hunter presses a gentle kiss to my knuckles.

Goodness gracious. My knees are about to buckle beneath me, and his lips haven't even come near mine...yet.

"Chloe," he says, his tone serious. "I must admit, I wanted to bring you here for purely selfish reasons."

"Shocker."

"Reason number one." Hunter gestures to my dress. "To see you all dressed up like this. To be honest, I'm speechless. You are the most beautiful woman I have ever seen in my life."

I arch an eyebrow. "I rank at the top of Hunter's most beautiful list? What a coveted position."

"Stop it." He grins. "I'm being serious. Trying to win you over with my words, here."

"You know how I feel about lip service."

Hunter's lips quirk into a crooked grin. "Now...what kind of lip service are we talking about? Because I'd happily let our lips do the talking right now, if you'd prefer."

I give him the satisfaction of laughing at his wit. "Please continue your spiel."

"Ahh, yes." He clears his throat. "Reason number two. To redeem myself for what happened in high school—and everything thereafter. I don't regret taking the path we did to get here, but I do sometimes wish I could have loved you much, much sooner than this."

Loved? LOVED?!

I cross one ankle over the other and brush a hand down the front of my dress, trying to keep my spinning head from taking over. I can feel my neck warming, probably reddening where my skin is exposed.

"Reason number three." He tugs at my hand, pulling me toward the canopy. "I wanted to dance with you again, like we did at the video shoot."

He ducks as we enter the covered platform, and I'm swept up in the glow of the dance floor, like I'd hoped to be at Preference. He's got a table set up on one side, filled with bowls of candy, delicate treats and pastries, and a crystal bowl of light-pink liquid.

"Is that..." I grin. "*Punch?*"

His expression grows serious. "Don't fret, my lady. Nobody's here to spike the punch at this dance."

I laugh, then keep laughing as I inspect all of the beautiful details of this night he's created for us.

"Who's going to eat all of these?" I ask, pointing to a mile-high stack of crinkly chocolate cookies.

"I have faith in us."

"I love your optimism," I snort.

I set my clutch down at the end of the table and turn back to face Hunter. He's got an intense look on his face, one that means business.

"Is that all you love about me, Chlo?" he asks, his voice growly as he closes the gap between us. "Because I could spend all night giving you a dissertation or Powerpoint presentation on all the things I love about you."

He's thrown the L word around a few times now, and I can't *not* acknowledge it. He's inviting me to step out to the edge, to join him as we jump together into this relationship. Head first. No doubts. All in.

Go big, or go home.

I draw in a deep breath before speaking, trying to gather my thoughts while Hunter towers over me, reaches for me, pulls me to him.

I take hold of his tie gently, working up the courage to meet his eyes.

"Hunter," I say, my voice nearly giving out as I glance up at his face. His head is tilting. He's leaning in and then stopping a breath away from my lips as he waits for me to speak.

"I love everything about you," I breathe.

"Now if that isn't true love, I don't know what is." I feel his nose scrunch up against mine, our breath mingling together. "I love you, Chloe Paulson. And I always will."

I tug on his tie, urging him closer. He responds slowly as I tilt my head back, and he traces a line down my nose with his.

We're still for a heartbeat before he presses his lips to mine, and I respond by kissing him back gently. I let the happiness that I've always hoped to find flow through me, filling me up until I'm ready to burst.

As our kiss deepens and he holds me tightly in his strong arms, it feels like my heart has moved to the outside of my chest, finally in a place where Hunter can see it. Where my true feelings can come to light. Where I don't have to hide behind fear, or what-ifs, or the anxiety that accompanies risk.

Because right now, this doesn't feel like a risk. This feels like coming home. Being swept up into his arms in the middle of a downpour. Being held under a blanket fort. Throwing on his worn and softened sweatshirt. And it tastes like Bud's biscuits and strawberry jam. Salted caramel. Cinnamon spice. Popcorn and peanut M&Ms.

Hunter slowly pulls away, and I taste his smile one more time, relishing in the way his touch, his kisses, and his strong hold ground me.

I feel more beautiful, more confident than ever before. And it's not because I know with certainty that Hunter loves me, but because I'm truly in a place where I'm able to *love him*. To let that love blossom in its full expression, to grow with time, to deepen and change and become more and more beautiful, just like our friendship has.

"Miss Paulson," Hunter says, dropping into a bow with one hand behind his back. He takes my hand and brings it to his lips again. "May I have this dance?"

"But of course," I say, allowing him to draw me toward the middle of the platform.

It's not until we're wrapped in each other's arms, swaying back and forth, that I realize what song is playing. Connor's song. The song that brought us together.

Our song.

Hunter starts singing along, his off-key voice skipping from high to low in the space over my head. I laugh into the lapels of his suit jacket.

"You'd better let Connor sing this one, honey."

"You sure? 'Cause I think I can nail that high note right at the end of the—"

"No, no." I squeeze his shoulder where my hand is resting. "I think he's got it."

He sighs. "Fine."

Epilogue

Hunter

I look up at the gray, gloomy skies, punctuated by the circle of nearly bare trees surrounding us. There's wind, the impending threat of rain, and yet, I feel like it's seventy-five and sunny. A gorgeous morning.

Apparently, this is what you sign up for when you decide to hold your wedding ceremony outside in December.

"You okay?" Luke asks from behind my shoulder. I turn slightly so he can hear me speak.

"Never been better."

"You just had to beat me at something else, didn't you?" he teases. "First one to kiss a girl, first one to break a bone..." He claps a hand on my shoulder. "And now the first one of us to get married."

I feel like I've successfully consumed the entirety of the kitchen sink from Rosie's, and my pulse starts reacting as I'm reminded of the miracle that is happening to me today.

I'm marrying my best friend.

Sure, waiting until the spring or summer would have been more practical, but since when have I ever been *practical*?

After Chloe's birthday last month, our relationship careened at breakneck speed out of the friend zone, briefly entered the dating zone, and zoomed straight into *let's get married* a few weeks later.

We've known each other for so long, waited for so many years to be together, that it just didn't feel right to put things off, to wait for reasons that didn't make sense for us. We already work together and spend most of our daily life together. Committing to move forward and do life together as husband and wife felt as natural as it had to dance under that starry sky on the football field at Ridgeview High.

When you know, you know.

The "Make Up" music video premiered a week ago along with Connor's single. Since then, Chloe and I have been barraged on social media by avid shippers and strangers who are dying to know if we are a real-life couple.

Little do these fans of Connor's know that they'll be getting a wedding at the end of our story, should we decide to share it.

"Mom's giving you the signal," Luke whispers from behind me. I catch Connor Cane's eye from his position off to my right, where he's standing, acoustic guitar strung over his shoulder, ready to play as Chloe makes her grand entrance.

We're situated in the middle of the backyard of our family home. Lainey somehow worked her event-planning magic over the past few weeks, creating a gorgeous archway and aisle in the backyard for us to say our vows under. Luke, Jax, and I are standing and waiting on one side of the archway, while Lainey is positioned on the other side. Dad's good friend Doug, one of the top investment advisors from L.M. Ward, the family firm, is officiating the ceremony.

My mother makes her way down the porch steps and up the aisle to stand next to Lainey as part of the wedding party. When you have an intimate guest list, nearly everyone present gets to participate in the ceremony.

Mama stands on her tiptoes to give me a hug and plants a kiss on my cheek, her eyes already filling with tears.

"Love you."

"Love you, too, Mama," I whisper back.

She clings to me for a moment longer before letting go. "You ready to see your bride?"

I exhale a whoosh of air, nodding. The anticipation is *killing me*. Sean grins at me from behind one of the cameras he's set up on a tripod. This video will, by far, top the list of my favorite projects to work on.

Mom had been right. The house had sold within a matter of weeks after Luke had helped her list it. When Chloe and I had talked about where we wanted to be married, it only felt right to do it here—a place where so much of our story took place.

I'd battled with feeling bitter and sad about losing the house I grew up in, the place that encapsulated so many of my memories with my dad. It's fitting that the final memory we're creating here will be the absolute best moment of my life so far, something that I can carry with me that will only continue to sweeten with time.

Darlene pokes her head out of the back door of the brick house, giving me a wave. I wave back, grinning, then turn to Connor and nod.

His fingers meet the guitar strings, his song carrying across the yard to give Chloe her signal to make her grand entrance.

At first, I listen to Connor's smooth timbre as he starts singing, the way it weaves between the notes he's picking on his guitar. But then Darlene emerges from the house with Chloe on her arm, and it's like everything in existence around me fades into the background.

Chloe meets my eyes as soon as she reaches the aisle, and I feel my throat knot. I try to swallow it down, but the emotion keeps swelling until it reaches my eyes. Tears gather in the corners as I take in the sight of my soon-to-be *wife*.

She's breathtaking. I allow myself to take in the sight of her simple gown, the lace sleeves that end at her wrists, her delicate train trailing behind her as she walks toward me. She's got her hair pulled back, revealing the sweep of her neck and the outline of her collarbones.

Her lips are painted a deep berry red, a shade that's grown to be a favorite of mine. She draws closer, and the smile she throws my way nearly stops my heart.

Darlene deposits Chloe at my side, giving both of us a tight squeeze before stepping back and taking a seat beside Ella Mae.

I slip my hand into Chloe's, and she grips my fingers so tightly she just about cuts off my circulation. We share a look filled with emotion, anticipation, and adoration.

Are we doing this?

We're doing this.

I lean closer so that I can whisper in her ear, "You are so beautiful."

A blush spreads across her cheekbones as she looks down, her lashes thick and full. She's really outdone herself today. Every feature is enhanced in the most natural, subtle, yet stunning way.

Doug clears his throat, and we hold onto each other for dear life as he begins the ceremony.

I'm able to hold it together until the time comes for Chloe and me to read our vows to each other. I'm up first and take my time slowly unfolding the already worn piece of paper where I've captured the promises I want to make to the love of my life.

"Chloe," I begin, "I have waited for this day for as long as I can remember."

And that's where the control I've been holding onto ends. I'm shocked at how my chest tightens, my throat closes up, and my eyes burn, blurring the words on the page and preventing me from speaking.

This overwhelming feeling, this love and pure devotion that I feel for her...how could I possibly verbalize it? How can one put into words the deepest feelings of the heart?

Chloe gives me an encouraging, watery smile, clearly affected by my show of emotion.

"Whew," I sigh, sniffing and trying to gain some composure. I swallow a couple times and take another breath before attempting to speak again.

"From the moment I first met you, I was awestruck by your courage. Your compassion and kindness. Your quiet way of making everyone around you want to be better."

I glance up from my paper to look at Chloe, and she's swiping at her eyes, gazing skyward to prevent her artful makeup from smudging. She fans at her face, and we laugh together.

"Though it took me forever and a day to build up the courage to make you mine, I've loved every moment of our journey, every part of our story. The long talks we'd share during our walks around the track during gym class. The copious amounts of biscuits consumed at Bud's. The laughter over the most ridiculous things that only we would find funny. The way we can speak to each other without really speaking. The heart-to-heart conversations. The way we work together seamlessly. The appreciation we have for each other's creativity."

She clasps her hands in front of her dress and gazes up at me shyly.

"Chloe, I promise to fight for our marriage every day of my life. To honor and respect and cherish you. To create more moments and memories together that will last a lifetime." I pause. "Though I am far from a perfect man, and our life together will not be perfect, I promise you that I will do my best to make you laugh every day. To help you see the good, even when it's hard. And to strive to be the kind of man who's worthy of your precious"—I swallow—"perfect love."

I make it through the rest of my vows, then my pulse picks up again as Chloe pulls out a leather-bound notebook to read hers.

"Way to show me up," I groan. "I bring a loose-leaf sheet of paper, and you bring an entire notebook."

Chloe laughs, shaking her head. "My vows only take up the first couple of pages. I'm going to fill the rest of it up with letters to you."

I hear the gals seated near us sniffling, clearly touched at Chloe's thoughtfulness.

Chloe reads her vows to me, and I'm blown away again at the way she sees me. The boy who'd helped her pick up her pencil in chemistry class the day we met. The kid who collected eye rolls every time he tried to flirt with her. The idiot who'd chosen to take someone else to the dance when she'd asked him first. The man who'd dated countless women, bounced from relationship to relationship, and had his fair share of casual flings. The man who tried his best to take care of her and failed miserably along the way.

Who I used to be doesn't seem to matter to Chloe at all anymore. What Chloe sees in me is the kind of man I want to become. And *that's* how I know that she's the one for me.

Doug declares us man and wife, and I waste no time sweeping Chloe into my arms and pressing a tender kiss to her lips.

She pulls back as our intimate circle of family members and friends cheer.

"I'm so sorry." She rubs a thumb along my bottom lip. "This is a—"

"Long-wear lipstick," I finish. "Couldn't care less."

And I kiss her again, tasting her smile and holding her to me like we're the only two people out there, shivering in the cold, December air.

THE END

Enjoyed Chloe and Hunter's story? I'd love for you to leave a review on Amazon or Goodreads!

Other books in this series:

The Retreat
The Holiduel - Coming November 2022

A Note from the Author

Though *The Make Up* is entirely a work of fiction, in many ways, Chloe's story is my story.

I was diagnosed with idiopathic scoliosis when I was thirteen, and then spent several years wearing a bulky, hot, uncomfortable prosthetic brace.

My friends could wear tight-fitting clothing, do sit-ups in gym class, and get hugs from cute boys without giving any of those things a second thought. I, on the other hand, worried constantly about what people would think about me once they saw my brace and the physical limitations it placed on me.

Despite my hopes and best efforts to correct my scoliosis, at some point I had to accept that my crooked spine wasn't going away.

I can honestly say, all these years later, I'm grateful for my scoliosis. My condition, while uncomfortable, has made me more empathetic and has taught me to find contentment and confidence in my own skin.

My crooked spine is a part of me, but it's not *who* I am.

I actively choose to dwell on all that I *can* do, rather than what I can't do because of my scoliosis. I can taste, smell, feel, and see. I have a healthy and strong body that allows me to run, dance, sing, laugh, read, write, love, and completely embrace and enjoy my beautiful life.

If you share any of these experiences relating to scoliosis with me, or anything else surrounding body image, I want you to know that you are not alone.

I wish that there would have been a story like *The Make Up* for girls like me when I was a teenager—one that normalized scoliosis and all of its many subsequent gifts. My hope is that Chloe's story offers you hope and reminds you that ***you are beautiful*** just as you are. You are worthy of every good thing, and you are oh-so much more than just your body.

Acknowledgments

Writing this second book in the Falling for Franklin series felt MUCH more difficult than the first. I wanted Chloe and Hunter's story to do the friends-to-lovers trope justice, and especially wanted it to have both humor and heart. Some aspects of the plot took more time and effort for me to formulate, but I'm grateful for the process of creating this story. It truly made me a better writer.

I also want to thank everyone who's read my books thus far, who has encouraged me both online and in person. Thank you to all of my sweet family members and friends who've taken the time to not only read my stories, but to love them enough to pass them along to others. Your support means the world to me!

Thank you to my beta readers, Laramee, Lanae, and Amanda, for your thoughtful notes and amazing suggestions in that early draft. You truly helped me feel more confident as a writer and storyteller. I'm so grateful for each of you!

To Heather Austin for being the incredible editing genie that she is. I owe you biscuits for LIFE. Thank you to Jenn Lockwood for your wonderful, final cherry-on-top edits.

And of course, thank you to my dearest, darling-est husband for inspiring so much of the romance in these stories. I lucked out BIG TIME when I married you.

About The Author

Hailey Gardiner writes cheeky, sweet romantic comedies inspired by the hilarious and awkward moments that make up her real life. While she is best known for her career as an acoustic folk singer/songwriter, Hailey has been writing stories as long as she's been writing songs. Hailey is a master at quoting movies, a dark chocolate fanatic, and lives in Utah with her husband and son.

Official Website: www.haileygardiner.com

Instagram & TikTok: @authorhaileygardiner

Made in the USA
Coppell, TX
20 February 2025